PALE TIDES

CASS TELL

PALE TIDES

LOVE AND LOSS IN A CULTURE SEDUCED BY LEGALISM AND RELATIVISM

destinēe

Also by Cass Tell:

SOCIAL CODE

Cass Tell has completed five other novels, to be published by Destinée Media.

Published by Destinée Media: www.destineemedia.com
Written by Cass Tell: www.casstell.com
Cover and formatting by Per-Ole Lind
Fonts: Bembo and Akzidenz

ISBN 978-0-9759082-6-6

Inspired by a true story

"Woe to you hypocrites . . .
for when you make a convert
you make him twice as much
a son of hell as yourselves . . .
Upon you may fall the guilt
of all the righteous blood
shed on earth".

Matthew 23

"Fallen! Fallen is Babylon the Great,
which made all the nations drink
the maddening wine of her adulteries".

Revelation 14

PROLOGUE

Present Day

Below, the expanse of Los Angeles County spreads out into the distance. I flew from Europe to see this, particularly Pasadena, one of those ambiguous cities hugging the base of the San Gabriel Mountains. It's been tens of years since I've been here, never wanting to return. But now it's time to confront this Medusa's head of anger.

I usually take an aisle seat where I read a book or catch up on sleep. This time I'm fairly certain of an eastern approach into Los Angeles International Airport, so I had purposely reserved a window seat on the right side of the airplane, first class. This view sets the stage, an overview before the details.

To the west the sun is setting over the Pacific Ocean and the haze over LA has a blood red hue, like an insidious shroud covering the city. We descend and through the airplane window I imagine I spot Pasadena, but it is difficult to distinguish one city from another in this ever-connected carpet of lights. I feel apprehension and wonder how to face this memory.

It's amazing how the mind works. At my age you'd think the painful memories should have faded, like a dissipating cloud on the horizon. Monique told me this isn't always so. As much as redemption can be real, we may still carry our hurts and anger even until death.

I hope not.

I don't know how long I will be here, maybe a week, maybe more. I've ordered a rental car and plan to drive north. My goal is to visit places from the past and hopefully meet some people. Before coming here I had a long list of names, but narrowed it down to three; Eddie Bailey, Ronita Jansen and Georgia Rose. I tracked down Eddie and have an appointment with him in a few days. The other two are yet to be found.

Some might assume that this quest is nothing more than an older person's curiosity of what happened to friends from the past. Maybe there's some of that. But more so I'm hoping they can provide insights.

Also, I'm thinking to attend an event this coming weekend, a homecoming.

More than anything, I need to return to the scenes, to better understand the destructive forces at play and to face this internal fountain of anguish.

Monique advised me to do this trip and to take all the time in the world. If anyone would know, it's her. One of her books is in my carry-on bag. It talks about what goes on inside people's heads, their behaviors, and healing.

#

The airplane continues its descent and I attempt to recall the world back then, but it makes me feel unsettled. It was a long time ago and subconsciously I know I'm avoiding the details.

So, instead of trying to remember exact events of the past, I reflect on the young man. What were his values and how did he see the world? His culture was that of California of the late 1960's. It was a time when the older generation sought the great American dream. Whereas, the younger generation was attracted to surfing, hot-rods and rock and roll . . . unaware of a menacing philosophical change taking place.

Like many people the young man was caught between conflicting cultures, diametrically opposed to each other, and through this he had to navigate.

I carry suspicions about him. I'm wondering if the hurts he experienced were caused by the sinister institutions around him, or was the enemy entirely different. Was it something internal, an innate rebellion that was leading to self destruction?

How would he have told his story back then, in his own words and through his limited viewpoint?

How was the world perceived through the naivety of a teenager not understanding the devastating power of the beast?

CHAPTER 1

In the Last Months of High School - 1965

The first hymn ended and I groaned when I thought how much more of the service remained.

I sat down and noticed movement on my left. There was a tall, blond girl starting down my row. When she noticed that Eddie and I were already sitting there she began to back up, colliding with the girl following her. This caused quite a bit of commotion as more girls were coming in, like a bunch of female bumper cars. Finally things settled down and they filed into the row in front of us.

They tried to look composed, but I spotted some nervousness, guessing it was because of their late arrival to the church service, and the disconcerting way they came into the sanctuary. They were the Women's Choir from Purity-Christian College, and were there to provide the special music for the service. All three hundred people in the congregation turned around to look at them.

The tall, blond girl was no longer in the lead. She had gotten mixed up in the shuffle and ended up right in front of me. Before sitting down she narrowed her eyes and stared at me. I dropped my head and felt my face turning red. I knew I was not too good around girls.

I counted sixteen of them. They wore identical pink button-down dresses, high-heels, and beehive hairdos, the preferred fashion of women in our church. 'Bouffant style' as some of them called it, sculpted and teased hair with massive amounts of hairspray making rigid towering helmets on their heads. They reminded me of pictures I had seen in Life Magazine when Elvis Presley went off to the army in 1959. There was this crowd of girls crying when he got on the bus, and they all had their hair done up like the girls in front of us.

At the end of the row an attractive lady sat down, maybe like twenty-five or thirty years old. I figured her to be responsible for the choir. Her long gray cotton dress contrasted with all the pink dresses. Her hairdo was the tallest. I was impressed how she could stack it so high.

Then I realized that it wasn't easy to see the podium up front because of the beehive hairdos in front of me. Even though I was tall I still had to bend my head to the side to look through the open spaces between their heads.

Two men in dark suits walked in just after the choir. Reverend Finch up on the podium waved his hand and signaled for them to come forward. Both of them had stern tight faces, probably feeling stressed from being late. They quickly walked down the long aisle and made their way up the steps to the podium where they took the special seats of honor. Reverend Finch shook their hands with a look of relief on his face.

The music leader announced the next song. We all rose while the pianist played an introduction, and the congregation began to sing.

My eyes left the hymnbook and I looked at the choirgirls in front of me. All were pretty, college students, older than Eddie and me. We were seniors in high school. I was just barely seventeen, the youngest in my high school class, and I would graduate in less than a month with the class of 1965.

Sitting there I sensed something sweet, like roses and irises, a blend of girlie smells. I observed the neck of the blond girl in front of me, her ivory skin picking up the color of her pink dress. Her hair was golden and it glistened when it reflected the light, like the sparkles in metallic paint on a hot-rod. I slowly scanned from the top of her perfectly styled beehive hairdo to her narrow ankles that disappeared into pink high-heeled shoes. Eddie says I *gawk* when I look at girls.

I sure liked looking at them, but I'd never been on a date with a girl. And Eddie said I'm not too good at talking with girls.

Distracted by the girl in front of me, I forgot where we were in the song and searched the words on the hymnal. I heard Eddie next to me softly singing, but he wasn't using the right words. Instead he was singing, "La-Ti-Da-Di-Da," or something like that.

The girl in front of him heard him and turned around with a condescending look on her face. Eddie looked at her cross-eyed. She flipped her head away so fast her beehive threatened to topple over.

Eddie tuned up the volume on his "Da-Di-Da" and sang slightly off-key. Several girls shifted uncomfortably.

I turned around and looked at the clock on the back wall. It was seven-fifteen in the evening. One more hour, maybe an hour and a half, and another Sunday would be over.

Every week, my family followed the same pattern: Sunday school in the morning, followed by the service that lasted until noon, a formal lunch at someone's house and maybe a little free time in the afternoon. At five-thirty we had the Young People's meeting and then the Evening Service started at seven o'clock. We even had church services on Wednesday evenings.

The Sunday Evening Service was the "evangelical service" which always ended with an altar call. The altar was this long low bench in front of the church, just in front of the podium, and you went up there to get saved. We could get saved whenever we backslid. If you backslid, then it meant you were on the road to hell.

It was usually the same people who went forward to the altar each week. I had been down there and gotten saved a few times, but not since my first year of high school. Back then I was starting to look at girls in magazines, and was imagining things about some of the girls at my school.

Reverend Finch said that was sin. He and the other pastors in our denomination said that God condemned the lust of the eyes, and that thinking any un-pure thoughts was sin. He often said, "To get into heaven you need to purge those evil thoughts from your minds and attain sanctified lives." And when he preached he tried to be helpful in this regard, always constructing his sermons on three steps such as Three Steps to Sanctification, or Three Steps to Holiness, or Three Steps to Missionary Giving, or the Three Steps to Being Accepted by God. Everything had three steps, and he jumped around to lots of stories and verses that explained his ideas.

Holiness and sanctification were words used a lot by people in my denomination. It was something like being proud of the fact you were behaving perfect before God. The church leaders would often prance around on the podium and say, "I've been saved, and I've been sanctified." If you were sanctified, then God would let you into his kingdom on judgment day. Those kinds of sermons about judgment day were scary.

The times in the past when I went down to the altar, I asked for forgiveness for my sins. I told God I was absolutely going to be a good guy for him, to be as perfect as I could be, and I meant it. The problem was, that never lasted very long. It was hard to keep up my motivation, but I still wanted to feel God in my heart.

Eddie Bailey was also a high school senior. I had seen him around at church, but he had his own group of friends. Then, a few weeks ago, we ended up sitting next to each other in church, and we hit it off. Eddie made friends easily. And we had something in common. We both knew what it was like to jump around all the time to a bunch of different schools. His dad was a chaplain in the U.S. Navy and my stepfather was a construction supervisor. Both jobs meant our families moved a lot.

When the congregational song finished, Reverend Finch introduced the women's choir from Purity-Christian College, saying, "We warmly welcome you to the San Diego Purity-Christian Church."

Everyone turned around again to look at them. Reverend Finch continued with something about "the college from our denomination, training workers for service to the Purity-Christian denomination, directed by Miss Nancy Walker."

Reverend Finch and the others often spoke about training everyone to serve our denomination.

Miss Walker, in the gray dress at the end of the row, stood up while motioning with her hand for all the girls to remain seated. She smiled, and took a small bow, her beehive hairdo remaining stiffly attached to the top of her head. Then she sat down, her back as straight as a flagpole.

Eddie leaned over to me and whispered, "Nice bod."

Reverend Finch continued, "And also from Purity-Christian College we are especially privileged to have Dr. James Arlin, Professor of Theology. And Mr. Champ Smyth, the men's basketball coach, who led the Crusaders to a winning season last year." Reverend Finch graciously waved his hand in the direction of the two men.

After the introductions, Miss Walker rose again, lifted one hand in the air, and the entire row of girls stood up in perfectly timed unison. She motioned the girls forward. They marched single file in precise cadence to the front of the church and formed themselves into two neat rows on the platform, standing ramrod straight exactly like Miss Walker. Miss Walker sat at the piano, struck a chord, and they began a soft and contemplative rendering of "Shall We Gather at the River."

When they finished, the girls quietly returned to their seats while the room remained silent in preparation for the evangelistic message.

Dr. Arlin took over. He was a good speaker, giving lots of little stories and illustrations to develop the points he was making, although I had a difficult time following exactly how the points linked to each other and where he was going. He highlighted his words with an entertaining repertoire of facial expressions. In the middle of a dramatic story, he raised his eyebrows so high that they almost touched his hairline. And near the end of his sermon, lamenting the tragedy of people who had neglected the call of sanctification here on earth, he filled his eyes with a look of deepest sorrow and wrinkled his face into the mournful expression of a pug dog. Some of the stuff he said made me feel all emotional.

I knew the final prayer would take awhile, almost like having to listen to another sermon, so I rested my elbows on my knees, and put my head in my hands when something bumped my leg. I opened my eyes and saw Eddie's rear end sticking out from underneath the seat in front of him. He popped up with a high-heeled shoe in his hand, grinned and went back under the next seat.

I immediately understood what he was up to and went to work in the opposite direction.

Sliding silently down onto the floor, I saw a perfect row of empty pairs of pink pumps, the stocking feet of their owners resting in front of or beside them.

Reaching around their legs, I carefully grabbed their shoes so as not to touch their feet, switching one shoe with another, and hiding some. There were now some pairs of two right shoes, two left shoes, or pairs of different sizes. I managed to get eight pairs of shoes switched around and popped up in my seat just in time for Dr. Arlin's booming, "Amen." Eddie had also managed to switch all eight pairs on his side of the row.

Dr Arlin solemnly asked for the choir to come forward to lead the song for the altar call, and the girls bent down to put their shoes on. It started slow, but in a moment things got agitated in front of us with sixteen girls groping around in an attempt to find the shoes that belonged to them.

At this point Miss Walker was at the end of the row, standing stiffly straight and raising her hand for the choirgirls to stand up.

The movement of the girls became even more frantic, like an anthill poked with a stick. They began getting more and more irritated and even started pushing each other intent on grabbing shoes out of other girls' hands.

Miss Walker glared at the writhing mass, reached across and pulled the choir girl next to her out into the aisle and angrily signaled the others to follow. The girls madly straightened their dresses and smoothed their hair as they limped toward the platform, no longer walking in unison.

One girl was wearing two left shoes and another girl was wearing two right ones. Several girls seemed to have shoes of different sizes, one shoe flopping back and forth on a foot that was entirely too small for it. Some girls had no shoes at all.

There was some unusual shuffling around as they took their original places in the two rows up front on the podium.

We were instructed that the choir would sing the first verse, and the congregation would join in on the second. Miss Walker sat at the piano and hit the first chords of "Almost Persuaded." I could have joined the slightly strained voices of the choir without looking at a book. "Almost persuaded, now to believe…almost persuaded, almost but lost." I knew all the verses by heart, having sung them so many times before.

I carefully observed the choir. They didn't have the same composure as before. Their voices weren't together. Some had forgotten to take their hymnals so they had to double or triple up. One hymnal was shaking, and one girl had to lean in an awkward position to see the words. Another girl's face was bright red. It looked like she was ready to cry.

Miss Walker hit a couple off-notes on the piano.

Dr. Arlin spoke softly asking if there was anyone who needed to come forward to the altar.

The beehive hairdos on two girls had come undone and hair was randomly streaming down the sides of their faces.

Some people in the congregation began to giggle.

Dr. Arlin droned on, pretending things were in order, as he paced back and forth in the front, looking at the congregation, but occasionally shifting his eyes toward the choir. He turned to the congregation and said, "I know, I know there is someone, someone out there tonight, some backslidden person who needs to come forward."

At the end of the song's six verses, the altar at the front remained empty.

During all of this the congregation was extremely attentive, watching all that was going on up front.

Eddie poked me in the ribs and pointed to the floor and to his left foot. Three pink shoes next to his made a considerable contrast to his black Converse high-tops.

I had a difficult time to keep myself from laughing, but was feeling guilty because we were in the serious part of the service.

"Search your heart. Ask yourself, 'Am I a sinner, backslidden? Will I be cast into the fiery furnace forever?' Come forward and bow at the altar where our brothers and sisters will meet you. Confess and promise to lead a life of sanctified perfection so that you may be saved." Dr. Arlin intoned as he motioned for the choir to start the song over from the first verse.

No one came forward, and eventually Dr. Arlin gave up and turned the podium back to Reverend Finch. Eyes drawn down, they both had looks of disappointment on their faces.

The service finally ended, and Eddie and I slipped outside before the bee-hived heads had looked up from the last amen and came back to their seats.

We walked out to the edge of the church parking lot and stood beside Eddie's 1940 Chevrolet. He punched me on the arm, and we began to laugh.

I heard movement behind us, a dark shadow, and a voice said, "Is one of you Robert Macon?"

I glanced over at Eddie. The figure approached, and I recognized the man Reverend Finch had introduced as Coach Smyth. "That's me," I said.

"I hear you're a pretty good basketball player," Coach Smyth stated.

"I like to play." I had finished top in my high school league in scoring and rebounding.

"We're looking for good players for the Purity-Christian Crusaders. How would you like to play there?"

"I don't know, Mr. Smyth."

"Just call me Coach Champ. Do you want to play?"

"Actually, I've been thinking about San Diego State. They contacted me at the end of the season."

"Why would you want to go to a non-Christian school?" Coach Smyth challenged. "No telling what they will teach you. Your education will be much better at Purity-Christian College. We score in the top percent of schools. Come and play for the Crusaders—for PC Cru."

Eddie broke in, "Hey, I'm going to PC Cru. Why don't you go too? We can be roommates."

"I'm not sure I can afford it," I responded.

"Don't worry about that," Coach Smyth replied. "Based on your basketball abilities I can arrange a full scholarship."

"A full scholarship?" My voice squeaked like a frog.

"Everything paid. Tuition, room and board," Coach Smyth said, and gave me a congratulatory pat on the shoulder.

"Wow," I breathed, wondering if this was one of those too-good-to-be-true type of things.

"You're coming to a fine school," Coach Smyth affirmed.

"Well...I guess," I stammered. "How does the scholarship work?"

"Don't worry. When you get to school come and see me. We'll take care of it. It's a deal?"

"Yeah, uh, Mr. Smyth." I didn't know what to say.

"I said to call me Coach Champ. Look, if you have any questions, give me a call. Otherwise, see you in September."

Coach Smyth waved and walked back toward the crowd of people gathered in front of the church.

"Champ, is that you?" a lady's voice cooed in the distance. I turned and saw Miss Walker.

I leaned back against the cool metal of the car and stared out into the black night. "What do you think, Eddie?" I asked.

He slapped me on the back. "I think it's great. We're going to PC Cru."

Coach Smyth joined Miss Walker who was talking with a couple of the choirgirls, including the tall, blond who had sat in front of me. Dr. Arlin was standing next to Miss Walker. She had her hands on her hips and was bent slightly forward. I could hear her shrill voice across the parking lot.

"Someone did this?" she questioned.

The blond girl pointed in our direction, and Miss Walker, Coach Smyth and Dr. Arlin turned and looked at us.

We quickly got into Eddie's car, and drove away.

CHAPTER 2

Freshman: 1965-1966

I threw the last pair of basketball shoes onto the floor behind the driver's seat, hopped behind the wheel of my 1954 Chevrolet and revved the engine. Soon I was speeding along the interstate from San Diego to L.A.

I passed Camp Pendleton, a large Marine training base and saw groups of men in dark green pants and green T-shirts. Some were running and others were standing around a dusty military truck. I even imagine I recognized a couple of guys from my high school who said they were going to join the Marines and go off to Vietnam. I knew there was a war going on, and a lot of eighteen year olds were going over there to fight the communists.

But, to be honest, I really did not know much about the war. We never talked about it in my family, in school, or at my church. All I ever heard anyone ever say was to, "Stay in college. You don't want to go over there." Other than that, I didn't have strong feelings either way.

In some ways it gave me the creeps to see those guys in thinking about where they were going, but right then my mind was on Purity-Christian College and the full basketball scholarship Coach Smyth had offered. I loved basketball and spent all my free time playing the game. It was about the only thing I was really good at, and I looked forward to play ball at college level.

I felt some anxiety about heading north to Pasadena on my own, but the words of Coach Smyth went through my head about the importance of going to a Christian college. I hoped I could find out something more about God, to deepen the religion in my life. I believed in God, but lately he seemed far away.

#

For a long time I drove alongside the Pacific Ocean. It was a warm Southern California day. The sea was a pale blue and the tide was out. I wished I had time to stop, to feel the sun on my body and swim free in the ocean, but I had to get to the college to register.

I made my way through Los Angeles impressed by the size of the city. Then, following directions someone in my church had given me, I took the Pasadena Freeway. The Freeway ended and I passed through some shopping streets and residential areas where the streets were lined with palm trees. Brown scrubby mountains rose to the north behind Pasadena.

Purity-Christian College was supposed to be somewhere in a residential area of the city, but after half an hour of driving around, I still hadn't seen anything resembling a college campus.

The houses looked like they were built in the 1920's. I was about to knock on a random door and ask for directions when I spotted the sign. The metal post stood slightly askew, and I could barely see the tiny arrow next to the faded lettering, *Pasadena: Purity-Christian College, Crusaders.*

I parked in the school parking lot, which was next to a large building that looked like some kind of an auditorium. On the side of the building just above the wide main entrance was a sign that said, *Registration.* In front there were groups of students standing around chatting and laughing.

I stepped inside and before my eyes adjusted to the dim light inside. I smelled something like sweat and old socks. Sure enough, a large basketball court filled the opposite half of the room, though the dilapidated wooden backboard and faded floor suggested that basketball wasn't a high priority here.

For the moment, the auditorium had been converted into a sort of registration center. I took a paper from a stack on a table marked Registration Instructions, and moved toward a long line of people in the section for freshmen. Most everyone stood silently; apparently I wasn't the only one reliving the nervousness of the first day of kindergarten.

Actually I should be used to it. Because of my stepfather's work we moved every year and there was always a new school to attend. I got tired of never staying in one place long enough to feel like part of the group, and eventually gave up trying to fit in. Being an only child only added to the agony. But college lasted four years, and I anticipated it with a tiny flicker of new hope.

"Next," a woman said in a sugary sweet voice.

I moved up to the table.

"Your name." She had a smile that looked glued to her face.

"Uh, Robert."

"*Last* name." She rolled her eyes impatiently.

"Sorry," I stammered. "Macon."

She flipped through a file of papers, pulled one out and handed it to me. "Take this and go stand in line over there. That's the counselor. He'll help you choose your classes."

After an hour, my turn finally came. The guy motioned for me to sit down.

"You have to choose an elective course, one that fits the schedule of your other courses. What's your major?" the counselor asked without any introduction.

"I don't know." Was I supposed to?

"Fine then, what do you like?" His voice had some kind of arrogant authority like he knew things that nobody else did.

"Sports and I'm pretty good in math."

"Okay, do Physical Education. Why would anyone want to do math?"

"Physical Education?"

"Yeah, all athletes do PE. For your elective, you can take Physiology of Exercise."

"What's it about?"

The counselor looked at his watch and the line of people behind me. "How to build muscles and things like that. Things you need to know if you do sports."

"I need to take that? I'm not sure what it is."

"You'll find out more when you take the course."

"What if I haven't decided on a major?"

"Look," the counselor said, clearly frustrated. "Just take it and see if you like it. You can change your major any time. Now let's move on to the other stuff. You need all the general electives as well as the religion courses."

"Religion courses?"

"Yeah. This is a Christian college." He looked at me like I was stupid. "Most people like to get those courses out of the way when they are freshmen and sophomores, so they can concentrate on their major after that."

"OK. What should I take?"

The counselor scribbled something on a piece of paper and pointed to another line of people. "Next stop is the financial table." He seemed relieved to have me off his hands.

I looked down at the paper and saw a list of classes, my first semester schedule; Physiology of Exercise, English 101, The Teachings of John Wesley, Purity-Christian Church Theology, and The Basics of Holiness.

A woman wearing black horn-rimmed glasses and a long cotton dress sat underneath a sign that said 'Financial Department.' She looked at my list of classes, muttered, "Fifteen credits."

She scribbled a few calculations on something like an accounting paper and handed it to me. "Here's the total amount that you owe. You can pay now or anytime in the next two weeks."

"Excuse me, ma'am." I wasn't quite sure what to say. "Mr. Smyth said I was going to get a full scholarship."

"Just a minute." She shuffled through a stack of papers. "You're not on the list."

"What list?"

"The basketball scholarship list. The list given to us by Coach Smyth."

"But he told me I was getting a scholarship." I felt stunned. There must have been an oversight. I stared at her, feeling lost.

"Well then, you'll have to go see him." She paused when I didn't respond. "His office is in the next building. Out the door, turn left, straight ahead."

I followed the woman's directions and found an office labeled Sports Department. A woman was clicking away on a typewriter. She glanced up, and I immediately recognized her as the director of the women's choir that had sung at our church the previous spring, Miss Walker. It was impressive how she could make her beehive hairdo stand up so high.

"What do you want?" she asked, hands poised over the keys. She sat ramrod straight and I wondered if it wasn't an effort to keep the hairdo from toppling over.

"Do you know where Mr. Smyth is?" I asked.

"Of course I know. I'm his secretary." She stared at me with narrow eyes and tight lips. It came across as contempt, or something like that. She turned away and began to shuffle through stacks of sheet music were on her desk.

"Can you tell me where I can find him? I'd like to set up a meeting with him."

"He's not here right now. Why do you need to talk to him?" She looked at me again and took a deep sigh.

"He promised me a basketball scholarship. A full scholarship."

"What's your name?" she asked.

"Robert Macon. My name wasn't on the scholarship list."

"Oh," she said. She looked at me again, only this time more carefully, and in her eyes I felt she knew something.

"Is it possible for me to see him?"

Her smile seemed to mock me. "You'll have to wait. Basketball practice starts in three weeks, and he doesn't come until the week before."

"But the Financial Office needs to know about the scholarship."

"I really can't help you. Why don't you just pay what you owe them and then you can discuss it with Mr. Smyth when he is here." She dropped her hands onto the keys in irritation.

"Could I at least set a time to meet with him?"

"Not really. I don't know his exact schedule, so any meeting would most likely have to be changed anyway. Just come back in a couple of weeks."

I figured I was out of options, so I went back and wrote a check for the amount the lady had given me. Just about everything I'd earned from working the past four summers disappeared in one moment, to cover the expenses of one semester.

Eager to get out of the stuffy auditorium and the endless standing in line, I turned to head for the door. A voice called out behind me, "Excuse me, young man, you need to sign the Community Living Covenant."

"On the table in the corner," the lady added as I stopped and turned back to her. She was another face with pasted smile, birds nest hairdo and horn-rimmed glasses. She said, "Please read the entire covenant carefully and sign your name at the bottom."

I scanned the purpose of the school, something about "education in an environment vital to the Purity-Christian tradition." It continued:

By signing this form, I commit to support the ideals of Purity-Christian College:

To be supportive of the College and all persons involved and to observe dorm hours,

To give thorough attention to the development of my whole person, including chapel attendance as required,

To abstain from alcoholic beverages, tobacco in any form, dancing, card playing, attending movies, and profane language,

To abstain from participating in behavior that detracts from spiritual growth and breaks down proper moral standards, and to follow the dress codes.

I commit myself to abide by the holiness standards of the college and I realize that in violating any of these standards, I surrender the privilege of being a student at Purity-Christian College.

It seemed a little excessive to me, but I hadn't been allowed to do any of that stuff growing up anyway, so I scribbled my name at the bottom.

"Thanks. Now you can go check in at the freshman dorm," the lady said.

I felt numb. I had been promised a full scholarship and now my name wasn't on the list. I imagined that Mr. Smyth was a busy man and maybe he just forgot. Something slipped. We could surely get it straightened out. Still, it left a hollow feeling in my core.

I took one last glance at the basketball hoops on my way out and headed to find my room and Eddie Bailey, the one familiar face in this place.

3

I found the dorm and Eddie, and I got settled into our room. The next few days were a process of learning where things were: classrooms, cafeteria, student center, etc. Most of the buildings had names, which I learned came from the people who had donated the money to construct the building, or after someone important in our denomination. So, there was the initial confusion of learning an entirely new jargon.

But I had been through this many times before. My parents and I had moved around a lot when I was growing up and I always had to learn a new school system, not that I ever really fit in.

The dorm for the freshmen men seemed to be one of the oldest buildings on campus—a two story rectangular wooden structure that looked like an old army barracks. The wooden floors creaked whenever anyone passed, which was often. Our room was on the ground floor and faced the library. We could look in and see rows of books and people hunkered down over wooden tables.

On the upstairs floor I met a friendly guy named Leyland McGrath. Even though he was a freshman, everyone seemed to know him. He was from Tulsa, Oklahoma and it turned out that he was the son of the top guy in our denomination.

Leyland got me involved in intramural sports. Eddie was only interested in golf.

One day Leyland and I were walking across the campus to the student center to sign up for sports, when we ran into a couple of guys he knew. He asked them for any advice about the school and they said that we absolutely needed to attend the kick-off social event on the Friday evening where "all the cute girls get snatched up."

One of them said, "If you don't score there, then you are out of luck for the rest of the year and you'll get stuck with the ugly ones."

Leyland laughed and said, "I'll be there. Good tip. Anything else?"

One of the guys looked around and lowered his voice. "Twenty-five cent movies in L.A."

Leyland held a finger to his lips and said, "I already heard about it."

"You're fast. You always were," one of the guys said.

They walked away and I asked Leyland who they were.

"Couple of Juniors. I've known them since elementary school. All of our dads have leadership positions in the Purity-Christian Church headquarters in Tulsa. Those two guys are pretty popular on campus, and they offered to get me hooked up. People here have their little groups, you know, and if you want to break in, it helps to have some connections."

Inside the student center, some tables were set up for different sports. Leyland seemed to know what he was doing, so I followed him around, signing up for everything possible along the way—tennis, ping-pong, wrestling, racquetball, volleyball, and flag football. In high school, I preferred sports to studies; I worked just hard enough to pass my classes and filled the rest of my time with sports.

The two sports I was really interested in were tennis and flag football. I was a little bit worried that I might injure myself with football, but was willing to take the risk and signed up. On the wall behind the desk I happened to notice a poster that announced a mandatory cross-country race for all athletes trying out for the basketball team, so I made a mental note.

When we left the student center and got to a place where we couldn't be heard I asked Leyland, "With those two guys, your friends from Tulsa, what was that about twenty-five cent movies?"

He laughed sarcastically. "There are these movie theatres in downtown L.A. that run old movies twenty-four hours a day. You pay twenty-five cents, and you can stay as long as you want. Want to go sometime?"

"You go to movies?" I asked.

"Sure, I like movies," he replied.

"But what about that Community Living Covenant thing we signed?" I interjected, feeling a bit confused. "Doesn't it say that movies are a sin and that we promised not to go?"

"Oh that." Leyland rolled his eyes. "Well, I already said it. I like movies. They're fun."

"But the rules? We had to sign the paper. And, and, what if God came back to earth and found you in a movie theatre?" I didn't know exactly why I said this other than repeating the argument that Reverend Finch used when he talked about the sinfulness of movies.

"I'll run out real fast if he comes back, and then he won't catch me." He laughed. "Anyway, I try to do more good stuff than bad stuff just to keep the scale tilted in the right direction." He turned to me with a frown on his forehead and said, "It's not healthy to think about those things."

We walked on and as we approached the dorm he asked, "Robert, aren't you sick of all the religious stuff?"

"Church is pretty boring," I replied.

"No not just church, but all the rules. I've had it all my life, growing up in the church headquarters in Tulsa, with everyone watching me and my friends. Having to carry the burden as the preacher's kid, the leader's kid, the missionary's kid, the church secretary's kid. No matter what you are, there is some special behavior that is expected. Everyone always breathing down our necks saying, 'You can't do this. You can't do that.' My two friends back there and me, we're fed up. I came out here to California to get away from all that."

"Why didn't you go to a state college?"

"My parents insisted that I go to a college in our denomination. I picked PC Cru because it is the one farthest away from Tulsa."

"I didn't have it that bad," I said.

He reached into his pocket and pulled out a folded piece of paper and handed it to me. "Here. Did you get this? It was on one of the tables in the student center."

On the top it said 'Student Rules', and then a list.

First there was a list of dorm rules: No females inside the front door. No rock-and-roll music. Be in your rooms by 10:00 p.m., and the list went on.

Below that it was another list for dress code: No Bermuda shorts. Girls could not wear pants but had to wear dresses that came no higher than half way between their knee and ankle. Appropriate hairstyles are mandatory.

And below that was another list about dating and stuff like that: No freshmen or sophomores allowed being alone with someone from the opposite sex. Freshmen and sophomores can only date on Friday nights unless especially approved by the Dean of Men and Dean of Women. Only double dating for freshmen and sophomores. Juniors and seniors could date. Next to that rule there was an explanation that this was an important time for juniors and seniors to find a spouse before entering into Purity-Christian service.

And again, the list went on.

"That's what I'm talking about," he said.

"It's tight, but not that bad," I replied. "Every place needs rules."

"Makes me sick. Good luck, holy man," he said, and took the wooden stairs up to his room.

4

What Leyland said kept going through my mind and it made me uneasy. I didn't think he was right. My family had always attended Purity-Christian churches in all the different places we moved, and the teaching was consistent. To do right is to abide by God's law and not do evil acts, and then he loves you. The evil acts are the things taught against by the Purity-Christian Church. There are many forms of evil, and movies are one of them. Yet somehow I thought it might be fun to go to a movie, and I was wondering what could be evil about it.

I also thought about what Leyland's two friends had said about getting the pretty girls before they were taken. It made sense to me.

I was seventeen and had never even been on a date, or even kissed a girl. Some of the guys in high school had talked about making out with girls and bragged about how far they had gotten. One guy I knew said he put his hand under a girl's bra while making out with her in the back seat of his parents' car. When I heard him tell it I had mixed feelings. I got extremely interested, but it made me uneasy, with this dirty feeling inside of me.

I hardly even knew how to act around girls, being tall and gangly, wondering if my zits were flaring up, and not knowing what to say. And, in high school, the girls in my class were always older than me and didn't give me any notice. Whatever school I went to, I was always the youngest in my class, way younger.

Over the past few days, I had seen a number of really cute girls, especially some of the juniors and seniors in my high school, but most of them seemed to have boyfriends. Anyway, what would cute girls want with me?

Nevertheless, on Friday night I allowed Leyland to drag me along to the social. "You've got to come," he insisted. "Otherwise you'll never meet people."

I followed him through the maze of people, weaving through the tight little groups until we found his two friends. They waved to Leyland, and their circle opened up to allow us in. Leyland joined in on the conversation, but I didn't know what to say.

I stood and listened, shifting my gaze from person to person and then back out into space, towering above everyone else and feeling like I blended in about as well as Bigfoot among the Munchkins.

A voice came over the microphone from the other room, and the crowd started moving in to find seats. The tension in my shoulders loosened as I took a chair next to Leyland and everyone's attention shifted toward the front.

I looked around and saw lots of cute girls dressed up for the evening with cotton dresses buttoned to their necks and bouffant hairstyles sprayed into place. Most of them had shoulder-length hair that swirled out above the shoulders like rigid little wings flowing out from their necks. It was like their hairdos came out of the same mold and their clothing off the same clothing rack.

"This evening, two groups will be performing," the clean-cut guy holding the microphone announced. "First we will have the Purity-Christian Ramblers with a medley of spirituals, and after them a skit organized by members of Circle K."

I wasn't sure what he meant by Circle K? The girls in the room had sweet smiles on their faces, eyes wide, looking at the guy up front.

Two girls and two guys stepped up to a loud applause. When it died down, they opened with the first song in the arrangement, "Give Me That Old-Time Religion." They sang without instruments, harmonizing like a barbershop quartet.

When the Ramblers finished, there was another round of applause. The girls in the room were really into it.

After the singing group, a guy and a girl took positions on the stage. It looked like they were preparing a skit. Identical pasted smiles were on everyone's faces in the audience.

From the corner, a voice asked in the tone of an advertiser. "Are you skinny and run down? Are you so thin you have to wear skis in the bathtub to keep from going down the drain? When you turn sideways and stick out your tongue, do you look like a zipper? When you drink StrawBailey pop, do you look like a thermometer? Then you need FAT-RICAL—the drink that adds weight to your body."

The guy and girl up front then started their part and got into a skit about Trigger Mortis, the Frontier Mortician: Have Hearse, Will Travel, who lived in Sparerib, Texas.

"What's wrong with you, daddy?" the girl asked. "What's your ailment?"

"I swallowed the thermometer, and I'm dying by degrees."

A universal laugh erupted in the room, but I felt awkward for missing the joke and not laughing.

I noticed one girl in the front row, and began to stare at her. It's funny how in a sea of faces one girl will stand out. That's what happened when I looked at her. She had the same style of hair as all the other girls and wore a similar style cotton dress, but her laughter seemed spontaneous and genuine, and most of all she had large breasts that pressed against the front of her dress.

A half hour later all the skits were finished, and I made my way to the refreshment table. While nabbing a few cookies, I observed groups of people forming, while talking, and laughing. At the same time I noticed a number of girls standing by themselves who seemed uncertain of themselves. They looked nervously around. After a few minutes of standing on their own, one by one they left the room.

Across the room I spotted the girl from the front row. She was with a small group of older students. A guy was standing next to her tying to catch her attention. Her figure even looked better now that she was standing up.

She seemed to ignore the guy next to her, for each time he came close to her she moved away from him just a bit, so much so that she eventually turned her back to him. He was an okay looking guy, maybe a senior. I thought about moving over to her group, but what chance would someone like me have with her?

Leyland was with his two friends from Tulsa and they had rounded up some of the cutest girls in the room. Rather than join them, I took a couple of cookies and a glass of punch, and slipped out into the warm evening air.

5

The next day I was lying on my bed attempting to read a biography of John Wesley. But mainly I was worried about my scholarship, and thoughts of that girl I saw at the Friday night social were filling my mind. I was imagining what it would be like to be with her.

After attending the social, I was also anxious about whether I would fit in at the school and live up to the standards of everyone else.

All I could do was try.

Eddie had disappeared to who-knows-where earlier in the morning; he seemed to have a habit of wandering off early and returning rather late, with no explanation of his activities or whereabouts.

There was a knock on the door.

"Come in," I called, too lazy to get up. Who was knocking anyway?

Leyland always came right in, and I didn't know many other people.

The door opened, and our dorm assistant, Donald Bonen. He was wearing a polo shirt tucked into khaki pants. Donald came by each evening at ten o'clock to check that we were in our rooms. He was the one who made sure everyone was living by the rules. If rules were broken, then Donald wrote it up and sent it to Mr. Grazer, the Dean of Men.

"Hello Robert," Donald said. "We're looking for volunteers for the prayer chain."

"The prayer chain?" I rolled over and sat up on the bed. "What's that?"

"You don't know about the revival?" Donald asked.

"Sure. They announced it in chapel." Every day for the past week, I wanted to say, and there were posters plastering the entire campus: 'Fall Term Revival. Starting the School Year Right. Evangelist Jacob Yokes.'

Donald spoke in a serious, condescending voice. "Every year before the revival, the school organizes a week of continuous prayer to prepare for it. We want to see Christian values upheld on this campus, and the more people who are involved, the more blessing we will receive. We are commanded to pray without ceasing and for the next seven days, we will have a chain of people praying day and night."

"That's impossible! You mean people will pray twenty-four hours a day for a week?"

"Exactly," he answered.

"How can anyone stay up for twenty-four hours a day with no sleep?" I asked.

Donald realized my misunderstanding. "Oh, it's not like that. We're setting up a special prayer room and asking each person to volunteer to pray for thirty minutes. When your thirty minutes is finished, someone else will come and replace you. The college considers this a valuable development of spiritual discipline and therefore of the whole person."

"Well, sure. I guess I can handle thirty minutes," I said. "Sign me up."

Donald scanned his notepad. "This school is overflowing with students eager to fulfill this responsibility. We only have a few time slots left. Could you take next Tuesday at four a.m.?"

"Four o'clock!" I exclaimed. "You mean like in the middle of the night?"

"It's an excellent time to meditate without distraction."

"Okay, I guess, if that's all you've got." I didn't like being forced into something I didn't have the motivation to do, but if it enabled me to become accepted by other students then I was willing. Anyway, since coming here I was starting to feel more spiritually alienated than ever.

Yes, I would do it.

Donald tore a small piece off his notepad and handed it to me. "There's your date and time. Don't forget to set your alarm. It is of utmost importance that the prayer chain not be broken. The success of the revival rests on this."

As they left, I had some strange mixed feelings of heaviness and hope. The prayer chain seemed extremely important to Donald and I felt a weight of spiritual responsibility on my shoulders. But I also felt hope, thinking this might be my chance to be accepted by some of the other students. And there was another kind of hope. Somehow in the bottom of my soul I had a yearning for God and maybe the prayer chain would help.

Combined with these feelings, there was something else that was making me extremely anxious. I wondered how long I would be a student at this school. I didn't have the finances to stay here long term. I really needed that athletic scholarship and decided to be diligent in tracking down Coach Smyth.

6

For the tenth time in two weeks, I entered the sports department office. The sterile white walls greeted me with about as much friendliness as the frozen smile on Miss Walker's face. "He's not here yet."

"Do you have any idea when he'll be back?" I implored with as polite a tone as I could muster.

"Are you majoring in Physical Education?"

I nodded.

"Then you are probably taking Physiology of Exercise. He's the professor for that class, and you'll know he's back when you see him in class. Until then, I can't help you." She looked down, and the furious clacking of the typewriter resumed.

Walking toward the front door, I had a hollow feeling in my stomach.

Previously that morning, I had been to my Physiology of Exercise class. The substitute professor had announced a quiz for the next class session, so I figured that meant he'd still be teaching then. Since the class only met twice a week, I'd have to wait at least another full week before I had a chance of seeing Coach Smyth.

I glanced on the wall and noticed the same poster I had seen
before, announcing the mandatory cross-country race. It was that
afternoon, and I had almost forgotten. There was too much on my
mind.

At three o'clock in the afternoon I made my way to the auditorium where there was a large group of athletes. There were all the
players from the senior basketball team and about twenty-five guys
who were trying out for the freshman basketball team. Track and
field athletes were also there, as well as athletes from other varsity
sports. I didn't realize so many athletes were participating.

The race was to take place in some hills above Pasadena and a
coach asked for volunteers to transport athletes. I raised my hand.

I drove my car with four other guys packed in, and we followed a
convoy of cars north to a starting point in the hills west of Pasadena.

One of the guys in the back asked, "So you guys know much
about this Coach Smyth?"

The guy next to me in the front responded, "Not really. He showed
up at my church one evening and somehow he must have known
about me. He spoke with me and offered a partial scholarship."

"You're kidding," the guy in the back said. "Something like that
happened with me. He said that if I played well, then they would
increase the scholarship in the second semester."

A guy sitting in the middle in the back said, "I got everything paid."

The guy in the front turned to me and asked, "And what about you?"

"I'm still working on it." I said, feeling empty, knowing that most of
these guys at least got something.

"Oh," was the reply from someone in the back seat.

I parked my car in a large dirt parking lot and we joined the other
athletes near the starting line. We found out there were several other
schools there and it made quite a large crowd. It was a big pre-season
cross-country race with about sixty or seventy runners. The race was
seven miles.

Seven miles didn't sound that bad. In high school, we ran five or six
miles at least once a week during practice. I knew that I had to do well. If
there were twenty-five guys trying out for the freshman basketball team,
they would only end up taking ten or twelve. If these other guys were
already being given scholarships, then why would they take me? I had to
prove myself.

The race took place on a dirt road that wound its way into the hills
and eventually returned to the starting point. It was a hot day and I felt

something burning into my eyes and nose.

"What's that smell?" I asked a guy standing next to me.

"Smog. Look into the distance."

I looked out into the valley and there was a thick red haze where the houses disappeared into a smoky fog several miles away.

"Pace yourself," the guy said.

Before I could ask what he meant, the starting gun sounded and I began to run. At first we were packed together, but gradually the runners began to thin out.

I set my pace to keep up with the leading group, my feet pounding on the dusty trail. After the third mile, my eyes and lungs began to burn. I lifted my shirt to wipe the sweat off my forehead and tried to breathe more rhythmically, but by the fourth mile, tears were pouring from my eyes and I was gasping for air. I dropped back, and the guy I spoke with came up beside me.

"Smog," he panted. "It'll make you sick."

About one hundred feet from the finish line I felt my stomach tighten. I slowed down and a couple of runners passed me, but I managed to stumble across the finish line and bent over by some shrub brush at the side of the road.

For three minutes I emptied my lunch, deep uncontrollable vomiting, the smog burning into my eyes while I gasped for breath.

The coaches from PC Cru stood and watched.

A coach from another school came over and asked, "Are you OK?"

"Yeah," I managed to say, while wiping a long stream of phlegm from my mouth.

He patted me on the back and said, "Good race, kid. We shouldn't have you guys out here when the smog is this thick."

"Thanks," I said. My stomach contracted several more times.

7

That evening I didn't make it to dinner, but lay on my bed, dizzy and nauseous. After a trip to the bathroom I found a note pinned to the outside of my door: Prayer Chain, 4:00 a.m. I set my alarm at five minutes before four, flopped down on my bed, and spun into oblivion.

I awoke to an incessant beeping, the red numbers on my clock glowing in the dark.

"What's that?" Eddie mumbled as he rolled over and pulled the covers above his head.

I groped around for my shoes and staggered down the dimly light hall-way and outside. On the second floor of the student center, a small sign hung from a door.

Prayer Chain in Progress: Do Not Disturb.

I opened the door. In a corner, a female student kneeled on the floor, her elbows resting on the seat of the chair in front of her and her hands folded in front of her face. She didn't move.

I didn't know how she could have held that position for thirty minutes.

I straightened my rumpled t-shirt and waited. Maybe she hadn't heard me come in. My stomach felt queasy.

I tiptoed toward her and tapped her lightly on the shoulder.

"I'm here to replace you," I whispered.

Without looking up, she raised one finger for me to be quiet. A moment later, slowly and silently, head still bowed, she left the room.

When I prayed, which was mostly at home before a meal, I generally didn't kneel. But maybe if you did then God listened more or something, so I knelt by the chair and began.

"Dear God, Bless this school and the teachers and students, and the revival and the sports, and . . ."

I'd never been a very wordy person and especially in my prayers. Suddenly I wondered if I could actually pray for half an hour. My knees were starting to ache, but mostly I was exhausted and sick from the race. I lay down on the floor, and tried to think of something really genuine to say. "God, I want to be good so you accept me," were the only words that came out.

I shut my eyes and couldn't stop myself from nodding off to sleep.

Some time later, in the distance, I heard a guy's voice. Then somebody was shaking me.

"You broke the prayer chain."

"Huh?" I sat up feeling dizzy. My lungs still hurt.

"You broke the prayer chain. That's not supportive of the college."

"I, what?" I said, slightly more conscious.

"You fell asleep. You broke the prayer chain!"

I don't know who the guy was, but I left the building and found my way back to my room, collapsed into bed and forgot to reset my alarm for class the next morning. I woke up just before lunch. The dorm was empty, so I walked to the cafeteria alone. I got my food and sat down at a table where I recognized two students from one of my classes, a guy and a girl. They looked at me disappointedly, shook their heads, and stood up.

One of them stared directly into my eyes, wrinkles on his forehead, his eye lids raised. "You broke the prayer chain. Haven't you been listening in class?" he said. "A fundamental basic of holiness is to remain unwavering in prayer."

"And watch and pray," the other said.

I wasn't sure if she was quoting from a Bible verse or just repeating something she had heard in church.

They took their food trays and moved to a different table.

8

Through the following days I noticed that some of the students in my religion courses were ignoring me, some were giving me stern looks, and others rolled their eyes upwards with smirks on their faces. This made me feel lonely and rejected. I guess I was wrong to fall asleep at the prayer chain, but I was physically not feeling too good. It was because of the long cross country run in the smog that I wasn't prepared for. The place I felt most comfortable was in the gym, so I spent most afternoons playing basketball.

One afternoon I was in the gym playing basketball with some of the guys on the senior team. They were good, but I played at their level, if not even better. It gave me some confidence, and I needed it, to at least feel good about something.

As we played, a group of students buzzed around the auditorium—hanging banners with slogans, setting up book tables by the entryway, and arranging microphones and speakers on the stage. The fall revival would begin that evening with a kick-off service. Leyland had told me that as a tradition, many members of the local Purity-Christian churches came on the first night, often to revive memories of the days when they were students and to socialize with others from the Purity-Christian Church.

Every student was required to attend the Friday evening revival kick-off. Then, the revival would continue over the following week during the daily chapel services.

At eight o'clock Eddie and I walked to the auditorium. Small groups of people stood outside chatting and laughing. Above the door, a large black and white banner proclaimed, *Advancing the Kingdom: Called Unto Holiness. Purity-Christian College Fall Revival.*

We went inside and took our pre-assigned seats where we sat alphabetically by name, Eddie Bailey closer to the front and me in the 'M' row not too far away from Leyland McGrath.

Row Monitors came by and a sheet of paper was passed down each row where we had to sign in our names. If we missed too many times, then we had to go see the Dean of Men,

"Good evening, brothers and sisters," the speaker began. "What a blessing to see so many of you gathered here tonight. Heavenly eyes are upon you and I am convinced that there will be a mighty work among us. We are called unto holiness and sanctification, and that is the theme of our revival."

He handed the microphone to a striking young lady. A belt was cinched in the waist of her cotton dress, setting off her shapely figure. She looked down, closing her eyes for a moment, and I recognized her as the girl who was just before me in the prayer chain who had been praying from three thirty to four o'clock in the morning. The pianist played a short prelude, and the girl looked out to the audience and opened in a meditative tone.

"Turn your eyes upon Jesus. Look full in his wonderful face, and the things of earth will grow strangely dim in the light of his glory and grace." Her voice was solemn. At times she looked at the audience and at other times she looked upwards, smoothly waving her hand as she sang, melodramatically raising both hands into the sky, and then bringing them together as though she were praying. There was one moment I thought she was going to cry and the crowd became quiet, mesmerized by her performance.

The words were so familiar to me, a song we sang regularly at the Purity-Christian churches I had attended. It was core to our beliefs that the things of this world, all the physical things were not important and were even evil when compared to the spiritual things.

The girl's sweet voice captivated me and I began to realize that because I knew the song so well, I wasn't really concentrating on the words, but more on her delivery. Her waist was unusually small, making her appear delicate. She finished and walked off the stage, a sweet smile on her face, and her hips gently swaying.

I looked around in the auditorium. Maybe over a thousand people were there. The girls were still dressed the same as at the Friday night social; the guys all had similar crew-cut haircuts. Black horn-rimmed glasses were the style. I had a fleeting impression that they all came from the same cookie cutter.

Turning behind me I recognized the girl I saw at the Friday night social, a week ago. She was a couple of rows behind me, and I guessed it was the 'O' row. She looked at me and I saw something in her eyes, like a twinkle, or more like an intent seductive glance.

I immediately turned around and looked at the stage; my cheeks and neck felt like they were burning.

Since first seeing her on Friday night I had been thinking about her and maybe my thoughts weren't pure. Now that she looked at me I didn't have the courage to keep eye contact. Yet my mind was filled with her.

On the stage in front there was the president of the school and next to him was the Dean of Men, Mr. Grazer. Someone had already pointed him out to me one day on campus. He had a face that was rigid and when he smiled it looked like he was breaking concrete on his jaws.

Dr. Arlin was also on the stage. He had been the special speaker at our church when the PC Cru girls' choir had come, and he had given the altar call. He was the head of the theology department.

Jacob Yokes, the evangelist, was introduced. He was from Tulsa, based at the central headquarters of the Purity-Christian Church. The announcer said he was a close friend of Dr. McGrath, the president of the denomination, and that seemed to give him special credibility. They did that a lot in the Purity-Christian churches. If someone knew someone who was important, then it made them important too.

Jacob Yokes took the podium, and he preached with fervor. He gripped the podium firmly with both hands. He commenced with the story of the Prodigal Son, putting it into our modern times, telling the story of a young man who as a child received instructions of the church. Hardened by rebellion, he chose a life of sin, wiling away his youth in movie theaters and bars, smoking, drinking, and engaging in debauchery. Many godly people pleaded with him to repent, but he persisted in the indulgence of the flesh. His mind was filled with sinful things of the flesh. His loving and holy father could not tolerate such wantonness, but the Prodigal Son recognized his folly, returned home, repented of his waywardness and vowed to lead a life of perfection.

"Tonight, you are being called to turn away from your wickedness and walk with purity of heart and life," he said. "Abstain from the desires of the earthly man, and follow the steps upward to sanctification where you may earn your heavenly reward."

I had heard this message many times before. It was a favorite among preachers in the Purity-Christian Church. Reverend Finch used it many times. All the preachers could really get wound up over it, and it provided the springboard to go into other stories and Bible verses. Most often the preachers picked verses from here and there to make their point. They used stories to get you feeling emotional.

And as Jacob Yokes spoke, somehow it touched me, and I desired to be good so that God would accept me.

It seemed Yokes could sense the emotional buildup in the audience, and he continued. "Do not forsake the assembling of the believers, but be faithful to the church . . . and we can be most thankful for the Purity-Christian Church."

He began to softly sing, "I'm so glad I'm a Purity-Christian. I'm so glad I'm a Purity-Christian, I'm so glad I'm a Purity-Christian, singing glory halleluiah, I'm a Purity-Christian."

The audience joined in, singing softly. It was a song I had sung many times in the different Purity-Christian churches I had attended, where we learned that Purity-Christians were the best Christians, much better than the Baptists and the Presbyterians. Baptists believe you can only get to heaven if you are baptized, and it only works if you are completely dunked under water. Presbyterians were false Christians because they drank and smoked and didn't believe in backsliding.

Yokes raised his hands and then lowered them and the audience became quiet. He was coming to the end of his message. "The students of this institution are setting an example for the world. You are the Purity-Christian Church of the future. I thank you for your diligence in prayer for this revival, and know that we will see mighty works during the coming week. Some students were diligent in forming a continual prayer chain, and I would like to thank them, for they know a chain should not be broken. There should be no weak links."

When he said this, he was looking at me.

I felt like the spotlights on the stage were rotating around, focusing all of their glaring light directly on me. My face burned in shame, and my throat tightened. I caught the eyes of a few students from my religion classes looking at me.

Mr. Grazer, the Dean of Men seemed to be glaring at me.

"Those who are faithful are honored." With each word that Yokes articulated, I felt the pressure of the stranglehold increasing. "Let us pray, that we will not fall into temptation and succumb to the weakness of the flesh. Jesus died for our sins. Now it is time to repent from backslidden ways, to repent and to lead lives of purity."

There was an altar call and at least a dozen students went forward and kneeled down at the long, low wooden bench in front. Groups of students kneeled around them, putting their hands on the backs of the repentant students. The girl who sang the special song went forward and kneeled next to a backslidden girl who was crying. She kneeled upright next to the girl, and unlike the other students assisting sinners, she kneeled with her back straight, putting one hand on the crying girl's back and raising the other into the air, her head tilted back, her blue eyes staring toward the ceiling.

Throughout the altar call I kept my head lowered, feeling the shame and rejection for being the one who broke the prayer chain. More than that, I felt alone and my soul was hollow.

The instant Jacob Yokes sounded the final amen I headed straight for the door. I passed the row where my favorite girl was seated and indeed it was the 'O' row. I glanced quickly in her direction. She was talking to a girl next to her.

I stepped outside, gulped fresh air, and quickly walked away from the auditorium. I needed to get away from the school. Emotions were rushing through me, but most of all I felt anger. I wondered how they could do this to me. I kicked the edge of the curb so hard that it actually hurt my foot.

I approached my car feeling deeply humiliated and told myself to get out of there and forget it.

9

The following morning I skipped breakfast, afraid to face any disapproving stares from my fellow students, and drove my car away from campus. To the west of the school I had spotted a city park with outside basketball courts. I thought it would be a good place to practice my jump shot.

After parking my car, I saw that there was a group of five colored guys playing half court basketball. We called them coloreds and that's what they called themselves, but I often felt it had a bad meaning when normal white people used the term. The colored guys were standing under the basket. One had a basketball under his arm and he was pointing at the face of another guy, swearing at him. The other guy was swearing back. I stood on the side and watched.

When they saw me, they immediately stopped. "What you want?" the player with the ball asked.

I felt uncomfortable. "Nothing. Can I shoot some baskets?" I pointed to the basket at the other end of the court that was not being used.

"Sure," he said. "You wanna play?"

I nodded my head, and in a minute we were playing three on three half-court.

They were great players, older than me, maybe between twenty-five to thirty years old. It was fun to play with them. When someone got fouled, it usually ended up in a heated argument, with one player accusing and the other contesting, but usually the ball went to the team that deserved it.

I never played with that many colored guys before. I mainly kept my mouth shut. They all seemed to know each other, and cursing seemed to be part of their way of acting toward each other.

No one cursed at me, maybe because I was younger than them, or maybe because they didn't know me. Or, maybe it was because of me being a white guy.

We played about two hours. I got banged a few times real good, but I found myself giving more effort than I had at any time over the past two weeks at PC Cru. I was relieved to be away from the school.

When we were finished, one of the colored guys said, "We play on Sa-deday mo'nin. You welcome to play."

"Thank you. I'd be happy to come," I said. I had a little bit of difficulty understanding him, because he spoke the way the colored people do, but I was thankful for his offer. It felt nice to be wanted by someone.

"You from round here?" he asked.

"I'm a freshman at Pasadena College,"

"That religious school?"

"I guess so," I replied.

"Ain't got no coluds in dat school. Wha-cha doing in dis neibo-hood?"

"I just want to play basketball," I said, thinking about what he had said about no colored people at PC Cru. There was one colored guy on the senior team who was a super basketball player, but he was the only one I saw in the school.

It also struck me that I hadn't been around colored people very much, except when we lived in Oakland for a few months when I was in grade school. But we never had any colored people in our church.

Once I overheard two men in my church talking about colored people. One said, "In the Bible the Negroes were cursed, and this curse goes on to all generations."

So from that I guessed that colored people were not allowed to be Christians.

The two men also said that the colored race is inferior and therefore intermarriage is wrong, and one of them said, "It's like marrying a monkey. Keep them on the trees." I remember that they both laughed.

That kind of talk made me uncomfortable, and I wondered if coloreds shouldn't be treated as normal, but wasn't sure about that. It was certainly interesting how these guys behaved. They seemed to laugh easily—so spontaneous. I somehow wished they would accept me, that might be friends.

"You be careful on dis side d-town," he said. "But, you come to play ball and we take care-ah you."

"You guys are great players," I remarked. "I learned a lot today."

"Come back. We teach you some more. We teach you bout life." He laughed.

I went back to my car, wondering if I had done the right thing by coming here. I was unaware that this might be a bad part of town, yet it was less than a mile to the west of PC Cru.

I drove back near PC Cru, found a small grocery store and parked my car. I headed for the front door, intending to buy a Coke and a package of Twinkies, considering to skip lunch at the school. The revival from the previous night was coming back into my mind and I didn't feel like going back to the school.

The door of the store opened, and a man came out carrying a brown paper bag. He looked familiar, and as I was about to pass him, I realized it was Coach Smyth.

"Hello Mr. Smyth," I said.

He stopped with a surprised look on his face.

"Hello," I repeated. "Robert Macon. I'm a freshman at PC Cru—from San Diego Purity-Christian Church. We talked about the basketball scholarship." My stomach felt tight.

"Right, right," he said, acting like he remembered.

I wasn't so convinced.

"Great, you made it here. Do you want to play ball?"

"Sure. That's why I came. In fact, I've been coming by your office almost every day. I wanted to talk about the scholarship."

"What about it? You want to play for PC Cru, right?"

"Of course." I had just told him that.

"Why don't you come by my office on Monday morning and we can talk about it. We start working out the line-ups the first day of practice, Monday afternoon. Be there." He started to walk off.

"But, the scholarship?"

"Like I said, we'll talk about it. We're having some trouble with funding right now. Think about the values you will learn at PC Cru. It's an important decision in your life. I've got to go. See you Monday."

I watched as he crossed the street and got into a car. Someone with a large beehive hairdo was waiting in the passenger seat but I couldn't see who it was.

10

As I drove back to the dorm, the encounter with Coach Smyth kept going through my mind and it made me feel uncomfortable. Today he wasn't as friendly as he had been when I first met him in the parking lot of my church in San Diego. In fact, it seemed he hardly recognized me. Maybe he had things on his mind. There was someone waiting in his car, so he probably had to go somewhere.

At the same time he had offered to see me on Monday, which gave some hope. But being back at the dorm made me feel uneasy and I definitely didn't want to meet any students. I dreaded having to go to the revival chapel services all of next week, especially with the way that some of the students and teachers were looking at me.

I was determined to live it through. My experience from all the different schools I'd attended was that the storm would pass if you kept a low profile. At least most of the time that seemed to work.

There was a knock on my door and it opened before I could say anything. It was Leyland McGrath. "Come on. You need to get out of here," he said.

"Where we going?" I asked.

"Drive me somewhere," he said.

"Where?"

"I'll navigate, and you just drive." He smiled.

We drove through Pasadena and he directed me to downtown Los Angeles, and then we parked in an area with dilapidated old buildings.

Leyland turned to me with a smile and said, "Movie-time. Twenty-five cent movie-time."

"But we can't." I said, " I don't feel good about it. And what if the school finds out?"

"How can they find out? Anyway, it's the weekend. The rules don't count as much."

"What kind of logic is that?"

"Leyland logic. It's just over there. Let's go."

Across the street was a run-down movie theatre.

"What movie is it?" I asked. I had never been inside a movie theatre, although I had seen plenty of movies on television.

"Around the World in Eighty Days. It's supposed to be a great movie."

Leyland insisted on paying for my ticket, and we went inside.

It was dark and smelled stale. My eyes adjusted, and I saw that the theatre belonged to a different era. The inlaid motifs on the walls and once ornate balconies were now faded and crumbling.

Stumbling over a snoring body sprawled out on one of the worn velvet seats, I kicked an empty bottle and sent it clattering across the floor. Apparently a collection of skid-row bums had decided that the twenty-five cent, all-you-can-watch entrance fee offered the most comfortable shelter for the price.

I felt excitement when the movie started. It was in color. I had never seen a movie in color. I had read an article in Popular Mechanics about scientists making color TV's, but they said it was a long way off and they would be very expensive to buy.

The movie was based on a Jules Verne novel and it was wonderful. It had transported me into a world I only dreamed of, a world of freedom and excitement, where the main character, Phileas Fogg had the courage to defy social norms and break out to a realm with unlimited possibilities for adventure. I wanted to stay and let my mind run free. But there was a gnawing sense of guilt and Reverend Finch' warning of what would happen if the Lord came back and he found me in a movie theatre. There was also the fact that I was purposely breaking one of the rules of the Community Living Covenant that I'd promised to adhere to.

I had to get out of there. I didn't want to be caught in sin.

#

On Monday morning, I was still thinking about the movie. I had enjoyed it. In fact I laughed when I thought of how Phileas Fogg and his valet had done so many fun things. It was exciting and wonderful. Somehow it also gave me a sense of guilt, like I had back-slidden. Reverend Finch and the other leaders in the church said that movies were sin and this was also reflected in the community covenant I had signed. If you backslide you go to hell and the thought of that terrified me. I vowed that I would put myself on the right track and from now on keep all the rules.

But in the bottom of my heart I knew I wouldn't mind seeing more movies like that, if I had the chance.

I had a one-hour break between classes, and I headed straight for the Athletic Department offices.

I walked in and smiled at Miss Walker in an attempt to be polite. She didn't look up until I stood directly in front of her desk.

"Hello, Mr. Smyth asked me to see him on Monday morning. Is he here?"

"Let me see." She hoisted herself out of her chair with a sigh and disappeared into an adjacent office.

After several minutes she came back, sat down and motioned with her hand toward Mr. Smyth's door. "Go ahead," she said.

Plaques and framed certificates hung on the walls, and a collection of polished trophies rested on top of a filing cabinet.

Smyth looked up from his desk.

"Ready for practice this afternoon?" he asked, with no mention of our encounter on Saturday. Today was the first formal day of practice.

"Yes, sir," I said. "As we talked about, I'm here to see about the scholarship."

"I spoke with the committee this morning. Unfortunately, they had quite a few unexpected expenses this past year. The good news is that they talked about it and agreed to give you a scholarship for one fourth of your tuition."

"One fourth? I came here because you promised me a full scholarship."

"It didn't work out." Smyth shrugged his shoulders.

"I don't have enough money. Does that mean I have to pay for the rest of my tuition and my room and board?"

"The Finance Department said you already paid for it."

"I did, but I expected I would get some of it back. That was all the money I had."

"I've done everything I can for the moment. We'll have to go this semester with the way things are right now—see how the team does and how well you play. Maybe next semester will be different. Think of it as a trial period."

I was stunned and didn't know what to think. This news caught me completely by surprise. My mind went blank and all I could say was "Okay."

"One other thing." The sharpness in Smyth' voice pierced me. "We demand the highest character from our athletes. The other students are watching you, and we expect you to demonstrate the highest standards of moral and academic leadership. We don't want any unfounded rumors going around."

"Yes, sir," I said, wondering if he knew that I went to see a movie. Or, was it something different?

"Practice starts at three o'clock. Don't be late."

"Yes, sir."

"Good. See you then," Smyth said, terminating the discussion.

As I left the office, Miss Walker looked up and asked, "Are you from San Diego Purity-Christian Church?"

"Yes. Why?"

"Just wondering. I'm the director of the PC Cru Women's Choir that sang there last May."

CHAPTER 11

Present Day

The airplane lands at Los Angeles International Airport and I clear customs and take a shuttle bus to an upscale hotel. I spend a fitful night. In the morning after a hot shower and several cups of coffee I check out and then drive away in the rental car that was delivered to the hotel. It is a Porsche like the one I have in Paris, a bit expensive to rent but I can afford it. It's what I'm used to driving, with the switches and a shift lever where they should be. But maybe it is more than that. It's having a familiar shelter for traveling through a foreign land.

I drive north on Highway 101 amazed at the stop-and-go traffic in LA, wondering how people can spend years of their lives existing like this. I drive carefully. Because of jetlag one's reactions can be slow. My head feels fuzzy.

The nine-hour time difference between Europe and California is a shock to the body clock, but it isn't only the time difference working on my mental condition. To be here in California after being away for so many decades makes me uneasy. I'm not sure what I'll discover, if anything. Hurts have been suppressed. Now it is time to deal with them.

Monique thought it would be helpful to revisit places and reflect on past events. It might give a new perspective. And even more helpful would be to talk with some long-lost people. She thought they might help put things into context, but she said I needed to be ready to face the truth because some things may be difficult to confront.

It is Tuesday and I have four days before I need to be in San Diego, to meet Eddie Bailey and attend a homecoming. He is one of three people on my list, but he is the only one I have been able to contact. For the next four days I plan to visit places and do research to try and find the others.

I reach Ventura and feel groggy so take an off ramp and head for a coffee shop on the opposite side of the street. I go inside and order a coffee, and a cinnamon roll that seems to be primarily made of sugar. Any French chef would be horrified by this and would call it candy rather than a pastry. The coffee is watered down compared to what they serve in Europe, but it is hot and gives me time to relax before heading north.

I reflect on the drive to Ventura. Things have changed. Years ago there were many more orchards and vacant fields between Los Angeles and Ventura. Now it seems like everything is houses and shopping centers and office buildings.

I think of the past and try and recall some of the scenes in the young man's story. Sometimes I like to think of him in the third person. It is a way of separating the present from a very different past, maybe it's a defense mechanism. When I attempt to recall the past I feel apprehensive, just as Monique predicted.

I remember how the athletic scholarship was denied to the young man and how that was the start of a downward path. Yet, it also began a spiritual quest.

But still I cannot really remember all the details, and again I wonder how the young man would tell his story, in his words and through his mental framework. Maybe after being here for a few days more memories will come to mind.

I pay for the coffee and cinnamon roll, hoping the caffeine and sugar will give me a boost to reach my next destination.

I head back to the car and after I unlock the door a girl approaches me

She says, "Are you heading north?"

In one hand she carries a small backpack. She's wearing sandals, tight low cut jeans, and a low cut cotton top.

I hesitate and then reply, "Yes. Going north."

She asks, "Do you have room for a hitchhiker?"

"Where are you going?" I ask.

"San Francisco."

"I'm not going that far, at least not today," I said.

"It's okay. As long as I can get further north."

I look at her and I'm not sure I want company, especially a young woman dressed as she is. But, having someone to talk with might keep me awake. In fact, it will only be for a couple of hours before I have to turn off from Highway 101, so that should be okay.

I give in. Maybe I'm vulnerable because of jetlag and because of what I've gone through in the past few months. "How about San Luis Obispo?" I say.

"That would be great," She says.

After we get in the car I start it up and head up the onramp and onto the freeway.

I turn to look at her and notice that her cotton top has dropped quite a bit and is revealing much of the top of her breasts. There is a snake tattooed on one of them. There's also a butterfly tattooed on her arm just below her left elbow.

"This is a super nice car," she remarks.

"Thanks," I reply.

"I've never been in a Porsche before. I guess they cost a lot," she says.

"More than most cars, but this is a rental."

Her eyes grow wide. "You rent this? That must cost a fortune."

"Some," I reply, trying to keep it vague.

She turns to me, smiles and says, "Do you need a girlfriend?"

I don't know if she is kidding, coming on to me, or what, and I wonder what I've gotten myself into.

CHAPTER 12

Freshman: 1965-1966

When I left Coach Smyth's office, the reality of what he said was sinking in. My chest felt heavy. I had trusted him when he said he would give me a full scholarship, even turning down a chance to play at San Diego State. And now he changed his mind so flippantly, and then he lectured me about character. Hadn't he in fact lied? Why were others getting athletic scholarships and not me?

It seemed like some people were turning against me, both students and teachers. Miss Walker always looked at me in a mean way. In walking across campus I had seen Mr. Grazer a couple of times and he always seemed to stare at me, which made me feel uneasy.

I thought about whether I had any alternatives and what to do. I had already paid my full tuition and I don't think they would give it back if I left the school. I was stuck. It was too late to go anywhere else. I'd started to make some friends here, so I figured I'd just have to work hard, do my best, and see how it went. Maybe the school really didn't have the money to give the scholarship. But if they didn't have it now, how were they going to have it next semester?

In fact, the more I thought about it the more a sense of deep anger welled up inside me, like a big wave. I told myself that I am trapped, they took advantage of me, and there seems to be no way out.

I was stuck, but vowed to prove myself on the basketball court. I knew that every school has its social sport, the one that gets a disproportionate amount of attention. The players are campus stars. Perhaps that was where I might win the favor of the students and staff.

The freshman basketball team practiced every day for two hours. I rarely saw Coach Smyth. I assumed he devoted most of his attention to the senior team. The coach of the freshman team was Mr. Brock, and he was the assistant coach to Coach Smyth at the senior games.

After a few days I realized that the practices were much easier than what I'd had in high school. In high school we worked on fundamentals. Here, the coach just threw out the ball and we played full court. That was okay for me because I like to play, but I knew I wouldn't progress enough. On weeknights after dinner I went to the gym and worked on my shooting. Saturday mornings with the colored guys was also helpful.

It allowed me to vent my anger, and the feeling of physical exhaustion seemed to release some of my emotional exhaustion. It felt good.

I attended the first practice game of the senior team against Westmont College from Santa Barbara. And, I was surprised to see the best players didn't start the game.

After awhile, I got to know some of them, and we began playing against each other on weekends.

One late evening at the gym, I happened to talk with the starting point guard on the senior team. I had regularly been watching the senior team practice and it seemed that Coach Smyth wasn't at all the practices. Instead an assistant coach had been running all the drills.

"Why does Coach Smyth miss so many practice sessions," I asked.

"Oh, Smyth? The invisible coach? He laughed. "Honestly, I don't understand it. We've always been told that he has a lot of fundraising responsibilities—networking and the like, you know. But still, if he's the coach, you'd think he'd be around more." He shrugged his shoulders. "On the other hand, I'm not complaining. I came here to play basketball, and he plays me, so what does it matter? With that, he picked up a ball, dribbled to the top of the free throw line and threw up a jump shot. He missed the rim.

I turned to leave the gym when I heard the player's voice behind me. "Hey. Here's some advice. He'll play you if he likes you. You have to brown-nose him."

What he said didn't make sense, or did it? But somehow I thought he might be right and in realizing this, confusion and disbelief fell on me like a cement block.

Some days later at another senior team practice I sat next to a student who wrote the sports column in the school newspaper.

He introduced himself as Mark, a senior, and said he'd been watching me play. "You've got a good shot, and you're tough on the boards. You keep your head up and watch what's going on, anticipating—not like many of the other players. What position did you play in high school?" he asked.

"More or less everything," I responded. "I went to four different high schools because my family moved all the time, and every coach put me in a different position. I can bring the ball down on a fast break, shoot from outside and inside, and I like to bump inside."

He said, "I've been watching the players. The freshman team looks pretty strong, that is, if they put the right guys out on the floor. I have my doubts about the senior team."

I thought I understood what he meant by that. I said, "At the last senior practice game against Westmont College I noticed that they didn't start all the best players, at least the ones I thought were best. They lost when I think they could have won."

Mark looked both ways. "I once interviewed Smyth for an article in the school newspaper. His line is that he plays the older guys because they have more experience. He says they may not be as athletically good as some of the sophomores and juniors, but experience counts."

"Does that make sense?"

"Yes and no. When you're in a tight situation, experience is important. You want people on the court who aren't going to get nervous and turn over the ball. And it is preferable to put guys on the floor that play well together."

"But why do you say no?"

"Oh, just sort of my own little theory."

"Which is . . .?"

The sports writer looked around again, and lowered his voice. "I probably shouldn't be saying this, but I've been observing the same thing for the past four years. Between you and me, Smyth plays his favorites."

"What do you mean?" I looked at him quizzically.

"I've been around here awhile, and I know these guys. If you watch closely, you'll see that most of the guys who get playing time are those whose parents have some kind of connections inside the Purity-Christian Church."

"Connections?" This was sounding stranger by the minute.

"That's what I said. Their dads are high-ups in the church organizational hierarchy, pastors or missionaries . . . or their parents give money to the school and the church. If these guys aren't the greatest, Smyth will add one or two solid players on the court. More often than not, the team wins because of the superior skills of those solid players. In the end, it's more a game of politics than basketball."

"Come on, he wouldn't do that," I said, really hoping this guy was wrong, but it made me nervous. My parents attended the Purity-Christian Church, but we didn't have much money because my stepfather worked in construction. And, they didn't really have any connections. Now, Leyland's father was high up and Eddie's father was a Purity-Christian chaplain in the Navy. They had connections, but of course Leyland and Eddie didn't play basketball.

"Like I said, it's just my theory. Don't pass it on, or at least don't tell anyone it came from me." He stood up.

"Sure, whatever," I replied.

"And you might also want to think about your own future here in the school as a basketball player. See you later."

When he said that, I felt even more anxious. The doubts increased in my mind on whether I did the right thing by coming here. I resolved more than ever to prove myself, to be a great player and to get the scholarship.

I went back to my room and Eddie wasn't there again. I noticed he wasn't around very much and he didn't tell me what he was up to.

After trying to study for a while I picked up the latest copy of *Sports Illustrated* and became engrossed in an article about the Los Angeles Rams professional football team. At eleven o'clock Eddie crawled in through the window of our room, as the front doors to the dorm were locked at ten.

"Where've you been?" I asked.

He had a grin. "Treasure hunting," he said. In his hand he had a cloth bag full of something and he went over to his desk and poured out a pile of coins.

"Where'd you get that?" I asked.

"Huntington Gardens," he replied.

"What's that?"

"Down in South Pasadena some rich guy turned his yard into public gardens so that he could show off his huge house. People stroll around there on the weekends and admire the flowers."

"But, why the coins?"

"They have a large fountain, a wishing fountain where people throw their pennies, dimes, quarters. It's there just there for the taking. You can go in through a hole in the hedge. There's no one around at night, and all you need to do is wade in and fill your pockets."

"You're taking the coins!" I exclaimed.

"No, I'm helping the gardeners clean the fountain." He laughed.

After counting all the coins he had twenty-six dollars and thirty-one cents.

"Not bad for a few minutes of work. You've got to come with me next time."

"No way," I said.

After a few seconds I laughed, poking him in the arm, calling him "Eddie the fountain-fisher."

13

We had our first game. It was against Cal Tech, and I was nervous. Coach Brock didn't start me, but after ten minutes he put me in as a substitute to relieve another player. "Take a break," he said to the other player. "In two minutes you're back in."

The first time I got the ball out on the forward position I made a fake step left and the guy went for it. I quickly dribbled, stepped past him and had a clear path to the basket. After two dribbles I went up over the rim and dunked the ball. One of the Saturday morning colored players had used that same move on me over at the park, and then afterwards he showed me how to do it.

I was so surprised. It was the first time I had ever dunked in a game. Sure, I did it lots during lay-ups, but to do it in a game was something different.

During the two minutes I gave it everything I had, blocking shots, stealing the ball once, getting rebounds and scoring eight points.

I had a feeling the Saturday morning basketball guys would be proud of me.

In the locker room Coach Brock congratulated us on our first win, and told us how important it was to remain focused for the rest of the season. He pulled me aside and said I would be getting more playing time if I continued to play like today, but he reprimanded me for forcing my shots after getting offensive rebounds. Instead, Coach Brock wanted me to pass it out to one of our open guys so they could take the shot. He named off a couple of names, saying I should be giving the ball to them.

While the other players showered and got dressed, I went back to the gym and shot baskets, losing track of time, needing to get over what Coach Brock had said to me. I was disappointed in how he coached basketball and disagreed with him. In high school I was taught that when you had an open, high percentage shot, you took it. If you got a rebound under the basket you went hard back toward the basket either for an easy lay-in or to draw a foul. It was stupid to throw the ball out to some poor shooter at the top of the key who would force a dim-witted shot.

I suddenly realized it was ten minutes before ten o'clock, the dorm curfew. I broke into a run across campus to get back to my room in time.

When I went through the front door Donald Bonen, the Dorm Assistant, was there with a clipboard in his hand.

"You're late," he said.

"I'm sorry," I said, looking at the watch on his hand and seeing it was one minute after ten o'clock. There was no way it would have taken me eleven minutes to run from the gym to the dorm. It was more like three.

"Is your watch on time?" I asked.

"Stupid argument, Macon. I have to tick your name. Two more and you have to go see Mr. Grazer, the Dean of Men. You're already being watched because of breaking the prayer chain . . . and other things."

I wasn't quick on the uptake. Other things? I wasn't sure what he meant but was afraid to ask, not wanting to get further into trouble. Instead, I watched him write my name down and then put a tick in front of it. He had a satisfied look on his face, like he had just won a small prize.

I walked toward my room and met Leyland in the hallway, wearing a bright blue t-shirt with a K inside of a circle emblazoned on the front.

"You look sad," he said.

"Just got written up for being late. My first tick. Two more and I have to see the Dean of Men."

Leyland looked down at his watch. "It's not ten yet. Was it Donald?"

"Yeah."

"He's an ass. I'll go talk to him."

"I don't want to get in trouble," I stated, feeling uneasy that Leyland might start a stink, and then I would be even more worse off.

"Wait here," Leyland said.

#

Five minutes later Leyland came back. "It's fixed," he said. I was so relieved. "How did you do it?"

"Showed him my watch, said his was off, and then started to talk about the Purity-Christian Church, the headquarters in Tulsa, and about introducing him to my father the denomination president . . . things like that."

"Why do that?"

"Just trust me. Your tick was taken off against your name, but be careful of that guy."

I felt relieved. "Thanks so much." Then I saw something on his t-shirt that caught my attention. "What's your t-shirt about, the 'K'? I saw a few of them around campus."

"You haven't heard about Circle K? Didn't you see the signs in the student center?"

I vaguely remembered seeing something, but I didn't really take notice.

"They were looking for a few new members. You remember my two friends from Tulsa, the two guys we met on the way to sign up for intramural sports? They're both in it, and they introduced me to other guys in it. I decided to join. Seems to be the thing to do. The teachers look favorably at the Circle K guys."

"What is it exactly?"

"Theoretically it's some kind of service organization, but in reality it's more of a social club. Get to know the right people, if you know what I mean. We meet every Wednesday at five p.m. with the idea to raise money for good causes. If you want to join, next week's meeting is the last opportunity for this semester. But you have to be sponsored by one of the members."

"Sounds interesting, but I can't. I've got basketball practice on Wednesdays."

"Too bad. Circle K members get the best-looking girls. But don't worry, basketball players are next in the pecking order." He laughed and went up the stairs toward his room.

I went in my room and saw Eddie sitting at his desk, his back turned to the door. He rarely sat at his desk.

"What are you doing?" I asked.

"Playing a game," he answered.

I reached for my soap and towel, and noticed a deck of cards spread out in front of him.

"That's against the rules!" I exclaimed.

He looked up at me. "C'mon, Robert, don't get so worked up. It's only Solitaire. Anyway, they made the card-playing rule because they don't want us to gamble, and I'm not gambling. See?" He lifted up his hands to prove it.

"Right," I said, stretching out the word. "What if someone finds out? Like that dorm attendant; Donald, for example. Maybe you shouldn't play in the room."

"Yeah, yeah, whatever. Thanks for the thought."

On the way out of the room, I walked past Eddie's open closet. An unpleasant odor greeted my nose. I had smelled it in our room before.

"What's that smell? Have you been around people who smoke?"

Eddie laid down the cards and turned to me. "Can I tell you something, a secret, and you can't tell anyone?"

"Sure, I guess," I said.

"You don't tell anyone."

"What is it?" I asked.

Eddie shot me a deprecating look.

"Fine, fine, I promise."

Reaching over, he took a book off the shelf and opened it. A rectangular space had been cut out of the middle, exactly the right size to fit the pack of Marlboro cigarettes hidden inside.

"I smoke," he said.

"You smoke?" His revelation hit me hard. Guys who hung out at bars smoked. Lower class people smoked. It was dirty. The church listed it as one of the worst sins.

"Since my second year of high school."

"Why don't you stop?" I asked, knowing that cigarettes were addictive, having been taught that it was the devil's way to control your soul.

"Don't want to," he replied. "I could stop, but I enjoy a cigarette from time to time . . . never more than two or three a day."

I didn't know what to say. I knew that Eddie was fun to be with, and he did goofy things, but this was difficult to take. I raised my hands in the air and said, "Go ahead and kill yourself. How do you think that makes God feel?"

"What? Loosen up my friend. You gotta try one." He took one out of the pack and tried to hand it to me.

"No way!" I exclaimed, not wanting to touch the filthy thing.

He laughed and put the cigarette pack back in its place in the book and then slid the book back into its place on the shelf. He gathered his cards into a pile and started shuffling them. "Okay, Robert, but understand that I don't see things the same way."

"Sure," I conceded. "As long as you keep this place aired out and don't smoke on campus. Oh, and one last thing," I added. "Remember that form we had to sign at orientation? It said if you smoke or do any of those other prohibited things, you surrender the privilege of being a student at PC Cru."

Eddie banged the stack of cards on the desk to straighten them and laughed. "Strange way of saying they'll give you the boot . . . but try and understand that there are some people who don't get kicked out."

14

The revelation that Eddie was smoking was a shock to me, and that he was playing cards. He would definitely get in trouble if they found out. More than that, I felt sad for him. He had definitely backslidden and if God came back and found him doing those things, then Eddie was bound for eternal fire.

At the same time, part of me secretly admired him for breaking so many rules seemingly unaffected. I wondered how he could do that and felt he was an incredible guy. When I thought that a big smile came on my face, and my next question was, "what about me?" But no, that wasn't a good answer.

The problem was that I didn't know what to do about Eddie. It was hard enough to keep my own life on track. I came to the conclusion that the best way to help Eddie was to provide a good example. That's what I would do.

The fall revival came and went, and the next big event at the school was Homecoming. Regular announcements were made in chapel. Even Mr. Grazer, the Dean of Men, took the podium and commanded that all students be on their best behavior during the Homecoming weekend: to keep their rooms clean and to make sure they "dressed appropriately." He wasn't clear on what appropriate dress was, but it seemed most students understood what he meant. He instructed us in a severe and commanding way, and it got everybody's attention.

I found it amazing how people often referred to him, especially Donald Bonen, who used his name as some kind of threatening club.

I discovered that Homecoming was the weekend when alumni, parents and church members came from all over the country to connect with acquaintances and friends in the Purity-Christian circle, and to relive their college days.

Leyland said that, "the wealthier ones came to evaluate the recipient of their donations or to consider becoming substantial benefactors, and the church leaders would use the event to inspect the spiritual condition of the school."

Sometimes Leyland could talk real eloquent.

He also said that's why the administration and professors were so nervous.

On Saturday evening was the Homecoming basketball game, which I planned to attend. Eddie was gone most of the day on one of his mysterious disappearances, so I spent the morning shooting baskets until I was kicked off the court because it was reserved for the alumni practice. Before the Homecoming game there was the alumni game where players from the previous PC Cru teams played against each other.

For the rest of the day I hung out in my room, or walked around campus to watch all the alumni and dignitaries who tended to stand around in little groups either talking about the good old times, or what happened to so-and-so.

During the day I saw my mystery girl again, the one from the "O" row in chapel. Leyland told me that her name was Pamela Owens and that her father had some kind of important position in the church hierarchy. She was standing with a group of older people and looked bored. I tried not to 'gawk' at her, as Eddie said I was inclined to do around girls. But I couldn't help but notice her fine complexion and shapely body. She did look over at me but I turned away and continued walking to the dorm. Her image often rested in my mind, as it did for the rest of the day.

Shortly before the senior game was to start, Eddie came into the dorm room carrying a brown paper bag.

"Where you been?" I asked.

"Playing golf," he said.

Eddie often played several times a week, and some other students who played with him said he was really good. He had discovered right away that golf wasn't my game, so he quit asking me to join him.

"Did you win?" I asked.

"Yeah. Won some money today."

"You bet on your game?" I questioned.

"It was just a small alumni versus students tournament. I played with three alumni guys and challenged them before the game, making a little wager—ten bucks each. Beat all three of them." He smiled.

"You made thirty dollars! That's great," I exclaimed. Then I realized something different and asked, "Isn't that gambling. The Purity-Christian alumni guys gambled?"

"If you want to call it that. These are all rich guys who give money to the school. They are not bad to get to know, and golf's a good way to do it." He pulled three ten-dollar bills out of his pocket and waved them through the air. "I'll treat you to the twenty-five cent movies."

"We can go for a lot of weeks with that kind of money," I said, letting out a laugh.

"What's in the bag?"

He reached in and pulled out a swimmers mask and snorkel and then a flashlight.

"What's that?"

"An underwater flashlight. While playing golf today I got an idea."

"What's the idea?"

"You'll see."

I shrugged my shoulders, knowing that Eddie kept his ideas to himself. "You going to the Homecoming game?"

"No, I'm going to try out my idea."

#

PCCru played against another small Christian college. The auditorium was absolutely packed when I arrived. I saw that a lot of guys came with dates. I came a little late and all the seats were taken, so I sat on steps in the back of the auditorium not far from the entrance door. I had a good view of the court and the stage on the opposite side.

On the stage were a row of seats where the president of the school sat, along with Mr. Grazer, the Dean of Men, and a whole string of dignitaries from Tulsa, including Leyland's parents. Below them, next to the basketball court, the basketball team sat on a long wooden bench, with Coach Smyth having a chair right at the end of the bench next to the officials' table at half court. The layout of the entire building gave me the sense that this was a carefully drawn architectural concept where everything centered on Coach Smyth.

I watched the two teams warm up and felt someone brush by me. I looked up and was surprised to see Pamela Owens.

She turned and said, "I'm sorry," giving me a sly smile, her gray-blue eyes staring deep into mine.

She looked beautiful, not one hair out of place, her face a fair, perfectly clear complexion. She wore a light blue cotton dress with a white collar, the dress coming down to her calves. From where I was seated I saw the shape of her legs that disappeared into round hips and a narrow waist. "Ga-a-a, it was fine," I stammered, feeling my heart melt and wondering what shade of bright red my face was becoming.

She smiled, turned and walked down the steps.

A guy walked past who I thought was a senior and he looked down at me, his face stern, and his eyes glaring. He caught up with Pamela and put his hand on her arm. They made their way to the front row where someone was keeping two seats free for them.

I watched them sit down feeling a mix of emotions, but mostly jealousy. I didn't like the way the guy looked at me. But, the way she looked at me stirred my inner being.

The game started. The opposing team was terrible and from the first minute it was obvious that PC Cru would win. That gave Coach Smyth an opportunity to play his favorites, the sons of pastors and wealthy donors.

At halftime they crowned the Homecoming king and queen. It was Donald Bonen and the girl who sang the solo at the revival. The eyes of all the students were locked on them like they were something special.

I was glad when the teams came back on the court, but wasn't too impressed with the quality of the game. PC Cru blew a fifteen-point lead, and I wondered when Coach Smyth would put some of the best players back on the floor.

With three minutes left, PC Cru was only ahead by three points. Coach Smyth put the two best players into the game, and PC Cru ended up winning by seven points. The crowd gave a large applause at the end of the game.

Mr. Grazer along with some dignitaries from Tulsa made their way off the stage and gathered around Coach Smyth. They congratulated him, patting him on the back, laughing and putting on a show for all spectators.

I didn't care too much for that. My eyes were fixed on Pamela Owens.

15

The following Monday, while on my way to the Physiology of Exercise class, I noticed a few stray streamers scattered around in the grass. They were the last lingering remnants of the weekend's excitement.

I was relieved that Homecoming was over and even now found it difficult to relate to the event. It seemed to have little to do with most of the current students, unless you were part of the social elite. It was definitely a great event for the alumni and dignitaries, but it seemed a time where many of the students were alienated. If you were a girl and didn't get asked to the dinner or the game, then you were really at the bottom of the social ladder, and there were a lot who were not asked.

And me? I had never been on a date, and certainly wouldn't even know how to act around a girl if I had to take her to the Homecoming events. I was just glad it was over.

I walked past the library on my way to class and realized that after more than two months at PC Cru, I still hadn't the slightest clue what the inside of the library looked like. Grades were never that important to me. I usually did enough work to pass, and left it at that. I considered myself an athlete, not an academician. The only courses I had ever liked and done well in were math and algebra, but at PC Cru I didn't take anything in those subjects.

When I was honest with myself, none of my classes really interested me. Physiology of Exercise was hard to endure, mainly because of the way Coach Smyth taught it.

He rarely greeted us as he entered, flopping his disorganized notes on the desk. His lectures often diverged into irrelevant basketball illustrations that he carried on in great detail. When the class ended, he grabbed his scattered papers and disappeared out the door.

This morning he showed up with empty hands. "Please put your notebooks back into your bags, because we have an exceptional opportunity to see in real life what we have been studying."

Everyone in the class sat up.

He looked around the room, his face in its usual stare, but this time it seemed more intense.

"In the Biology lab, the pre-med students have been studying the human form, and we have an opportunity to learn from their work. I assume you all know the term 'cadaver'?

He paused, seeming to enjoy the confused expressions on our faces.

"We have an opportunity to study muscle groups and movements by seeing a real life example. I believe this will greatly enhance your understanding of human physiology."

The class was quiet.

"I must say that this is optional, but what you learn today will be helpful on Friday's exam. If there is anyone who would not want to participate, you may do so on your own volition. If you want to refrain from going, please raise your hand."

The eyes of everyone in the class surveyed everyone else.

Smyth smiled. "Then please follow me."

We followed him to the front of the science building, a massive brown brick structure and the newest building on campus.

Smyth led us down a tiled hall lined with heavy wooden doors. Some had small windows in them, allowing a glimpse of orange-carpeted offices, or rooms lined with cupboards, cabinets and strange metal machines. The rest were solid. I pictured laboratories full of beakers of bubbling liquid and strange concoctions.

We stopped in front of a solid door and waited for Smyth to unlock it. An eerie blue light illuminated his face as the door swung slowly open to reveal a windowless room. In the middle, a white cloth covered a long form atop a gleaming metal table. No one spoke a word as we gathered around the form. Smyth shut the door with a heavy thud, and abruptly switched on the lights. I squinted while my eyes adjusted.

In a casual tone, as if he were giving a regular lecture, Smyth began, "While for most of you, seeing a dead person is not an every day occurrence, it is a normal and important part of the study of human biology and physiology. It is much easier, for example, to understand the way that a tendon connects bone and muscle when you see it in real life than when you hear words like 'junction' and 'axis'." He paused.

"The woman whose body lies under this white cloth" . . . he motioned with his hand toward the table . . . "died of lung disease not long ago. She was thirty-six years old and a heavy smoker. You will see that her lungs are an abnormal color, but I would ask you to concentrate on her muscles rather than other internal organs."

Smyth walked to the head of the table, grasped two corners of the white cloth, and slowly lifted it off the body.

Several students gasped in revulsion. I swallowed, trying to push my stomach out of my throat. In front of me lay the pasty white form of a naked female. A neat incision stretched from the hollow of her neck all the way down to her dark pubic hair. On her right side, the skin remained in place, a flaccid white breast resting like a slightly mounded pancake on her chest. The left side had been carved into an uneven terrain of internal organs and substances. Smooth, dark, reddish-brown interspersed with bubbly gelatinous gray. Little chunks of pinkish-white flesh lay on the table beside it, remnants of the excavation.

A torrent of conflicting emotions churned inside of me, but at the same time a grotesque fascination kept my eyes fixed on the body.

Smyth pointed out the woman's lungs and heart. "In a healthy person, the lungs should be pink, but lung disease turned them almost black."

I followed his finger trace above her left lung. A gooey mass rested just underneath his finger, looking like runny purple peanut butter loosely held into an oblong shape.

He said, "It's unfortunate, but this is what happens if you live in sin, and in the case of our denomination her lifestyle is forbidden. We must live lives of purity."

He was looking at me when he said this.

My neck and cheeks felt hot. I thought of Eddie, smoking. Did Coach Smyth know about that? Was it now guilt by association because I was Eddie's roommate? Or was he looking at me because I had not told the authorities about Eddie's behavior? Or, was it something else.

The way Smyth stared at me gave me a deep sense of guilt. There were so many things I could feel guilty about, but I didn't know if there was something specific that warranted his somber face, eyes glued to mine. That gave me even more anxiety.

I almost wished he would talk to me directly, ask me questions, and try to understand me. These hints over a dead body are just sickening, I told myself as I took another step back and tried to hide myself,

Smyth looked back at the dead woman and moved on to the real purpose of the lesson, Smyth showed us exposed muscles in the woman's neck and the front of her body, naming them and explaining their functions. He continued with the major muscle groups in the left leg, which had been peeled of its skin but otherwise remained fully intact.

"Now let's talk a little bit about movement. God created the body with all kinds of special connections between muscles and bones that allow for a great deal of flexibility. The rotation of the arms in the shoulder socket is particularly interesting." He moved the woman's left arm.

At the shoulder, the medical students had completely severed the arm from the rest of the body, and it was just stuck back in place. Smyth lifted the woman's left arm to a ninety-degree angle with her body, and then turned it outward to demonstrate the different movements.

He moved it back and forth as though she was running. As he brought it down, he lost his grip on her wrist, and the arm slipped out of his hands and bounced onto the floor with a dull thud.

A girl screamed and collapsed. Two guys caught her and carried her out of the room.

"That's what happens when your ligaments break," Smyth said, reaching down to pick up the arm. As he bent over, I caught a sickening gleam in his eye and his lips twisted into a sinister smile.

He stood up and resumed a stern expression.

For the next ten minutes he continued to explain muscle groups, but some students weren't even watching, standing there with white faces, as in a stupor.

Finally he said, "I think that just about does it for today, unless there are any questions."

The room was silent.

Smyth spread the cloth back over the woman's legs and pelvis area, but left the top exposed. "We've had enough with the cadaver. Class dismissed."

Students headed for the exit.

I stayed a moment and forced myself to look at the woman. On her right side the skin seemed so smooth. It was difficult to know what her face looked like, because it was nothing more than muscle and bone, her teeth exposed in an ugly grimace. Her lungs sickened me, charcoal-purple, the color difficult to describe.

I wondered who she was and what her life was like. What caused her to smoke, to continue with this dependency that eventually killed her? Did she love? Did she have children? What was her joy and sadness? Did she know God? Where was her soul?

It was difficult to imagine her as a real person, yet she had been. And while I understood the importance of medical students to learn about the human body, I wondered why we were here. What was the real reason for this experiment? Was it just to pass on a message to me? And why did Smyth and the other staff seem to single me out? What had I really done but fall asleep in a prayer chain?

Confusion and disgust mingled with the strange smells in the room. I felt sad for all the students who had seen this, but mostly for the woman on the table.

I walked from the science building and took a breath of outdoor air. It was a warm day and there was smog in the air, burning my eyes and lungs. It frightened me that the smog might be doing to my lungs what I had just seen. I felt nauseated, like the day I ran the cross-country race.

Smyth had continually used the words, "The cadaver." Was that all she was; the cadaver? Eventually is that all we are? More than ever I was terrified of death and it made me desire to do the right things so that God would accept me into his eternity.

The one thing I resolved was to be more diligent in following the rules of the Purity-Christian Church and in doing so I would not sin. More than ever I wanted God to accept me. Then, maybe these teachers would also accept me?

16

I managed to keep a regular routine until Christmas. My parents were in the process of moving to Santa Cruz, so we decided to skip Christmas as a family. Instead, over the break, I stayed in the dorm and worked for the main post office in Pasadena, sorting mail for ten hours a day. It was the busy season, so they hired additional people. In the evenings I went to the gym and shot baskets and on Saturday mornings I went to play ball with the colored guys.

When Christmas break was finished and Eddie came back from San Diego, I learned somehow he had managed to get a master key for all the professors' offices. He said this would help him gain access to "study material" before important exams.

Basketball intensified in January. The freshman team played in a couple of small tournaments, and we came in first place both times. Our reputation on campus grew, and more people started coming to the freshman games, which usually took place just before the seniors. Practicing shooting in the evenings had helped move me up to the position of top scorer, and I was emerging as a prime candidate for the coming year's senior team.

I still had the feeling that Coach Smyth and some of the teachers continued to inspect me, but I also sensed different eyes on me. The uncomfortable feeling of being watched by teachers had been swallowed up by respectful admiration from my peers. As I walked around campus, more and more people were starting to smile at me, even the girls. Instead of me gawking at them, I caught some of them gawking at me. I was now sensing a strange sensation that I had never much felt before. I was suddenly proud, and happy about being proud.

In particular, I was getting smiles from two girls who came to most of the freshman team games. One of the other guys on the team asked me if I knew either of them. I said I didn't, and he just smiled. After that, I often caught them clapping enthusiastically when I scored a basket, got a rebound, or blocked a shot.

Most of the time, when our games ended, I stayed to watch the seniors play but after one game I was particularly tired, and I needed to get back to my room. I had a six-page paper due in the morning, and I didn't even know the assigned topic.

Showering quickly, I dressed and headed for the exit. I had to make a quick trip to the convenience store to grab caffeine for the long night ahead of me. I didn't even see the two girls standing outside the gym until they called out to me.

"Hi Robert." They waved and walked toward me.

"You played fantastic tonight."

"Thanks," I replied.

"You were the best," one of the girls said. Her cotton dress bulged in soft rolls on her chest, but she was rather large around the middle with a wide waist blending with wide hips. Like many of the girls at PC Cru she wore a gold chain around her neck with a small shiny gold cross suspended on it. "I'm Sandy, and this is Alice." She motioned to the petite slender girl next to her. "We come to all your games."

I could hardly break my gaze from Alice's sparkling green eyes.

"I've seen you there. Do you like basketball?" I asked.

"Oh yes," Sandy exclaimed. She smiled, and the light reflected off her silver braces. "We love to watch you play."

"Where are you going?" Alice asked.

"Thought I'd go get something to drink," I said.

"Hey, that's great. We were going to do the same thing," Alice said, her full lips forming a perfect smile as she beamed up at me.

They both stood there, looking at me.

"So…" I hesitated, "Do you want to come with me?"

"That would be fun," Alice answered.

"We can take my car," I offered, moving closer to Alice so I could walk beside her. Sandy came around to my other side.

At the car, I unlocked the passenger door, expecting Alice to get in.

"Oh no!" Alice exclaimed.

"What?"

"I just remembered that I have a paper due tomorrow, and I haven't finished it. I've got to go."

"Hey, wait, I have a paper due tomorrow too, and I haven't even started it. We can have a quick drink, and then work on our papers together when we get back."

"Thanks, but I really better go. You two enjoy yourselves." She waved and walked off.

I watched her until she disappeared. When I finally turned around, Sandy was already in the front seat. I closed the door for her and went around to the driver's side.

"Where shall we go?" she asked as I started the car.

"I'm not sure," I said, concentrating on backing up. "We can get a Coke or something."

"Okay," she agreed.

We went a few blocks to the closest drive-through restaurant and I bought two Cokes and then drove back in the direction of campus.

"Have you ever seen the lights of Los Angeles at night?" Sandy asked. Without waiting for an answer, she continued, "I know a place where there's a really beautiful view. Go right at the next light," she directed.

I followed her instructions, winding up into the hills around Pasadena, the nervous feeling in my stomach rising with the altitude. I didn't even try to make conversation.

And then I suddenly remembered something that made me feel worse . . . the student rules: 'No freshmen or sophomores allowed being alone with someone from the opposite sex. Freshmen and sophomores can only date on Friday nights. Only double dating for freshmen and sophomores.'

"Here," she indicated. We were at the top of a hill.

Bouncing along a dirt path next to a construction site, I slowed and came to a stop at the edge of the lot. The view was magnificent. The entire L.A. area stretched out before us, a mass of tiny sparkling lights fading into a glowing haze in the distance.

"Isn't this nice?" Sandy broke the silence.

"Not bad," I had to admit.

"Why don't we listen to music?" she suggested, turning the radio to a local pop music station.

I tried to relax and leaned back in my seat. She started asking questions, and I managed to keep up a decent conversation for a while, ending on the topic of her friend Alice. Silence fell again, and my thoughts drifted.

"So what do you want to do when you finish college?" Sandy interrupted my reverie.

"I'm not sure. Play basketball, maybe. I haven't thought much about it."

"Don't you think you should have some objectives? If you don't think about the future, you might end up wasting your life doing whatever seems fun at the moment. Most men want to have a good job and a family."

"I guess so," I said, sitting up straighter and staring out the windshield. I was going to be eighteen years old next month and hadn't really thought much about jobs and family.

She scooted toward me on the seat until her arm pressed against mine.

"Um, how about you?" I blurted. "What do you want to do?"

"I want to have a good life. To raise a family and make sure my children are taught the right things." She shifted and rubbed against me.

A moment later, the lights disappeared as she came around in front of me and placed her lips against mine.

I slid backward in my seat, but she placed her hands on my chest and moved along with me. Her braces scratched my upper lip as she kissed me again. Rotating my shoulders, I crammed myself between the steering wheel and the window, my back pressed hard against the door. She leaned farther forward until her chest rested against mine.

Her unrelenting lips slowly roused my body into action. My mouth responded to hers, and I moved my arms around behind her, kneading her back in small massaging motions. Instinct took over, and the motion intensified, our bodies writhing against each other in a quest for more.

A flaming fire filled me as she moved her mouth around to my ear. Panting, she whispered, "Robert, do you love me?"

I wasn't sure what I should say, yet the emotional volcano inside my being told me that I must be feeling something like that, so I mumbled back, "Uh . . . huh, I love you."

A soft groaning sound came from deep in her throat, and she buried her face in my neck, which ignited the fire even more.

I brought my hands around in front and groped for the top button of her dress. My thumb got stuck in the gold chain around her neck. I untangled it and flipped the chain and cross to the side fumbling with the fabric, I undid it and began on the next one. Suddenly, she jerked off of me and grabbed my hands, pushing them away from her.

"No!" she exclaimed.

I leaned toward her, and she jumped back over into the passenger seat. "Didn't you hear me? I said no."

She looked down and buttoned her dress back up. "I'm saving myself for marriage."

"Huh?" I asked, wondering how things went from hot to cold so fast.

Smoothing her hair, she said, "That is something sacred and holy, reserved for marriage."

"Uh huh," I mumbled, when all my emotions were focused on what was inside that dress.

"You said you love me," she said. "Love is a commitment, you know."

"Ah." I thought back to just a few moments ago. Did I say that I loved her? What was I thinking? My mind had been engrossed with other things and who knows what I said. I looked over at her as she sat rigid, squeezed against the corner of the door and the car seat, looking at me with indignant eyes. I put one hand on the steering wheel and the other on the car key in the ignition and said, "Maybe we gotta go?"

On the way back down the mountain to the college, she launched into an explication of what an honorable man ought to be, using Bible verses and examples of different men in the Purity-Christian Church.

I parked my car and walked her to the front of her dormitory, trying to be polite. A few people stood around talking as we approached. At the door, she turned to me and said in a voice loud enough for everyone to hear, "Robert, it's so wonderful that you told me that you love me."

I opened my mouth but nothing came out.

She looked me deeply in the eyes.

"I'm not so sure right now," I stammered.

"What do you mean you're not sure?" she asked, hurt flooding her tone.

A few people turned to look at us, their attention attracted by the screech in Sandy's voice.

"I just need to think about it a little bit," I said softly.

"You mean you really didn't mean it?"

"Well, yes and . . . no." I didn't know what I meant. I liked the feelings that she had drawn out of me, but I wasn't sure what to do with them.

"Yes and no?" she squeaked. "I think that means no. You really know how to take advantage of a girl." Bursting into sobs, she ran into the building.

I stood there frozen, staring at the empty doorway. Then I realized that a number of students were looking at me, and I slid off into the shadows, thankful for the darkness.

The next day on the way to class, Alice caught up to me from behind. "Robert!"

"Hey, how are you?" I asked before I caught the angry look on her face.

"How could you do that to my friend?" she burst out.

"Do what?"

"You told her your loved her, and then you tried to do some sinful things with her. If I had known you were like that, I wouldn't have come near you. You had better fix your mistake and make things right as soon as possible."

"I'll try," I said, though I didn't really understand what I needed to 'make right' or how she intended for me to do that.

"You'd better," she said.

17

A couple days later Eddie walked into our room and said, "Hey Robert, have you been thinking about your future? Are you preparing yourself to be a good husband and father?" Eddie put his hands on his hips and assumed a high-pitched voice. "And don't ever forget . . . this," he cupped imaginary breasts, "is for marriage." He rolled onto his bed, roaring with laughter.

#

For a while after the Sandy event I felt like a lowly piece of cracked sidewalk that people avoided stepping on, but then I began to see humor in what happened. After all I was only seventeen and no one ever taught me what you are supposed to do around girls. I never learned those things at the movies or anywhere else. Certainly our church never talked about relationships, other than the sin of evil thoughts.

I figured Sandy had lured me to that parking spot and then my desires took control like a rip tide. I was flying on instinct, and it was actually quite an amazing thing. At the end of the day, I came to the conclusion that she was a Purity-Christian denomination nut-case, probably like a lot more girls at this school.

If the officials at the school found out that I had broken one of the rules I didn't know what the punishment would be. Freshmen were not allowed to touch girls or be alone with them on a date.

I decided to stay away from girls after that and stick to basketball. At the same time, whenever I saw Pamela Owens on campus I had fascinations about her, but never got near her. And whenever I saw Sandy she would stiffen her back and turn her head away from me. I began to chuckle about this and thought of her as an old maid school teacher.

By March I found myself suddenly floating free in an endless sea of time. I was now eighteen years old. Basketball season had ended. I never got the full scholarship for the second semester although Coach Smyth increased it a bit over what they gave me the first semester.

I finished the season as the top scorer and rebounder on the freshman team. I could have easily scored more points, but Coach Brock was always on my back about kicking the ball out to one of the guards to take an open shot. I did a lot of that, but most of the time they missed.

A few other guys on the freshman team had full athletic scholarships but their statistics weren't nearly as good as mine.

I wondered if I should transfer to another school because I didn't have the finances to make it another year at Pasadena Purity-Christian. I took out a loan to pay for the semester, and knew I would have to work quite hard in the summer to pay it off.

I often went to the sports office to try and talk with Coach Smyth, but was only able to speak with Miss Walker. After her repeated rejections I finally gave up on my visits and began to wonder what to do in the future. Basketball was the only thing I really enjoyed.

While I had been anchored to the court, everyone else had been going in different directions. They had formed circles of friends, joined clubs, and settled into social routines.

Leyland urged me to join Circle K during their second semester acceptance rounds, but I wasn't interested. Eddie and a few of his friends went cruising on California Boulevard almost every evening. On Saturday mornings I still went over to play in the park with the colored guys. I think they liked me, and sometimes they even swore at me. It made me feel uneasy, but good to be accepted by them.

Mondays and Thursdays I had morning and afternoon classes, so I ate lunch in the cafeteria. Once in awhile Eddie would join me, but I usually sat by myself, reading or reviewing notes.

Flipping through a religion course textbook while I finished my last-minute preparation for an exam that afternoon, I lifted a forkful of macaroni and cheese to my mouth. A girl stood in front of me, holding her tray of food. "Is this place free?" she asked, motioning to the empty chair on the other side of the table.

I nodded.

She smiled and sat down. Something about her face struck me—it was more than just friendly—safe, sincere? I couldn't say. Most of the girls around here seemed to want attention, or they wanted something from you; you could read it in their every motion. After my episode with Sandy I avoided encounters with other girls at all costs.

"Crowded today, huh?" I asked when I had swallowed my mouthful.

"Yes," she said after a moment, lifting up her bowed head and placing her napkin in her lap.

"Ah . . . my name is Robert Macon." I closed the textbook and pushed it to the side of the table.

"I'm Georgia Rose."

I hadn't seen her before around campus. "Are you a student here?" I asked."

She reached for her glass of water. "Only part time and I live off campus. I work full time for a company in Pasadena. One has to pay the bills," she smiled."

"Yeah, you're right. This school is expensive."

She nodded and then we were quiet. My stomach had the jitters. To make conversation I asked, "How do you like PC Cru?"

"I'm not sure." Her voice softened.

"Why is that?"

She paused, then said, "It isn't exactly what I expected."

Georgia had caught my attention. That's something like what I was thinking.

"Why not?" I asked.

She smiled. "I wanted to try a Christian college."

I looked up. "What for?" I said it as if it would be stupid to do that.

She laughed at my reaction. "Well, I know this might sound trite, but I really want to deepen my faith."

When I heard that, I didn't know what to think, but my instincts were to get up and run. Was this another one of those Purity-Christian girls? I had learned from experience that some of the Purity-Christian girls were dangerous. Yet, I was curious, and she had very fair skin, soft light blond hair, sparkling blue eyes and lovely pink lips.

"How do you deepen your faith?" I asked. "I tried everything and nothing seems to work."

She looked at me inquisitively. "What do you mean, *tried*?"

"Going to church, being good, being sanctified. All that. Some people seem to live the right way, but it just makes me feel guilty."

She took a bite of food, put her fork down and said, "I don't see it that way. I don't have much of a church background. So, I found the link with God another way . . . I guess that's one way to put it"

I was curious. "How in the world could you find a link with God without going to church and living up to the doctrines and rules? Without that you can't be holy and God won't accept you."

She laughed a bit, softly, not like she was making fun of me, but as though she held an important truth. There was something about her face that radiated.

"Church is fine," she said. "We need church, but there is something more than that. Finding the link with God doesn't have to do with living up to standards and rules. It is simply responding to God's love and his forgiveness, and then living your life with him."

"Well, I've been going to church all my life, but whatever you're talking about isn't something I've ever heard."

"Maybe you heard, but you didn't listen."

That's all I needed was another person to tell me what I was doing wrong.

My jaw tightened. "Listen. What you are saying is not enough. You have to end up living an absolutely holy life. You have to do the altar-call and then get sanctified. For me it's just not working."

"Maybe you need to just stop working and allow God to take you for who you are, and then, from that to engage him in everything in your life."

"Without following rules?" I asked.

"Something like that," She said.

"That's not true religion. You have to strive to be holy. You need self will and you have to try hard, to have endeavor, because God holds you accountable." I felt I was playing back the same concepts I had been taught so long.

"How good do you have to be before God accepts you?" She asked.

"Perfect," I stated.

"That's the problem, and Christ takes care of the problem."

I didn't get what she said and it made me feel nervous. She was speaking something wrong, maybe even heretical. How could God take me for who I was? God didn't create us as robots but as creatures with self-will and he asked us to not stray from the straight and narrow or we would pay the consequences. She sounded like a religious nut.

Things got quiet between us as I finished my food. I stood up. "Sorry, I gotta run. My exam starts in ten minutes."

She looked up and said, "Thanks for the discussion."

"You too," I said, still feeling uncomfortable about her religion ideas.

"Good luck with the exam," she said.

"Yeah, sure," I said as I turned with my food tray and walked away.

#

I thought about what Georgia Rose had said and it made me increasingly nervous. I didn't think I understood all the theology she was talking about, but from what our church had taught us I knew there was something wrong in what she said. I decided she was just another one of the crazy girls that were in the school and decided to stay clear of her.

One evening Eddie was hanging his black leather jacket in front of the open window to air out the smell of smoke embedded in its fibers. He had shown up with the jacket a few weeks before and I wasn't sure where he got it. He looked like someone from one of those motorcycle movies from the fifties.

Eddie remarked, "You know, Robert, you need to get out more. You should have seen the hot-pants down on Colorado Boulevard tonight. Girls like nothing else. Whew!" He let out a low whistle.

I had seen that girls were starting to wear very tight shorts, which were known as 'hot-pants', but definitely not at our college where they still wore the long cotton dresses.

"Hey, by the way," he said, "Leyland mentioned this place that he knows about. He and I were talking about going tomorrow. Why don't you come with us?"

"What kind of a place?" I asked.

"What does it matter?" he replied, pulling his special book off the shelf and dropping a new pack of Marlboros in the secret compartment. "Anything's got to be better than staying in here all the time."

"Sure, I'll come," I said. I tossed aside some hand written notes that I'd been blindly staring at. I looked up at him and saw a smile on his face.

"What's the silly grin for?" I asked.

"I heard a rumor."

"What am I being accused of now?"

"Nothing like that, but it is about you."

"Like what?" Man, I was curious.

"You know Pamela Owens?" He asked.

The mention of her name made me feel light. I thought of her all the time.

Eddie laughed. "You should have seen your face when I mentioned her name."

"So what," I defensively said.

"You gawk at her so bad, it is unbelievable," he accused.

"Okay, I think she's beautiful. What's the rumor?"

"She has the hots for you."

I was stunned. Eddie played tricks, and I knew he was setting me up. "No way," I countered.

"No. I'm serious. She told some girls that you were cute."

"Me, cute? I am anything but cute."

"I agree with you, but she thinks so, and that's all that matters. She told them she's tired of typical Purity-Christian boys."

"I don't know what she is talking about. Anyway, she's a junior, maybe two or three years older than me. What would she want with a guy like me? And, her father is vice-president of the school." Somehow I had the feeling that the teachers and people in administration were looking at me, so why would an older girl, the daughter of the vice president, take an interest in me? It just didn't make sense.

"She's like Leyland and me," he said. "We have been inside the church boundaries all our lives, and sometimes we need to get out."

"Well, if she thinks I am her way out, she's thinking wrong."

"Why don't you do something then?"

"Like what? She's two years older than I am. She's gorgeous and probably wanted by every guy on campus. And, there's no way I'd ever get past her preacher dad."

"C'mon, Robert, you're put off too easily. That's your problem . . . you always see the obstacles, never the way around them. Try this for once: think, 'What would Eddie do?'"

I looked at him like he'd landed in the cuckoo's nest.

"And don't give me that look. This is your chance. Practice. What would Eddie do?"

"He'd buy a Playboy magazine and imagine her face in the centerfold," I spat out.

"Okay, maybe." A lusty twinkle filled his eyes. "But let's say I wanted her for real."

"I don't know. I don't have your imaginative mind."

"That's why we're doing this exercise." He assumed the voice of a patient schoolteacher explaining the concept of one plus one equals two to an obtuse student. "Fine. We'll start this way: I'll tell you what Eddie would do, and then you can think about it.

"First, I would see what I had: I'm a basketball star. That's a start. Then, I would think about what she might want. What do girls typically want? A sensitive and caring guy who's interested in them. So, you invite her to a basketball game and then you take her out afterward to a nice coffee shop, buy her a dessert and ask her about herself. And then you go smooch with her, and get your hands on those big knockers." He laughed.

I smiled, but felt defensive when he talked about her body. Although, if I was honest, she was often on my mind. I imagined how it would be if I were with her—the things we would do, how I would act and how she would act with me. But reality didn't work that way. And Eddie made it sound so easy. "She'll probably laugh in my face," I mumbled.

"Never know until you try," Eddie retorted.

That's it. That was the problem. I knew I would never try. But I kept imagining that I would like to have an opportunity.

CHAPTER 18

Present Day

I drive north in the Porsche with the young woman in the seat next to me. She had asked if I needed a girlfriend.

I let it pass and ask, "What's waiting for you in San Francisco?"

"Friends," she replies.

"Is that where you live?"

She says, "I went to school up there and graduated last spring from San Francisco State. Then I went with a guy to L.A. It was okay for a while but we decided to experience other relationships. Now I'm heading back to San Francisco."

"What was your major?" I ask.

"Economics and a Sociology minor," she answers.

"That's an unusual combination."

"I took the economics because of my parents. I'm not sure I'm really into it."

" So, what do you do now?" I ask.

"What do you mean?" She replies.

"Like your next step or work?"

"I don't know. There are too many options and no options, if you know what I mean? I can't decide."

She reaches for the radio and turns it on, and finds a station and asks, "Would you like some music?"

"Why not," I reply.

It was a pop station and they were starting to play a song with a female singer. I didn't catch her name.

"This is a cool song," she exclaims.

The singer's voice toggled back and forth between a normal voice and a cracking falsetto. It sounded like a cat in heat.

The girl next to me starts to move to the beat of the song, her shoulders and breasts bobbling back and forth. I wasn't sure if the song really had a fixed melody.

It is strange to listen to the music. I feel no connection to it. It is like I had gone one way and California had gone another. Sure I had observed cultural happenings in the United States, but the fact is, I no longer feel a part of it . . . or at least I'm several steps removed.

"My name is Brandy," she says.

I tell her my name.

She sticks out her hand and we shake hands. Her hand is firm and her skin is smooth.

"Nice to meet you," she says. "Where are you from?"

"Europe," I answer.

"Wow. You don't sound European."

"We have good schools over there." I smile.

"I want to go to Europe," she says.

I'm wondering if this is just conversation or a lead in to something more?

We ride a while listening to the next song, which is similar to the previous one, disjointed and lacking melody.

We talk about music and what young adults are into today in California.

I notice that at times her voice tends to be whiny and gravelly, unnatural, as thought her words are being de-fragmented into a hundred pieces, especially as she comes to words at the end of a sentence.

In recent movies and TV series, I've noticed that many young American females spoke like that. From Brandy's voice it tells me that this way of talking has transferred from cinema over into the general culture.

It makes me wonder how we sounded back in our day, what expressions we used and how we differentiated ourselves from the generations before us. One thing is sure. The younger generation of today holds to a different set of behavioral ideals than those valued when I was young. And, it is likely that the next generation will conform to something different.

Yet, how we think and act cannot be divorced from those who lived before us, for I've seen that the thoughts of one generation become the actions of the next. So, indeed we are products of the past.

My train of thought is interrupted when Brandy reaches across to turn down the radio and I again notice the butterfly tattoo on her arm.

"What does the tattoo signify?" I ask.

She smiles and points to the butterfly. "This one signifies life as we float from experience to experience." Then she points to the snake on her breast. "This one represents danger. Don't touch . . . unless you're a rich man who drives a Porsche." She laughs.

"I appreciate that," I say.

"You're cool," she says.

I take the discussion in another direction and ask, "Why did you get the tattoos?"

Her eyebrows rise. "What do you mean? It's an expression of individuality. Everyone is doing it. It's body art. It's cool."

I wait a moment and then ask, "If everyone's doing it, maybe it's not individuality. Maybe it's a cultural conformity."

Her lips tighten. "Cultural conformity? What do you mean?"

I pause for a moment and collect my thoughts. "Cultures adopt different values, that is, different ways of behaving. To use your phrase, they conform to what is accepted as being 'cool'. This can be simple fads, like urban cowboys of the 1970's or a desire to collect cabbage patch dolls, or beanie babies. Or, even tattoos. Of course it goes beyond fads, into such things as our worldview. And think of moral conventions." I waited then said, "You know, I've found it interesting to think of the underlying presuppositions behind all these conformities."

"It's not a fad or a conformity. It's a cultural expression." Her voice is sharp.

"That's what I'm trying to say."

"You sound like one of my sociology professors," she says. "And you're European. What would you know?"

I smile.

Brandy pulls her cotton blouse up to hide the snake, but can't quite cover all of it. Then she turns and stares out the window.

I drive and try and keep my eyes on the road ahead. She's a beautiful young woman, shoulder length wavy brown hair and brown eyes. There must be at least a thirty-five year age difference between us, if not more. The thing that separates us most is a divergence of worldviews. I glance at her again and think about Monique and what she said about identity.

Monique's hypothesis was that in today's western society the body has become the primary canvas on which many people express their identities, especially girls. She said the idea of 'self' no longer has underpinnings, as it has become a relativistic feeling. When this happens, then people lose the foundation for their identity, and externals become the reference points by which they define themselves.

Monique commented that body shape, weight, hairstyles, and clothing, as well as material possessions become the means through which many people define themselves, in an effort to express uniqueness. But in so doing they are conforming to exterior ideals rather than being directed by one's true inner being. For instance, many girls compare themselves with the popular girls and will do anything to be physically like them. They exercise and go on crash diets, and become obsessed by food. And sexual attractiveness and sexual expression become a primary way of validating themselves.

Monique had numerous cases of young women who were dealing with these types of issues. She even wrote a paper on it.

We ride a long time without talking. Brandy finally turns away from the side window and looks at me. Her top has again shifted down below the snake. I wonder if she is really aware of the impact this has on men.

She asks, "So, what's your answer?"

"My answer?"

"To life, to all of this." She waves her hand in front of her.

I grin. "That's a big question."

"You seem to be the answer man. Give it a shot," she says.

I think for a moment. "I'm not sure I have all the answers, but perhaps I can tell you about someone I knew, a long time ago. It was someone caught between conflicting cultural systems. He was conforming to them in ways he didn't realize. He suffered from them and he was lost. He also had his own internal nature to contend with, if you could call it that. Then, he began a quest."

"What do you mean by that? A quest?" She asks.

"He began to seek something deeper beyond cultural systems. You might call it true spirituality or the divine, that is, to connect to the unique living God."

Her face becomes still, as though she is lost in thought.

After a while she says, "I don't believe in that."

"In what?" I ask.

"The unique divine," she states.

"Why not?"

"Because we are all divine gods. We can all make our own beliefs and morality."

"Where did you learn that?" I ask.

"You don't learn it. Everyone knows it."

"If everyone knows it, then it may be one of those cultural conformities I talked about, or more like a cultural paradigm. But who knows, maybe they are wrong, like when everyone believed the world was flat, when in fact it is round. I guess I'd ask the origin of the belief, because it seems to me that being divine has to do with being the sustaining force of the universe. I'm not sure any of us have that quality."

She raises her lip and says, "You and your cultural conformities."

She turns and looks out the side window and is quiet.

We approach San Luis Obispo and I see the sign indicating that Highway One is five miles ahead. I take the next off ramp and park. Across the street was the on-ramp to Highway 101 north.

"That might be a good place to catch a ride north," I say. I reach in the back, find a piece of paper, write something on it, and then fold it a couple of times.

"Where are you going?" She asks.

"First to Morro Bay. Then north."

"How'd you like to hang out for a few days?" She asks.

I look at her. "You know, maybe it might have happened in another time and place. But I'm getting over something and need to be alone.

"A relationship?" she asks.

"Yes . . . a loss . . . but more than that."

"I might be able to help you," she says, leaning toward me and giving a lovely view of the entire snake and more.

For a moment I feel desire and temptation.

I say, "Thank you, but I need to be alone. I have to go."

"A missed opportunity," she states. Her eyes are expressing something like disappointment or rejection.

"Brandy, you don't need me or anyone else to validate your identity. I wish you the best."

She opens the door, gets out, bends down by the open window, and says, "Last chance."

I use this as an opportunity to hand her the piece of paper that I had written on, and say, "Consider this."

"You're weird," she says.

She takes the piece of paper and then shuts the door quite hard.

I watch her walk away.

CHAPTER 19

Freshman: 1965-1966

The weather was getting warm in California, and it wasn't conducive to studies. Spring fever was hitting the students, and a lot of them were doing silly pranks around the school. I didn't participate.

Eddie was spending more and more time away from the school on "business projects," as he called them. I found out that he was still making the evening runs to the wishing fountain at Huntington Gardens, but his activities had greatly expanded. He was going to different golf courses in the middle of the night and snorkeling for golf balls that had been lost in the ponds. And then he would resell the golf balls. He started a small gardening business, undercutting the prices of the Mexican gardeners, and he started a car wash and polish business. He hired college students to do the labor and he just ran the businesses.

I worked in the afternoons for the U.S. Post Office, as they paid well.

Over time I'd also noticed that our room was filling up with more things and asked Eddie about them.

"Borrowed," he said.

"From where?"

"Thrift shops and other places."

"You mean you took them?" I asked.

"Yep." Eddie nodded triumphantly. "The nightstand, radio, bookshelves," he pointed to each object as he named it, "lamp, binoculars, and," he opened his desk drawer with a flourish, "five wooden pipes and a dozen pairs of glasses."

Observing my surprise, he added, "People don't buy this stuff, and what are the stores going to do with it? I'm just doing them a service. We spare them the trouble of having to haul it away."

Besides taking coins from a fountain and lost golf balls from golf courses I realized that Eddie was expanding his reach. I hoped he would set some limits before it got him into trouble.

#

Saturdays were lazy days, and I still played with the colored guys in the morning. One Saturday afternoon, Leyland came into our room and asked if we would like to do something special.

We got in Eddie's car, Leyland in the front seat and me in the back.

"Where we going?" Eddie asked.

"Drive. I'll navigate," Leyland commanded. "We're going to see a friend."

Eddie asked, "Who's the friend?"

Leyland said, "She seems pretty cool, and from what I can tell, she's not in your typical Purity-Christian Church girl. I talked to her, and she invited me to come over in the afternoon and bring a few friends along."

We drove west some blocks almost to the area where I played basketball on Saturday mornings.

Eddie parked in front of a duplex, the only building on the street that didn't seem to have its windows boarded up.

Leyland knocked, and a voice called out, "Just a sec."

I heard keys rattling, and three locks clicked before the door opened.

A tall girl with long straight hair stood silhouetted in the light behind her.

"Hi, I'm Trixie," she said, smiling. "Come on in." A snug shirt highlighted her form, flashing glimpses of her belly button when she moved.

"Here, sit down on the couch, and I'll go get something to drink." Long, smooth legs disappeared around the corner into the kitchen.

I sunk into the soft cushions, the music from the record player filling my head. *I wish they all could be California girls.*

Trixie came back with four bottles of beer and opened them with a metal beer opener.

"Wow," I heard Leyland say.

Eddie had a big smile on his face.

She handed each of us a bottle.

Some kind of shame filled me as I took the cold bottle in my hand, but there was also a strong feeling of excitement.

"So, tell me a little bit about yourselves," she said, stretching out on a chair across from us.

Eddie and Leyland gulped down their beers. I held mine, considering it. What could be so bad about beer? Could it just be enjoyed without getting drunk? Then I put it on the table.

My mind was racing about what was happening. Somewhere along the way, I caught that she was studying languages with an emphasis on Greek.

When my turn came, I managed to get out my name and that I was majoring in Physical Education.

"You're an athlete, aren't you?" she asked. "I could have sworn it the moment I saw you."

"Yeah, I play basketball."

She lifted one leg and crossed it over the other. "I like watching basketball, but honestly, I'm thinking more of taking up surfing since moving to California. Have you ever been?" She looked me in the eyes.

I met her gaze for a moment, and then shifted my eyes away from her. "I surfed quite a bit as a kid."

"Really? We could go sometime."

The thought sent a warm chill through me. Water dripping off her sun-browned stomach…. "Uh, I didn't bring my surfboard here." My mind flashed to PC Cru and I wondered if they had any rules against surfboards?

"Too bad," she said. Hey, do you guys like to play cards?" she asked, turning to Leyland and Eddie.

"Sure," Leyland said.

"How about poker? Do you know the rules?" She pulled a deck out of a drawer in the table.

Leyland and Eddie nodded. They were half way through their beer.

"I've never played," I said.

"No problem. I'll teach you." She dealt five cards to each person and explained the rules. I wasn't quite sure I understood, but I hoped I'd catch on. I didn't want her to know that I had never played cards before in my life.

"Before we start, we have to think of something to gamble. The game's boring otherwise," she said.

"Like money?" Eddie asked.

"Nah, that's not very exciting. How about clothing? Strip poker, okay?"

I shifted nervously, but Leyland looked excited. "Sounds like fun," he said.

"The rule is that if you lose a hand, you take off a piece of clothing. Are you ready?"

"Yep." Eddie scooted forward in his seat.

I lost the first hand and took off a shoe. At the end of the second hand, I lost my other shoe, and shortly thereafter both my socks. I started paying more attention, my body tensing as I concentrated on the game.

After an hour, the pile of the clothing on the floor had grown considerably. Eddie, Leyland and I were down to only our pants before Trixie lost for the first time.

"Guess I'm a little behind you guys," she said with a mischievous smile, lifting her shirt and slowly slipping it over her head. California Dreaming by the Mamas and the Papas played in the background. Now wearing only a small, white bra, she sat back down as if nothing had happened and dealt another hand.

I excused myself to go to the bathroom. Splashing cold water on my face, I tried to still the boiling muddle churning inside of me.

After the next three rounds, three pairs of pants landed on the floor, and three pairs of hairy legs stuck out of boxer shorts.

I tried to focus on the cards on the table in front of me, but I couldn't keep my eyes away from Trixie's chest. I didn't notice that she had lost the hand until she stood up and said to Leyland, "What should it be? The sandals or the shorts?"

"You know what," Leyland said. He leaned back into the couch, and folding his hands behind his head.

Putting her hands on her hips, she cocked her head to the side and asked, "What?"

"Oh, come on." He looked away, reddening slightly. "The shorts."

Her fingers reached for the button, and it seemed like forever before she slid the zipper downward.

I couldn't think. I fumbled with the cards in my hand and forgot how to play. The round ended, and I lost. I sat motionless, frozen to the couch. In an almost involuntary movement I took my beer off the table and took a sip. It was bitter and I couldn't say I really liked it.

"Are we still playing?" Trixie asked. "Take them off. We have to play one more hand after someone loses."

I dropped my boxers, and felt the flames rising in my face as Trixie looked at me. I sat back down as fast as possible and pulled my knees up to my chest, and lost the next hand almost before it was dealt.

Trixie announced, "That's it. Game's over."

Scrambling for my clothes, I dressed as fast as possible. By the time I had buttoned the last button on my shirt, Trixie was just stepping into her shorts.

"Hey, thanks for the evening," Leyland said. "That was fun."

"I had a great time," Trixie replied. "Come again whenever."

I had my hand on the door. She walked up and laid hers over it. "Robert." She looked up at me, and I glanced down, avoiding meeting her eyes directly. "Come back sometime. I can teach you a few more rules about poker."

"Okay," I mumbled and headed for the car. I wanted to get home and take a shower. The sadness and guilt were back in my head, but now there was another feeling—stupidity.

20

Eddie and Leyland were laughing as we went back to the car. It was early evening. I wanted to go back to the dorm and take a shower to try and rinse out what I was feeling. But Eddie asked, "What now?"

"Let's go to Hollywood," Leyland said.

Eddie laughed. "I know exactly what you're thinking. The Pink Pussycat."

"Oh no," I said.

"Come on Robert," Leyland said. "Lighten up."

But in my heart of hearts, I was interested.

A couple of weeks ago Leyland, Eddie and I had run into his two friends from Tulsa, and they passed on a tip about a place called The Pink Pussycat, a club on Sunset Strip. Evidently the club was not too tight about their rules and turned a blind eye to college students.

"How old do you have to be to get in?" I asked.

"Twenty-one, the usual," Leyland said. "My friends said we don't need to worry."

"There's no way I'll pass for twenty-one," I protested.

"Robert, give me a break, you're six foot five and a basketball player. If anybody gets in, it will be you."

"You guys are nuts."

Eddie drove to Hollywood and we cruised down Sunset Boulevard, taking in the sights.

Then I saw it. A pink building with a neon pink sign flashing an exaggerated outline of a female form. My stomach knotted in nervous anticipation.

Eddie parked along the street, and we strolled along the sidewalk until we reached the bright pink building. A row of spotlights illuminated the façade, focusing on another image of a woman with a cat's head. Her floor-length black evening gown revealed an ample bosom and cinched in to an extraordinarily small waist. From the back of the dress, a long black tail protruded into the air.

A real woman resembling the figure on the wall stood at the door. My heart pounded in my chest as we approached her.

"Can I help you?" she asked, her throaty voice coming forth in a purr.

"A table for us," Leyland said, lowering his voice and pretending he was in a movie. The endless hours in the theater had served at least one purpose.

She looked us up and down for a minute and then led us inside.

A single light lit up the pink wooden stage, where a comedian stood in the middle of a joke. I heard laughter and a smattering of applause before my eyes adjusted to the darkness. Groups of men sat around tables, chugging beer and grinning.

Leyland had spotted an empty table in a far corner. "This is fine back here," he told the lady.

She started toward it when a voice thundered from the front. "Bring 'em down here." The comedian motioned to a table attached directly to the stage.

She paused for a moment, then started toward the front, directing us to follow. We paraded behind her, every eye following our silent march through the room.

The comedian broke the stillness. "I guess I better go out and check the hubcaps on my car to see that they haven't been stolen." The place exploded with laughter.

"Have a seat, boys—uh, men," he corrected himself, leaning over and looking down at us. "Looks like we just lowered the legal age to thirteen," he commented to the crowd, as if we couldn't hear. The laughter rose again, and a few people clapped and stomped their feet.

"So, you're out for a cultural experience, huh? What is this, a field trip?"

The temperature in the room rose by the minute, and my coat hung on my shoulders like a lead x-ray protection jacket. A trickle of sweat rolled down each temple. I looked over at Leyland. He shifted uncomfortably. I was surprised to see that Eddie wore a nervous smile.

Turning to the crowd again, the comedian asked, "Shall we throw them out or let them stay?"

"Let them stay," someone yelled.

"I can't hear you," the comedian said.

"Let them stay," another voice called out. And then a chant began, "Let them stay. Let them stay. Let them stay."

My face burned, and my head threatened to explode. Weren't places like this supposed to have trap doors in the floor?

The comedian held out his hands for silence. "Okay. The jury has spoken. Enjoy the show, boys." With a lecherous grin, he left the stage.

The light dimmed and a soft swirl of colors played over the stage. Slow, rhythmic music pulsed in the background, the suggestive prelude tensing the listener in anticipation. From the back corner, a woman appeared, feathery wrappings fluttering around her body. Raising her arms above her head and rotating her hips to the music, she glided in smooth, seductive movements toward the front.

Pausing directly above us, she bent forward and grasped the edges of the feathers at her calves. A sensuous smile flitted at the corners of her lips, and she began unwinding the wrappings, slowly peeling them away from her skin. Her gestures set my insides throbbing and commanded my eyes to follow as a sparkling silver-sequined bikini slowly emerged from underneath the feathers.

Pressing her hips forward, she moved her body with the music. Her hands slid up the sides of her legs, around to her stomach, and up to the clasp between her breasts. The top of her bikini dropped to the floor.

She reached down to pick it up, two red stars sparkling on the tips of her bosom. Stretching out the elastic band of the bra, she aimed it at me. With a snap, it smacked against the side of my face. Instinctively, I drew back, covering my face with my hands, and the crowd burst into laughter.

Pulling the bikini back again, she popped it at Leyland, then at Eddie. Sequins and feathers swirled around our faces. We ducked down and put our hands over our heads, trying to fend off the attack.

The entire room shook, and everyone went wild, thoroughly enjoying our humiliation. She stood up, took a bow, and said, "Come back and see me when you reach puberty." Thunderous applause followed her off the stage.

Slowly, we raised our heads and saw the cat-woman from the front door standing in front of us. "Perhaps we should invite you to leave at this point," she said. "This table is reserved."

Leyland nodded, and we sheepishly slunk through the crowd as they cheered us out.

On the way back, we rode in silence. I closed my eyes and tried to ignore the strange sensations coursing through my body. Two red stars glistened and danced before my mind.

After a few miles Leyland spoke out from the back seat. "Did anyone collect any feathers as a souvenir?"

Eddie and I laughed.

I was riding shotgun and I reached across and whisked my hand across the top of Eddie's head. "Just getting the feathers out of your hair to get rid of the evidence," I said.

We laughed.

For the rest of the ride back to Pasadena we were making jokes about feathers and card playing and all the crazy stuff that happened that day.

I carried mixed emotions because of what we had done that day, but found all of this to be a heck of a lot of fun.

21

The next day, Sunday, was a day of torment. I got up in the morning and took a long shower hoping it would make me feel clean. It didn't.

I felt I had betrayed the school and myself. At the same time it was exciting to do those things, and I wasn't sure which one had left the deepest impression; drinking the beer, Trixie undressed, or the girl in the feathers dancing on the stage.

The guilt was starting to set in, because those acts went against everthing I had ever been taught or believed in. Fundamentally it kept coming back to God. If he was holy and perfect, then didn't we need to be perfect to be accepted by him? No matter how much I tried I could never attain that perfection, that 'sanctification' that our church leaders always talked about. In effect, I was headed for hell.

I recalled my discussion with Georgia Rose and how she had talked about true religion being something different. What she had said made me even more confused.

I needed to talk with someone to help think it through.

On Monday morning I found a time slot when Dr. Arlin wasn't teaching. I went to his office and knocked on the door.

"Yes," I heard him say.

I entered his office and he looked up from some papers and he said, "May I help you?"

I said, "I have some religion questions about God and wonder if you could help?"

"Please sit," he said. He motioned to an empty chair on the opposite side of his desk.

He looked at me carefully and a sign of recognition came into his eyes. "Oh yes. You are from San Diego Purity-Christian Church, right?"

"Yes. Robert Macon."

"Hum . . . Why did you want to see me?" His eyes narrowed.

I thought that professors were supposed to be excited when students wanted to meet with them personally. I wasn't sensing that. I began, "I'm a bit confused about this idea of backsliding and being sanctified."

"Yes?" He leaned back in his chair and folded his arms across his chest.

I didn't know exactly how to say it. "In our church the preachers and evangelists are always talking about backsliding. But I'm not really sure what it is. I guess my question is, how do you know when you are actually backslidden . . . and, ah, you've been rejected from heaven and are going to hell?"

His eyebrows came together, wrinkles forming on his forehead. He stared into my eyes. "Somehow I'm sensing there is something specific behind your question. Perhaps if you told me more about it, then I could better help you with your question."

His response to my question made me squirm in the chair. I didn't know what to say. Should I tell him about going to the movie, and the beer, and card game, and the stripper, and my thoughts about Pamela Owens and so many other things where I had fallen short from the rules of the school. I felt like being pushed into a corner.

"Ah . . . no, it's just a religion question," I stammered.

He frowned. "Backsliding is a spiritual state in which the converted has a still continuing tendency of the flesh to lust against the spirit."

"But what does that mean?" I asked. "If at any point someone lusts, then they are going to hell?"

"It needs a detailed theological exposition to fully develop this idea, but generally it is when one's heart strays from the spirit of God."

I thought for a moment. I'm sure he would lose me if he began to discuss theology. I know so little of it. I asked, "How do you really know when you have strayed from the spirit of God, that is, to cross the line into hell?"

"It is a matter of the heart. The doctrines of our church outline the biblical boundaries which must not be crossed. But the church does everything possible to help its congregation. If someone has experienced sin and backsliding, our denomination abundantly offers altar call services on Sunday evenings. It is a chance to go to the old rugged cross and confess and repent from any shortcomings one may have experienced during the week. Unfortunately not all people take advantage of this, for instance, last spring when I was at your church in San Diego."

I thought about that, how Eddie and I had switched the shoes and it upset the girl's choir, and then the entire congregation was laughing at the girls. I tried to hide my smile.

And then I remembered how Dr. Arlin had seemed so disappointed when no one came forward.

"What about sanctification? Does that keep you from backsliding?"

"Well yes," he stated.

"Is it really a state of sinless perfection?

His eyes shifted upward as if deep in thought. "Sin is a rare exception for the sanctified church member, but with entire sanctification a person is entirely devoted to God, and in no way is under any influence to original sin."

"So, the leaders of the church have gotten to that state?"

"That's correct. The lust of the flesh and the pride of life are no longer a factor in their lives."

"And you've gotten to that state?" I ask.

"I can humbly, yet proudly say that entire sanctification is possible." He gave me one of those glued on Purity-Christian smiles.

"How did you achieve this?" I ask.

"It is through years of discipline and living up to the doctrines of the church and through faith and love, and it is a gift."

He started to shuffle with some papers and I sensed our meeting was finished, and I thanked him for his time.

I left his office feeling worse than before. Here was a holy man yet I could never attain this level of holiness. He had come to a point of sanctification, a sinless perfection. I thought about the evils that I had done. This was falling so far short of church doctrines and rules. What was to stop me from doing these evils again and again? Why couldn't I have this gift like Dr. Arlin had it?

I walked across the campus with a resolve to follow the church rules and not sin, but deep down I had a shadowy doubt about the possibility of sinless perfection.

22

For a week after seeing Dr. Arlin I tried to keep my thoughts pure, but I kept coming back to images of the dancer at the Pink Pussycat with her long beautiful legs and fine waist. I was also thinking of Trixie and how we had played strip poker, and the excitement I had when she removed each piece of clothing.

I kept remembering the good time we had coming back in the car, and how we were joking and laughing about the feathers.

So, I found it impossible to keep those thoughts out of my mind no matter how hard I tried.

Beside that, something else was also filling my mind. I found myself in a state of doubt about what to do the coming year, whether to return to Pasadena College or go to another school. Thoughts of the military draft were going through my mind as the Vietnam War was gaining more news coverage every day. If I dropped out of school then surely I would be called into the military.

I decided to visit the sports department another time to try to talk with Coach Smyth about a scholarship for the coming year.

"Can I help you?" Miss Walker asked.

"I'd like to set up an appointment with Coach Smyth, if possible."

"Anything's possible." She smiled only this time it didn't seem like a pasted on smile. There was humor in her eyes.

She had never been that friendly before.

"Then can I fix a meeting?" I asked.

"Yes, when?"

"How about next Tuesday at two o'clock?"

"OK." She wrote something down in a little book in front of her.

"Thank you," I said.

I turned to leave, and she called after me, "Anything's possible, as long as you know how to play your cards."

I looked back and saw a smirk on her face.

#

I walked away from Miss. Walker's office wondering exactly what she meant by the remark about 'how to play your cards' when I heard a voice behind me say, "Robert Macon?"

A middle-aged woman approached me. "Can you come with me, please?"

I knew it wasn't a question.

"I'm the secretary for Mr. Grazer, the Dean of Men. He would like to see you."

I swallowed, remembering how I felt the first time I saw the flashing lights of a patrol car in my rearview mirror. "Do you know why?"

"It's something important."

"I just got out of class, and my next one starts in less than ten minutes. Could I come see him afterward?"

"I think it would be best if you came right now," she said firmly.

I followed her to the administration office, passing Coach Smyth on the way in. I felt his eyes on me, but when I looked up, he stared off in the distance, as though he didn't know me.

The secretary stopped in front of an open office door. "Go in," she said.

I entered, and she closed the door behind me.

An impressive mahogany desk occupied the center of the room. A man sat behind it, his forehead pressed permanently into a stern expression.

"Sit down," he directed. He folded his hands on the desk, white cuffs protruding from the arms of his navy suit.

I took a place in the straight-backed wooden chair directly across from him.

"I'm Mr. Grazer, the Dean of Men," he announced in a deep and commanding voice.

"Yes sir," I answered.

He paused, and I felt his eyes probing my face. Did he think that he could see through me, that if he looked long and hard enough, he could delve into my soul and discover a writhing mass of evil upon which he could pronounce judgment?

I focused on the bulging buttons at his stomach. If he ate too many more hamburgers, they were going to pop.

"I understand you're not a very good poker player."

"I'm sorry, sir?"

"I've heard that you don't play poker very well," he repeated.

I said nothing.

"Do you think that playing cards is a proper behavior?"

"No sir, it's against the rules of the school."

"Then why were you playing cards?"

"I don't know how to play cards," I answered.

Mr. Grazer cleared his throat. "This past week, a student in the Greek department left a book in class, and another student turned it in. It was a personal diary, written in Greek. When Dr. Arlin translated it, he discovered descriptions of indecent acts, which also mentioned names of other students at the school. We hope this is not true." He sounded quite convinced that it was.

My mind spun. What was I supposed to say? The memory of that night hung over my conscience like a mass of iron suspended by a tenuous thread, threatening to break at any moment. I wished I could confess the whole thing and free myself from the guilt, but I knew that the instant I made any mention of the truth to Mr. Grazer, I would be done for. His was not the compassionate ear of forgiveness and grace, but rather the ear of one intent on rooting out all evil and eradicating it through unmitigated discipline.

"I don't know any Greek." The words popped out of my mouth before I could think.

"I wasn't suggesting that you knew Greek. What I want to know is if this girl is fabricating a story. God despises a lying tongue, and there are severe consequences for speaking falsehood." He looked at me very deliberately. "She said that you lost your clothing while playing poker."

"That can't be, sir, because, as I already said, I don't know how to play cards."

"You don't, do you?" Mr. Grazer queried with a doubtful expression.

"Uh, no sir."

He contemplated my words for a moment. "So let it be," he said, apparently out of questions. "If you weren't engaged in this activity, then can we assume that the other individuals mentioned were also not involved?"

"I don't know any other names," I answered.

"Since it appears that you were not involved, there's no need to keep a record of this. The young lady has been asked to leave the school but when we pressed her she mentioned you. She said she was practicing her language skills by writing a novel in Greek, but I'm thoroughly disgusted by what she has written. Private diary or not, she blatantly violates the literary standards of this school and of the Purity-Christian Church." He seemed to need some object to denounce, a scapegoat to carry the un-holiness far from him.

"This is a clear transgression of the school's covenant code", he said. "You have not been here to see me before, but some professors have reported on you about other matters."

I still didn't know what he meant by other matters but thought it best not to ask.

"While the veracity of this young woman's acts cannot be substantiated, I am offering an option for you to leave school for one week to think about your covenant with the school. If you prefer to press this, then you will be asked to leave the school permanently.

"We have been informed that there may have been other students implicated by this young lady but it is difficult to positively identify them without defamation. We will not pursue them, but we hope that you will choose to be an example to them."

The dean looked at me solemnly and asked, "Which option will you take?"

"I'll leave for a week," I said.

"Do not take lightly the measure of grace you are receiving in this mild punishment. Go back to your room immediately, collect the things that you need, and get off of campus. Come back to my office at this time one week from today, and do not have any contact with anyone at this school until I see you again."

I nodded and stood up.

The sternness of the dean's countenance faded slightly, and he unsuccessfully tried to don a compassionate expression. "I must tell you that, from the very beginning, some of my colleagues had concerns about you. Nonetheless I like to give every student a chance. In fact, this is your chance to think about how you want to live. What kind of life are you going to choose?"

"Yes sir," I said, not knowing what to say to him. He was right. I had sinned, an awful sin, but no matter how hard I tried I couldn't seem to achieve the perfection required.

Maybe I was destined for a life of sorrow and heartache. I didn't want it, but nothing seemed to work. And the worse thing was that I couldn't talk with anyone because no one seemed to really care. I knew I had to accept my punishment.

"You are dismissed." The dean swiveled around in his chair and began looking through some papers that were on a side table.

I left without a word. Gathering a few articles of clothing, toothbrush and toothpaste, a razor, and a blanket from my room, I got in my car and headed away from the campus of Purity-Christian College.

23

After driving aimlessly along the streets of Pasadena, I eventually found myself following the signs to Highway 101, north toward San Francisco. I didn't realize how long I'd been driving until it struck me that I had the road almost to myself. The smoggy brown hills of Los Angeles had disappeared, and after half an hour I caught a first glimpse of the sea, a fuzzy blue horizon in the west.

I passed Ventura and at a gas station in Santa Barbara, I filled up the tank. The road had gradually drawn closer to the water, and as I pumped gas, I could see the tips of some sailboat masts poking up in the distance. I paid for the gas, bought a coke and a package of Twinkies and then drove my car to a parking lot near a boat marina.

I walked around the marina for a while, listening to the soft splashing of the water against the boats, and the creeks and groans of the moorings. I found a wooden bench and ate the Twinkies and drank the coke and just sat there for a long time and tried to reflect on my situation.

My mind was numb. I felt like my world was a constraining straight-jacket, but I wasn't able to give it more definition than that. I had difficulty to comprehend all the forces at play in my life, and why I was so inadequate at understanding them and facing them and being the good person I was supposed to be.

All I knew is that I had been instructed to leave the school for a period of time and I was now heading north, and I knew I needed to use this time to gain some perspective on things.

Back on the road, the lowering sun glared in my eyes, and I pulled the sun visor down. Eventually I'd have to find a place to stay for the night. I calculated that I had about seventy-five dollars in my bank account. That should be more than enough to last the week.

After passing Santa Barbara, I welcomed the peaceful emptiness that the barren landscape offered. In the east, bare brown fields slowly climbed into small hills that hovered in the distance. The deep turquoise of the ocean evaporated into an almost invisible glow, and endless gray cement stretched out before me as fast as it slid away underneath.

At San Luis Obispo I took Highway One to Morro Bay and a small sign caught my attention. It read, *Montaña De Oro*. I wasn't sure what it was, but turned off and went south about a mile or two and found an unpaved road that led toward some sand dunes.

I parked the car and wandered over the dunes to an immense stretch of sandy beach with not a person to be seen. It was becoming night and I was lonely and I gathered a few twigs and scraps of wood and made a fire. A cool wind blew in from the sea and the small fire did nothing to warm me. When the flames settled down into embers, I pulled a blanket out of the trunk, rolled up in the back seat, and fell asleep.

The sunlight and gnawing hunger pains woke me. I drove into town and found a supermarket. I could survive on bread and Spam, interspersed with a few Jack-in-the-Box hamburgers, for a couple days. But when I spotted the ninety-nine cent breakfast special at the diner across the street, I decided to get my empty stomach off to a good start. A thick pile of buttermilk pancakes soaked with butter and maple syrup, accompanied by crackling strips of greasy bacon, settled the growling and I drove back to the sand dunes.

The crashing of the waves seemed to be calling to me. The tide was coming in. I had grown up on the ocean, practically living in the saltwater, but in the last eight months at PC Cru, I had hardly seen the beach. I parked my car, changed into some shorts in the back seat, and wandered down to the beach, carrying my blanket.

I stripped off my shirt and walked to the edge of the water. The frigid temperature hit me like a wall when I dove in, and I sucked in my breath. I pumped my arms in fast strokes and kicked hard to keep the blood flowing, and swam out as far as I could before my lungs threatened to explode.

Panting from the exertion, I paused, and then watched for a good wave. I was an excellent body surfer and didn't need a surfboard to ride a wave. There is a technique that is difficult to learn, but if you gain some speed just as a wave is cresting, and then angle your body into the slope of the wave, it will catch you and propel you toward the shore.

I missed the first one, but on the second try I caught it and let the force of the water push me back toward the shore. I swam out again and again, relishing the exhilaration of riding the waves. When I had worn myself out, I went back to the sand, collapsed on the blanket, and fell asleep under the warmth of the sun.

After a couple of days of swimming, body surfing, and sleeping, the fresh air began to sweep away the guilt and shame that plagued me. I enjoyed the time alone and the release from the pressurizing presence of other people. I had forgotten how much the constant social interaction constrained me.

In the evenings, I jogged along the sandy beaches, then sat down and watched brilliant orange and pink streaks paint the sky as the sun sunk behind the horizon. I lay on my back and waited until darkness fell and the stars came out. Staring at the vast expanse of the universe, I felt small and insignificant.

I couldn't help thinking about everything that had happened since I came to Pasadena. I had looked forward to having real friends, finding a place where I belonged. I liked hanging out with Leyland and Eddie and I had made somewhat of a name for myself as a basketball star. Yet here I was, on the verge of losing everything I had hoped for. The week would be over tomorrow, and I felt rested and refreshed.

The thought of going back to see Mr. Grazer cast a heavy shadow over me, and I contemplated staying away. I could get a job, live somewhere by the ocean for awhile, do whatever I felt like without worrying about some rule that I might be breaking, or what some dean or other person thought. But a nagging voice inside me asked, what about basketball, my parents, my education?

Climbing back into my car, my legs filled with lead. I sat behind the steering wheel for half an hour before I finally turned the keys in the ignition. Along the highway leading south, I seemed to be driving into the eye of a storm. A pregnant stillness suddenly replaced the turmoil that had tossed me around seven days ago, and my heart pounded heavily under a silent weight.

I parked my car and walked slowly to the dean's office. Dean Grazer's secretary greeted me with an expressionless face and motioned for me to wait. An hour passed before he appeared in the door and said grimly, "Come in."

I sat down across from him. His eyes bored into my soul, and all the guilt that the waves had swept away came rushing back over me in a crushing force.

"Have you had time to think about what you did?" he asked after a long pause

"Yes, sir."

"And what have you decided?"

The intensity of his gaze pierced me. "I want to live a holy life."

Was I pronouncing my own sentence? For, when I said this I wasn't sure.

"Perhaps you are beginning to understand the gravity of your sin. I expect that you will not forget it soon."

"No, sir. I won't." Somehow I wasn't telling the truth and I felt my jaw tighten.

"You may return to school. But Robert, I want you to know that both God and I will be watching you to test the genuineness of your confession. You must demonstrate a commitment to change and a willingness to put aside your rebellious ways and submit to the authorities God has given you."

"Yes sir. I understand," I responded without emotion, feeling as though I'd fallen under the curse of the White Witch, who turned all her enemies to stone.

"You are dismissed."

With deliberately slow movement I stood up looking him in the eyes and then I turned for the door. I felt no connection with this man and resentment flowed through my veins like hot coals. How much longer could I play this game? It seemed that was what everyone else was doing, just playing a game.

I went to my car and collected my things. I hoped the room would be empty when I got back.

When I opened the door and saw Eddie and Leyland talking, instead of disappointment I felt only a hollow deadness.

"How was the week?" Leyland asked.

"OK. I spent nights on a beach up in Morro Bay," I answered flatly, my back turned to him as I put away the things I had taken with me.

"Did you see the dean?"

"Yes."

"Did you say anything about us?"

"No. Neither of you were identified."

"That's great!" Eddie let out a sigh of relief.

"Thanks so much for not saying anything," Leyland said. "We could really be in a lot of trouble."

I put the last shirt from my bag back in the drawer and closed it. "I guess it was better for only one of us to take the punishment. Anyway it wasn't too bad. I actually had a good time on my own and everything."

"And you got a great tan." A nervous laugh came from Eddie's direction.

I made a vague attempt at a smile.

It was quiet for a moment, and then Leyland said, "You know, it would probably be a good idea if we're not seen together too much over the next few days. If we're associated with you, the dean might become suspicious."

"I understand," I said, a layer of ice freezing over the stone statue that I had become.

I drifted through the next few weeks, isolated in a sea of people. Other students observed me from a distance, and I sat daydreaming in classes, hearing the teachers' voices as echoes far away.

Every night before I went to sleep, I imagined the deep blue of the Pacific Ocean and pictured myself floating along with the rise and fall of the waves.

24

Over the next few weeks, life slowly slipped back into a normal rhythm. I kept a low profile, walking like a zombie around campus, and playing basketball on Saturday mornings. The end of the term was coming up, and I anticipated working a construction job in San Diego, as I had the previous summer, but I didn't know where I would live. My parents were now living in Santa Cruz.

Leyland put more effort into Circle K to maintain a good front and to keep himself busy. Eddie was active with his different projects.

I spent increasingly less time on campus, going for long runs, driving up into the mountains, or wandering aimlessly around Pasadena.

To my surprise, I found Eddie in the room one afternoon when I returned from class. We rarely saw each other during the day. With his back to me, he bent intently over his desk and looked to be tinkering with something. I walked up closer. He was probing around inside an old telephone with a screwdriver. A fine layer of dust covered his arms and the thighs of his pants.

"A new bargain from the thrift store?" I asked sarcastically.

"Yep, but a lot more than that when I'm finished here. Wait a minute," he said. He went over to the hot air vent at the bottom of one wall, removed the cover, and reached deep inside. Pulling out two wires, he threaded them through one of the holes in the cover and replaced it on the wall. I watched as he attached the wires to the telephone, and put the receiver to his ear.

He stood silently for a moment, and then passed it to me. "Listen to this."

I heard a dial tone. "So?" I asked him.

"We have a telephone now." Eddie grinned.

"Ah . h. h . . . ?" I didn't know if I should be angry or astonished. "How on earth...?"

"I was bored one day and decided to go exploring under the dorm. There's a sort of crawlspace, full of dust and spiders and stuff, you know. Well, while I was down there, I came across this telephone line. With a little further investigation, I discovered that it runs down to the dorm supervisor's room. What this means, my friend," he held up the telephone and shook it meaningfully, "is that we're hooked on to his line. We can listen in on all his conversations. It'll be an invaluable source of information. And, best of all, when he's not there, we can make telephone calls." He set the phone down with a look of triumph. "Not bad, huh?"

"That's incredible," I said. Eddie had a way of getting me into situations where I couldn't help but admire the ingenuity of his actions, dubious as they were.

When I came back from shooting hoops that evening, Eddie sat in the corner, the phone pressed to his ear. He held his finger to his lips, and motioned for me to come over. He handed me the receiver. After a moment, I recognized the voice of the dorm supervisor. I listened for a couple minutes. He seemed to be talking to a friend.

Eddie watched the expression on my face. "Cool, huh?"

Eavesdropping on the supervisor's conversations became a regular habit over the next weeks. We usually listened in the evenings, when he made personal calls, until Eddie picked up on a discussion between him and the dean of students one afternoon. They were talking about the situations of particular students. After that, we listened regularly in the afternoons, reporting our discoveries to each other.

"Boy, have I got some news for you," Eddie announced one evening. "Donald Bonen—our beloved dorm attendant, Homecoming King, Circle K President, et cetera, et cetera, et cetera…." He rotated his hand in a rapid circle to indicate the long list of meaningless accolades. "Donald Bonen was caught intoxicated *and* in improper conduct with a girl last week."

"Wow," I let out an astonished whisper. "What's going to happen to him?"

"You gotta love the way these things work," Eddie said, shaking his head. "He 'confessed' his sin the following day and got off scot-free. Apparently his dad's a somebody in the church. Between that and Donald's position here, it would be too embarrassing if anything became public."

A dull thud struck me. "I see." I nodded slowly and sat down on my bed. "So that's the way it works . . . is that right?"

I stared off into space, my mind empty. Fire filled my being as I wondered, why me and not Donald?

"This is good stuff. I've got to hear more," Eddie said with a mischievous grin as he went back to the phone.

I don't know how long I had been lying motionless when I heard him.

"Pssst! Robert!" Eddie held his hand over the mouthpiece and beckoned frantically, his eyes wide.

The voice of the supervisor came through loud and clear. "Well, how do you want to treat it?" he asked.

"He doesn't fit with my system." My heart pounded when I heard Coach Smyth's sharp tone.

"So what should I do?"

"I just can't carry the expense next year. I need players who bring value to the team beyond their basketball skills. The school's running tight on money, and I've got a lot of pressure on me to help the fundraising efforts. Anyway, I didn't really like him from the start; there's something about him that doesn't jive with me. Keep an eye on him, and let me know if you find anything suspicious. I've got to find a way to terminate him from the team before next season starts. If he wants to stay in school, that's up to him, but it'll be on his own expense."

"Okay, we'll play it like that. I'll keep you posted," the dorm supervisor said.

Two clicks followed, and I laid the telephone down. "They were talking about some player or something," I said. I had a sick feeling in my stomach, imagining Coach Smyth' evil eyes searching out their victim. Whoever they landed on was about to get seriously screwed over.

"Do you know who they were talking about?" Eddie asked.

"No, but I didn't like the sound of it."

I lost interest in the telephone, and, since the supervisor was out of town for a couple days, Eddie used it in the evenings to call an old girlfriend of his in San Diego. Leyland came over and rung up high school buddies in Tulsa.

I had avoided making personal calls; it didn't feel right. Finally Eddie convinced me to call my parents. He capitalized on my guilty feelings for not making more of an effort to stay in touch with them after they moved to Santa Cruz. The phone rang ten times before my stepfather answered. He was on his way out to go somewhere urgent, so we only talked for about twenty seconds.

25

I spotted Coach Smyth walking across the school parking lot, and jogged up to him. "Hey, coach," I called breathlessly, "can I talk to you for a minute?"

He turned around and looked at me with a disgruntled expression. "I'm in a hurry. What do you want?"

"I was just wondering about playing for the team next year. I hadn't seen you in awhile, and was hoping to talk with you about it. You know I played well. I can be a real asset to the senior team. They need a strong rebounder."

"I've been wondering about the kind of example you set," he mused.

"I'm an excellent scor—"

"I mean off the court," he said. "I expect all my players to go to church. When was the last time you were in church?"

I paused. "Uhh…"

"Exactly," he said with an emphatic nod. "This is a Christian college, and for that reason our team is about more than just basketball. Our supporters are in the churches, and they need to know that our athletes are maintaining the highest moral standards in this institution. I believe we've talked about this before."

"Yes sir."

"Well," he shook his head, "I'm not sure I've seen enough of that in you."

"Could we talk about it, sir? I would be more than happy to discuss this with you."

"Not right now. I have to go. Make an appointment with my secretary." He started to turn away.

"I've tried to, Mr. Smyth, but she always says that you're busy."

"We'll talk about this later. My family's waiting."

"Sir . . ." I stammered, but he was already getting into his car. I saw the silhouette of a woman in the front seat and two smaller heads in the back as he drove away.

My fists tightened as I stood and watched the car disappear down the street. Why was he always too busy for his athletes, and especially me?

26

The next day I was headed to the Soda Fountain, a place on the campus where a lot of students hung out, where they sold coffee and ice cream and drinks. I wanted a milk shake.

Just as I got to the door a girl walked up and I opened the door for her. It was Georgia Rose, the one with the strange religion ideas that I had talked with in the cafeteria.

"Hi," I said.

She looked at me for a moment and then said, "Ah . . . Robert? Yes, Robert."

"That's right," I said. "The one with the religion questions."

She laughed. It sounded pleasant and made me feel good.

"You meeting anyone?" I asked.

"No. Just getting a milkshake before going to class," she said.

"Would you like someone to sit with?' I asked her. "In seeing you I've got some questions." There were some things she said before that had kept going through my mind.

"That would be nice," she said.

We found an empty booth.

The waitress came and Georgia said, "A chocolate milkshake please."

"Make that two," I said to the waitress.

The tall milkshake glasses clunked on the table as the waitress set them down in front of us.

Georgia took a straw and held it in her delicate fingers and she looked me straight in the eye. "So, you mentioned that you had some questions. But, I may not have any answers." She smiled.

Her directness surprised me. With the typical PC Cru girls, you had to play a game of cat-and-mouse. They evaded questions and dodged any slightly serious topics, batting their eyelids coquettishly and making you chase them. Every time you pounced, they'd jump away, unless, of course, they thought that you were about to pose *the question*, at which moment they became suddenly demure and attentive . . . like Sandy.

I took a vigorous swig through my straw that hollowed my cheeks with its force. "Um, faith, you know, some of that stuff you talked about when we were in the cafeteria."

"Why don't you tell me what faith means to you?" she said, encircling the base of her glass with her hands.

What a question, I thought. And I wasn't sure I had a ready answer. "I mean, I guess I've always thought it was everything religious—going to church, reading the Bible, following the rules, being a good church-goer, doing the right thing." The whipped cream on top began to melt. I scooped it off with the long-handled spoon and let it dissolve in my mouth. "What does it mean to you?"

"I can only share from my own experience and what I understand from reading the Bible. I'm not sure where faith starts, maybe by understanding that God is there and then seeking him, but there's more. You believe in God, don't you?" She asked.

"Uh . . . yeah . . . Since I was a little kid, I guess."

"Well I didn't, that is, I didn't grow up in a Church going family. But I began to question things, like why there is order in the universe rather than disorder, and what is the origin of personality and the basis for morality? And is there truth, I mean true-truth and where does that come from? I read a lot. I always have."

She caught my attention, like I was with someone a heck of a lot smarter than me. And I liked the way her blue eyes sparkled when she talked.

"So how did you come to believe in God, I asked."

She smiled again and looked me in the eyes, so much so that I had to glance away.

"It was more than just believing that a God is there," she said. It was entering into a relationship with him. And it wasn't through reading philosophy or complicated books on theology. It was rather simple."

"How was that?" I asked.

She explained, "In high school I was over at a girlfriend's house and we talked about spiritual things. Then my friend talked about God's love and how much God wants to be in a relationship with us. Then we talked about God's holiness and perfection, and I realized that I was anything but that."

I looked at Georgia. For me, she seemed about as perfect as anyone could be.

She continued. "My friend explained that God gave his son and by believing in him and by understanding what he did on the cross, then we can become children of God. And that's what I did. I didn't understand much of Christianity because of my upbringing, but I believed and I continue to believe. For me, that is faith. And the thing is, when Christ is in your life, God no longer condemns you because he sees you through the holiness of Christ."

My mind was racing and I felt uneasy because she was missing something. If what she said was true, then it seemed like it gave you a free license to go out and do anything you want. I know that God sends backsliders to hell, but she was describing something worse . . . to get a free pass any time you sinned and broke the Purity-Christian rules.

Before I could mention this to her she continued in her train of thought. "You see, God offers us a free gift of salvation. The Bible says we can never be saved by trying to gain God's acceptance through works. Otherwise people would become proud and boast. But when you understand the true holiness of God and one's complete inadequacy to ever be holy, then there is an ongoing thankfulness for what Christ has done. That's what happened to me."

She tinkered with her straw, looking down, sliding it into the glass and then delicately sucked on it. Her lips were pink and I was drawn to her lovely complexion.

A long moment passed. I didn't know what to say. What she said was so simple, almost stupidly simple, but wasn't there something missing?

Basically the way you get accepted by God is to go to the altar and confess that you've backslidden by breaking the Ten Commandments and the Purity-Christian rules, and then you cry and get emotional. And then after that you do your best to be a good guy for God. That was the example in our denomination. And I knew for sure that there were people in our church who had actually attained the state of 'entire sanctification' as they called it, like Dr. Arlin and Coach Smyth. They said it was a state of sinless perfection.

Also, I was confused over the way she was using some words, like holiness and salvation. She was using them in a different way than in our denomination. I was afraid that if our church leaders heard what she said, they might call her a heretic.

"But there's got to be more than that," I said. "Faith must surely include what you said, plus following the religious rules?" I thought of my discussion with Dr. Arlin.

She traced her finger down the condensation on the glass, leaving a clear trail behind it that slowly clouded over again. "Can we really win God's favor by following rules? Anyway, I think faith has more to do with relationship. And through that relationship my life will change and I will reflect more of the qualities of God. There's a saying . . . show me your friends and I will show you what you will become. My friend is Jesus Christ. It's a life time walk with God, through faith in a relationship with him."

"Relationship?"

"If I trust you, believe you, I will put my faith in you."

"So, do you trust me?" I said, trying to lighten the discussion.

She smiled. "If I don't know someone how can I trust them? But if that person demonstrated their love by giving their life for me, I would trust them. That's what Christian faith is all about."

For some reason that hit me. Was that the core of my religion problem? I didn't have faith because I didn't really know God. But there had been times that I had tried so hard.

She sipped the straw and I watched the level of her milkshake go down a bit.

"But, what about pleasing him?" I asked. "I've tried everything . . . but . . . I fail no matter how hard I try."

"It sounds like you might be focusing on the wrong things."

"What do you mean?" I asked.

"Robert, is it possible that God reaches out to us, rather than us trying to reach out to him through our efforts?"

"I don't think so," I whispered. I slurped the last of my milkshake and wiggled my straw around, trying to suck up the last few residual drops in the hollow of the glass. I looked up at her, but had a difficult time looking her straight in the eye. Something about her melted me inside, and what she said made me feel empty. "I refuse to think that you can get something in life without working for it—especially when it comes to God. You have to work for all the spiritual things the church talks about."

"That's one way to do it," she said. "But how far have you gotten by working to please God?"

"Not very far," I replied. "In fact I've gotten nowhere at all." I felt my eyes water up. She was right, I hadn't gotten very far. In fact, I was an absolute failure.

"Then, God has offered us an alternative," she stated.

We sat there not talking, and when she finished her milkshake she said, "Robert, I think I understand how you feel, because that's the way I felt for a long time. I don't make any claim to have all this figured out, and I'm not sure I ever will. It's just that I came to a certain position, and you are free to differ. I can only tell you that I believe in God because I think there's a spiritual part of who I am that relates to him. And so, belief for me is about trusting God to nurture that part of me—while praying and communicating with God when I can, allowing every part of my life to connect to him." She leaned slightly forward as she spoke, emphasizing the earnestness of her words.

I hadn't heard anything like this before and didn't know where to begin with it. It almost sounded like a foreign language. It was so far removed from sanctification, holiness, backsliding, and everything that went along with all of that.

We finished our milkshakes and went our separate ways. I wished I could know as much as she did.

27

The week before final exams were to begin I sat again in Mr. Grazer's office and heard him say, "You've committed a felony."

"I'm sorry. I've done what?" I asked.

"You've committed a felony. Wiretapping—using someone else's telephone illegally—is a federal offense."

I sat in the hard wooden chair, trying to process what Mr. Grazer was saying. His words fell soundlessly on my ears.

"There is no question about your behavior this time. You have received more than a good chance to prove yourself, and you have failed. The evidence is quite clear." He pushed a piece of paper across his desk toward me.

It was a telephone bill, including a list of all the calls that had been made from a particular number. I recognized a San Diego area code on many of them. One with a Santa Cruz area code number was underlined in red; my parents' number. I scanned across the line to the total charge for the call: fifty cents for twenty seconds.

"Because of the brevity of the offense, a federal judge would most likely not prosecute you. However, in our eyes, a sin is a sin, no matter how great or small. The issue here is your heart. You have willfully chosen to continue your ungodly behavior, and we will not tolerate it any longer."

I looked at the other telephone numbers and he caught my eye. "You are not the only one to make telephone calls," he said. "We will speak to the others, but you have already been dismissed from school for a week. This is their first time, so I will just give them a warning, like I gave you a warning."

I was thinking of Leyland and Eddie. They had done more than me. I just followed stupidly. Why did I do that? It was because I needed friendship, but was it? I tried to reason it through, and ended up missing some of what he was saying.

"Robert, Christianity is a system of belief." He picked up a booklet from a small table behind his desk and said, "This is from our church Articles of Faith." He read,

We believe that the grace of entire sanctification includes the impulse to grow in grace. However, this impulse must be consciously nurtured. Without such purposeful endeavor one's witness may be impaired and the grace itself frustrated and ultimately lost.

I wasn't sure exactly what it meant but nodded my head.

He continued. "You see, a true believer is saved and sanctified and this is demonstrated through a life of holiness. Unless it is learned and followed, it is frustrated and ultimately lost. Living by this system allows believers to be healed of their moral and spiritual ailments. You have failed to understand this and to pursue the true light. You have not come to the old rugged cross and pursued the path to perfection. You have not demonstrated this through you actions. From this moment, you are officially dismissed from Purity-Christian College."

"Dismissed?" I asked, leaning forward in the chair. My voice echoed in my ears. "For how long?" My head started spinning, feeling denial as a first reaction. This couldn't be happening to me.

"This is not a temporary dismissal. You have already received more forgiveness than you deserve."

I didn't want to understand him. "How will I take my final exams? I can't miss them. They are in three days."

"Robert." He spoke my name with a heavy finality, and I felt the iron wrecking ball swinging toward me. "You have broken the rules, and you were warned of the consequences. By your actions, you have demonstrated that you cannot live up to the standards of godliness embodied in this institution."

"But if I can't take the final exams, I'll fail. I've paid for this semester, and I can't afford to retake these classes." I pleaded, "Please let me take the finals, and then I will leave and not bother you anymore."

"This is the last time I will tell you. This is not a discussion. You do not belong here. Go, remove every evidence of your presence from your room, leave this campus, and do not come back."

An hour later, I threw the last pair of basketball shoes onto the floor behind the driver's seat, and slid behind the wheel of my 1954 Chevrolet. I turned onto a calm avenue lined with palm trees, and Purity-Christian College disappeared behind me. My life was crumbling all around me.

CHAPTER 28

Present Day

I drive away and see Brandy in the rear view mirror, standing by the side of the road looking lost and sad. In her hand she has the piece of paper I had given her and I see her opening it.

I'm not sure what to think about that experience over the last couple of hours. I assume it gave me some insights into the current culture in California, but I would need a larger sample in order to make conclusions. In any case, I need to press on.

Turning off of Highway 101, I take the Pacific Coast Highway, to Morro Bay and check into the best hotel I can find. Then I take Monique's book from my carryon bag, go back to the car and drive south a couple of miles to what is now Montaña De Oro State Park.

I pay the entrance fee and drive to the same area where I had camped so long ago. At that time it had been totally open with no state officials around. I park the Porsche and walk to the top of an immense sand dune, sit down and look out at the deep blue sea.

I try to reflect back on the circumstances of why I had originally come here, of what happened at the school and what that week here had meant. Many years have passed since then and the past is a bit of a haze.

What I do know is that being here initiated a life-change, although more significant events came later. What Morro Bay represented was a first taste of freedom from the beast, as strange as that might seem.

While I try to focus on those past events I am unable to do so. Instead, my mind is filled with something else. I keep looking at the book I am holding. It is a book on Psychology written in French by Monique. She was my confident and best friend. We were married for many years and while our careers were different, when not working we were together all the time.

I turn to the first page of her book and read the words she had hand written. They were in English.

To Robert,
My precious love. I wrote this book for you. Life in this broken world is temporal but we pass to a perfect world where life and love are eternal, as is the human soul and spirit. Those who are the children of God can look to the

future with confidence.

Therefore I am certain we will meet again and be forever together. You have been a wonderful husband and I have cherished every day with you. Please continue to gain the most from life and may God bless you every single moment.

Je t'aime,

Monique

My eyes blur. The title of the book is *Surmonter Chagrin et Tristesse*, which in English is translated to something like 'overcoming grief and sadness'. She was a Psychiatrist and wrote a number of books, mostly academic. But this one was written during the last two years of her life when she knew the cancer was advancing.

She wrote the book in simple French so even a plain guy like me could understand it. It is analytical for sure, but full of words of encouragement and hope.

And she wrote it for me.

I sit on top of the sand dune and my mind feels weary. I miss her so much. She's been gone almost four months now and every day I still have tears. I'm thoroughly grateful for my time with her and what we experienced. There are many things I miss about her, like her positive outlook on life, her insights into human nature, and especially her deep spirituality. I miss her presence.

I especially miss sharing this experience with her. Can I really face all of this without her?

In this moment I am unaware of my surroundings and all nature is but haze. I wish the sun would not shine, for the depth of pain recoils at its brilliance.

The afternoon shifts toward evening. I watch the sun set as it fills the western sky with magnificent colors of red and pink. Tears roll off my face as grief and sadness fill my soul.

How can I go on without her?

CHAPTER 29

Sophomore: 1966-1967

The crunching of the carrots between my stepfather's teeth as he deliberately ground them to a pulp before swallowing echoed loudly in the silence. I concentrated on shoveling forkfuls of peas into my mouth. The sooner they were gone, the sooner the meal would be over, and I could escape back to my room. My mom sniffed and blew her nose as the last of the peas disappeared.

The chair legs screeched across the floor as I pushed myself away from the table. On the way out, I dropped my plate in the sink, the collision of porcelain and metal filling the air with a raucous clatter.

The next few days continued in a similar fashion, punctuated by occasional outbursts from my mom or stepfather. I made every effort to avoid unnecessary interaction with them. I couldn't change the situation, and sooner or later they would have to accept that.

A knock sounded on my bedroom door, and a moment later it opened.

"Robert, we need to talk." My stepfather filled the doorframe.

A somber seriousness permeated his voice, and I sat up. "About what?"

"About your future."

No one had mentioned that thus far.

"What do you expect to do now? My job here in Santa Cruz is almost finished, and we'll be moving on soon."

I said, "I'm looking at construction jobs for the summer. I guess after you leave I'll find a place for myself." I had made some phone calls, and it looked like I would be able to get work.

"Is that all?"

"Yeah." What more was there to figure out right now? I had gotten kicked out of college just before the end of the semester, and I had planned to work during the summer anyway. The only difference was that I was in Santa Cruz rather than San Diego, and wouldn't be going back to PC Cru in the fall. Right now I wanted to get busy with *something*, and forget about everything else.

"You better get yourself back in school," he said.

I couldn't answer because of the lump in my throat.

"If you don't stay in college you will get called up to Vietnam and it's likely you will come back in a box. You don't know what that will do to your mother."

That hit me hard and I felt a surge of guilt for what happened at PC Cru. I had evoked enough sorrow on my mother by getting kicked out, but if I got killed? I could imagine how that would destroy her. But, maybe getting killed was the best thing. I had failed in college, and I doubted if I would ever graduate. What school would ever take me?

"Yes sir," I said, bowing my head.

He turned around and shut the door without another word.

#

I got a job with a construction company that laid asphalt. A few weeks into the summer, my parents moved to Sacramento where my father was to supervise a team that was putting up a new state government building.

Scott, a guy at work who operated the spreader, helped me find a cheap one-room apartment near the beach. My job consisted of walking along behind the spreader with a shovel and flattening any asphalt that came out unevenly, or shoveling excess asphalt that fell along the side of the run. It was hard work. The hot sun baked down on the boiling asphalt. Greasy steam rose up, infiltrating my nose and eyes. Each evening I would go home to my apartment and spend long periods in the shower, trying to rinse the oil from my hair and skin. It wouldn't go away, like the pain I was feeling from my failure at PC Cru.

On weekends I played basketball and started surfing occasionally. The more time I spent in the water, the more I longed for it. It brought back memories of Morro Bay and the hours of staring up at the massive array of stars in the black night sky. Somehow the expanse of the sea gave me an odd yearning for something spiritual that would give meaning to my life, but it seemed so far away.

Some Sunday mornings I went to a local Purity-Christian Church, but the things I heard never filled the emptiness in my soul. After I came back from church, I picked up my surfboard and headed for the beach.

Along the Santa Cruz Boardwalk, there was a long swath of sand. It was summer and crowds of people swarmed through the gaudy collection of amusement park rides, hot dog and candy stands, roller coasters, and game booths. In the evenings, the flashing colored lights reflected off the ocean, while music, laughter, and loud voices floated through the air. Masses of high school and college students from the Bay Area and the San Joaquin Valley packed the beach and the boardwalk every weekend, dancing and partying at the dance hall until early in the morning.

Besides surfing, I hung out on the beach, people-watching. Sometimes I hung out with Scott, who had grown up in Santa Cruz and was very much a part of the local scene. Through him it was easy to get to know people, but I tended to stay on my own most of the time.

It didn't take me long to realize that something had changed in the year since I graduated from high school. Life at PC Cru seemed sort of like an isolated bubble floating in its own little sphere. While I had been studying John Wesley and the basics of holiness, the surfing craze had hit California more than ever, and everyone wanted to be a surfer.

Throngs of pseudo-surfers drove over from the Valley, dyed their hair blond, mounted cheap surfboards on top of their cars, and blasted Beach Boys music on their radios. In contrast, the real surfers wore screen-printed t-shirts and colorful 'baggies' flower shorts from the surf shops, and some even made or designed their own boards.

I could pick the real ones out in an instant—they maneuvered the waves with agility and confidence while the other guys paddled around crazily and got pounded. I could sense the tension between the two groups too; resentment flowed from the original crowd toward the newbie's.

I didn't want to bother anybody. I just wanted to get on with things, and try to forget that agonizing year in my life.

Whenever I thought of PC Cru and the pressures that had been put on me to perform their religion and live up to their high holiness standards, it caused me to feel inadequate and I sensed anger toward them and toward myself. Why could they be so holy and sanctified, and why was I so utter unable to do so? Had God singled me out as an unforgiving backslider and was I bound for eternal damnation?

The more I thought about it, the more it was upsetting me, so I decided to put all the God and religion stuff behind me. I observed other things taking place in the world around me that were very different than the PC Cru way of life, and I suspected I may find my fulfillment there.

30

One Friday, at the end of a hard day of work when we were putting all the equipment away, Scott asked me if I wanted to drive up to San Francisco with him the next day. Over lunch he had been talking about some of the things taking place in San Francisco, the hippies and new ideas.

A few of them even showed up in Santa Cruz, and they looked much different than the surfers. The surfers had bleached blond hair and wore baggies and t-shirts with surfboards printed on them. This new group wore folksy clothing, beads, and headbands.

We talked about them over lunch, and Scott described some events called "Love-in's," but we didn't know much about them other than that it was a big gathering of young people. Scott thought it would be interesting to go up and see what was happening, so I decided to go along for the ride.

It was a beautiful summer day and the drive from Santa Cruz up Highway 1 to San Francisco was magnificent. There were very few houses along that stretch of road, except for the town of Half Moon Bay. The deep blue Pacific Ocean seemed to stretch into eternity. It was one of those perfect days where you wished you could be out on a boat, sailing away to some distant land.

We entered San Francisco, parked the car, and walked a couple of blocks to Golden Gate Park. I heard what sounded like music, but it had an unfamiliar beat—not like the fun sound of the Beach Boys I was accustomed to. At the entrance to the park, a tingling excitement began to creep into my limbs.

We passed through the gate, and a swirling mass of color and activity opened up before us. Guys with scraggly shoulder-length hair, wearing purple and orange pants danced with girls in flower-printed bikinis, wearing flowers in their stringy hair. Bongo drums and guitars banged and twanged as a group of informal picketers paraded past carrying hand-painted posters proclaiming, *Free Love* and *Make Love, Not War.*

There was a group of people under a tree sitting cross-legged on the ground. A guy held a cigarette to his mouth and inhaled deeply, then passed it to the person next to him. They all looked like they were in some sort of trance.

"Wow," Scott breathed, "This is amazing."

A girl in bell-bottom pants and a tie-dyed t-shirt came over to us.

"Hey, how are you guys?" she asked, sticking out her hand. Her eyes were glazed.

"Fine," I said. She wasn't wearing a bra, and the shirt hugged her chest, outlining every curve and contour.

Lifting her arm, she straightened the scarf around her head and nodded in the direction of a group of people. "My friends are over here. Do you want to join us?"

"Sure," Scott said.

I followed dumbly, overwhelmed by the pulsating sensations inundating me. We sat down and I wiped my hand over my face, feeling uncomfortable. What was going on here? I knew that there was a war in Vietnam, and that some people demonstrated against it, but this—

"We came in that car." She pointed to a VW van painted in a chaotic collection of garish designs. Red, yellow, and blue spun in psychedelic circles, and signs in the windows read: *Tune-In, Turn-On, Drop-Out* and *Do Your Own Thing.*

"That's some paint job," I said. "Where are you from?"

"Everywhere." She laughed. The goofy smile on her face seemed to last forever.

"No. From where do you come?" I asked.

"From nowhere. I'm a leaf in the wind," she laughed again, putting an arm on the ground to support herself, her head bobbing back and forth.

A guy with long hair said, "We're driving around the country, experimenting with a new way of life. The past is so confining. There's no freedom in the rules. Everyone makes their own."

That sounded foreign to me, but caught my interest. "How do you live?" I asked.

"From place to place," he answered. "We are gods to ourselves."

I saw that he misunderstood my question, but I let it pass. He was already onto another topic.

"We are spreading peace and love. We have a special experience that we share with anyone who's interested. A little drop of liquid can help you to see the world from an entirely different perspective. It's so far out." He showed us a small glass vial with some liquid in it.

"Is that LSD?" Scott asked.

"Yeah man," the hippie said, the words coming out slow.

"Too cool," Scott said.

The girl raised her head and lifted her hand into the air flashing a 'V' with her fingers. "Peace and love," she said.

She rose up and pushed the hippie guy on his back and lay on top of him and in a moment they became a tangle of tongues and limbs, seeming to forget we were there, or maybe they just didn't care.

A guy and a girl came over and sat down. They dressed similar to the two people writhing together in front of us.

"I'm Moon Beam," the girl said. "This here," she motioned to a guy with an overgrown beard wearing an ancient leather coat, wisps of its former fur collar matted into an extension of his greasy, disheveled hair, "this is Kosmic, spelled with a K."

"Are Moon Beam and Kosmic your real names?" I asked.

She laughed. "What is real? Everything is and isn't. It's what you want it to be."

It was a warm day and I wondered how he could stand wearing such heavy clothing.

He took a long drag from a hand-rolled cigarette and slowly rotated his reddened eyes upward to us. A glazed, lost look hung in his face, and he stared out at nothing. "Hhii," he slurred. "Expanded consciousness, man-n-n."

The smoke curling up from his mouth smelled strangely sweet, not like the acrid odor of tobacco that Eddie reeked of when he came back from his projects at night.

"Its hash," Moon Beam said, guessing my unspoken question. She dug in her pocket and pulled out a little plastic package filled with small greenish-brown chunks that looked like cow manure. "You roll your own joint and smoke it. Want to try?" Bending down, she picked up an imaginary object off the blanket and flipped it up into the sky.

"Are you kidding? Do I ever!" Scott exclaimed.

I felt uneasy. "Thanks, but I think I'll walk around a bit more," I said.

Moon Beam and Scott sat down, and she began explaining how to roll a joint.

A big crowd of people had gathered around a stage at the other end of the park, and I moved in that direction. A young woman with a wild mane of frizzy red hair falling in her face grasped the microphone, tossed her head around, and belted out a song.

"Everybody's got it, They're all trying to feel it. Everybody's dancing and singing romance, and they want to feel more, baby."

The people gyrated against each other and jumped up and down in a wild frenzy.

"Come on and do it. Come on, come on. Come on try it with me, try it with me, baby. Don't matter who you are, no, no. Don't matter where you come from. You just gotta try to feel it. C'mon, c'mon, c'mon...."

Suddenly a girl in a bikini top grabbed my hand and pulled me in. "C'mon," she yelled over the noise of the crowd.

"That's Janis Joplin who's singing."

I nodded like I should know, but I didn't know who she was other than she sounded like she was going to break her vocal chords. I stood there looking at the girl in front of me as she started to move her hips.

"Dance!" she commanded.

I didn't really know how to dance, but, keeping my eyes on the movement of her torso, I wiggled my hips and ricocheted off the people around me. She moved in closer, pressing her chest against mine, and I forgot about my gangly body and let the music take over.

"You want to do it with me?" she asked.

She said it like when you ask to borrow a pen from a classmate.

"You mean?" I questioned.

"Yeah, to do it with me right here on the grass."

I looked around. There were hundreds of people. I had thought about doing it with girls, but not here, like this.

"No, thanks," I said, stopping my movement which I knew was a lame imitation of dancing, anyway.

She cackled, "No spontaneity. No love." She moved away from me, her hands in the air, moving her hips to the music, disappearing into the crowd.

My senses felt overwhelmed and my nerves were rattled. Was this real? A girl had just made a proposition to me to do it right here?

#

I drove Scott's car back to Santa Cruz with him slumped on the passenger seat, a faint smile highlighting the peaceful expression on his face. Over the next few weeks, images and feelings from the day lingered in my mind. The people seemed so free, so relaxed and unburdened, sitting and lying around on the green grass under the trees. They drew me in, welcomed and accepted me without knowing the slightest thing about me. I relived the closeness of the girl's body against mine when we danced, the invitation she had extended to me to share in herself.

I had never before experienced such an openness and total lack of constraint. In that environment, I wondered if I could be completely me. I didn't have to perform or meet anyone's expectations, or hold back who I was inside.

31

As the end of summer approached, I decided to enroll in a local community college. I made an appointment to meet with the admissions counselor to sign up for fall classes.

Walking into the administration building, I remembered the first day at PC Cru, the intimidation of all the different tables and lines, getting shuffled around and standing endlessly in line.

A friendly face smiled at me as I entered. "Hello, can I help you find something?"

"I'm looking for," I looked down at the name on the piece of paper, "Judy Johnson, the admissions counselor."

"Room 209. Go up to the second floor and turn left." She pointed in the direction of the staircase.

"Thanks," I answered.

I knocked on the door and a voice called, "Come in."

"Hello, you must be Robert Macon." A lady in a warm orange sweater and brown skirt came out from behind her desk and shook my hand. Motioning to two cushioned yellow chairs angled toward each other, she said, "Please sit down." She picked a file folder up off the table and opened it on her lap. "Welcome to Cabrillo College. We're glad that you'll be a student here this fall. You need to choose your classes, is that correct?"

"Yes," I answered.

"And you're intending to major in Sociology?" she asked with such interest that she could have convinced me that she was considering the major herself.

I nodded.

"Okay, let's take a look at your transcripts," she said, sorting through the pile of papers in the folder and pulling one out. She examined it for a moment, and a furrow slowly dug its way across her forehead.

"These are your classes from your first semester—Physiology of Exercise, English 101, The Teachings of John Wesley, Purity-Christian Theology, and The Basics of Holiness?" she asked with a puzzled expression.

"Yes."

"Were you studying religion?"

"No, I was supposed to major in physical education."

"Physical education?" She looked up. "But you only had one class that would count toward that."

"There were a lot of basic requirements. It was a religious college and I took what the counselor told me to take."

"Hmm." She perused the transcript again. "What happened with your second semester? Did you have some kind of problem? It shows fifteen credits of 'F'." The tone of her voice made her question sounded genuine, not like she was condemning me.

I relaxed. Something told me I could be completely honest with her, and she wouldn't condemn me for my mistakes. "I was kicked out of school."

"Oh." She leaned back in her chair and thought for a moment. "Well, that's all in the past, so we don't need to worry about it. Unfortunately, however, none of the credits from these religion courses will transfer to a Sociology major. And, I'm sorry to say, we can't erase the failed classes, so you'll have to work extra hard to bring up your GPA. But if you're dedicated, I'm sure that you can do it." She smiled. "If you need help at any time, there are a number of groups on campus that offer free tutoring. I'll ask my secretary to give you their information before you leave."

Bringing out the course catalogue, she guided me through my options. Half an hour later, I left with a list of classes, and a seed of hope sprouting out of what had been a desert of despair. From an academic perspective, all the time and money I'd invested at PC Cru was a complete waste. I had no useful credits, and in their place a big black mark on my transcript that would take, what seemed to me, like an insurmountable effort to erase.

But Judy Johnson believed that I could do it. Coach Smyth, Mr. Grazer, Dr. Arlin and the Purity-Christian College Crusaders were now put behind me. With this new chance I resolved I would now get it right.

#

When school started, I picked up a job at the local gas station, which provided enough income to cover rent and food. Between work, school, basketball and surfing, I was always coming and going from my apartment.

The first few weeks I really hit the books, wanting more than anything to get my grade point average up so I could graduate some day. I was determined that nothing would get in the way.

One day, just after parking my car in front of my apartment, I saw a girl walking along the sidewalk. When she saw me looking at her, she smiled at me. My stomach lurched, and I quickly smiled back before she looked away. I watched her enter an apartment several building down from mine.

Over the next two days I saw her coming and going several times.

On the third day when coming home from school, I parked the car and flipped off the radio. I intended to work through the evening to submit an important paper that was due the following day.

Trudging down the street toward my empty apartment, I kicked a stone along and wondered what to eat for dinner. The refrigerator didn't have a lot of options to offer, and my cupboards were pretty bare. On top of that, crusty dishes filled the sink; I hadn't had time to clean up recently.

"Hi, neighbor."

I looked up from the sidewalk cracks. There she was.

"Uh, hi."

She stopped beside me, tilting her head upwards and smiling. "How are you?"

"Oh, fine."

"You don't look so fine. Long day?"

The note of caring in her voice loosened something inside of me. "Yeah, pretty much."

"Are you hungry? I've got some sandwich stuff if you want to come over."

That surprised me—that she would ask a total stranger. "Well, yeah . . . sure. That would be cool."

"My place is over this way." She started walking, but I already knew where she lived. I fell in step beside her.

The key clicked in the lock. I sensed a hesitation rising inside me. Maybe I shouldn't go in with her, I suddenly thought.

But she was already halfway across the room. "Don't just stand there; c'mon in," she beckoned while she flipped off her slippers.

I stepped over a pile of clothing and found my voice. "Do you live here alone?"

"No. I share the apartment with another girl and a guy, and ah . . . let's just say a few other people. We split the rent."

Throwing papers and books off the couch, she cleared a space. "Sit down, make yourself at home. We're not very particular about things here, as you can tell." She laughed.

The couch springs protruded palpably through the worn cushions.

She walked across the small room and put a record on the record player. The soft rhythmic harmony of *The Sound of Silence* by Simon & Garfunkel drifted across the room. *"Hello darkness my old friend . . ."*

She walked back and stood directly in front of me. "Do you want to dance?" she asked.

"Oh, I don't really know how." Her navel was directly in front of my eyes.

"Come on, I'll show you." She pulled me next to her and placed my hands on her shoulders. Sliding her arms around my waist, I felt her hands slip under my shirt and begin caressing my back. Her hips rubbed softly against mine, and my body began to respond to hers. We rocked back and forth slowly, melting into each other.

My whole body tingled as her fingertips skimmed the surface of my skin on their way around to my stomach. I tensed when she loosened the button on my jeans and pushed them down to the floor, revealing evidence of the desire coursing through me. She reached down and pulled off my tennis shoes, and then lifted my t-shirt over my head.

"C'mon, take it off," she said, pointing to her t-shirt and jeans.

My hands trembled, and I was too fast in yanking her t-shirt off. It messed up her stringy long hair, but she seemed to like it. She wasn't wearing a bra, and now my knees were shaking.

I couldn't get the button undone on her pants, so she had to help me, but a moment later she was naked.

She pulled me on top of her on the couch.

I wasn't thinking; there was an innate instinct that guided me. After a rush of gratification, it was over.

My body instantly relaxed, my heart pounding hard.

She immediately laughed. "First time?"

"Uh-huh," I murmured, a flame of red burning up my neck and over my face. There was a flood of feelings, mainly embarrassment—and guilt. Yet, her soft, naked body was a delight to feel against mine.

"That was the fastest I've ever seen," she said.

"I'm sorry," I whispered.

"No worries. You've got potential. Look, I've got to go, but it'd be great if you came back again sometime. Whenever you're ready. Okay?" She touched her lips to mine, and rolled out from underneath me.

"Sure, I'd like that." I sat up and reached over the crumpled newspapers on the floor for my underwear. "Sorry that I wasn't very good."

"Don't make a big deal about it. It's only sex," she said. "Next time I can show you some things to make it better." With a brief smile, she left the room.

My foot got stuck in my pant leg, and I twisted my shirt around when I tried to get it back on. Stumbling out of the apartment in a daze, I didn't even notice my bare feet until I was halfway home. Embarrassed, I snuck back into her place and grabbed my shoes. I didn't see her anywhere.

At home, I walked past the mess in the kitchen and headed straight for the shower, hoping for hot water. The building hadn't originally been designed to accommodate so many apartments, and the capacity of the water heater quickly reached its limit.

In the bathroom, I unbuttoned my pants, remembering the feel of her hands on my stomach only a few minutes ago. As they dropped to the floor, my naked body stared back at me out of the mirror in the corner. What was this mass of flesh and desire that I couldn't control?

And, she said, 'it was only sex,' so flippantly. What did that mean? It wasn't just that, or at least not meant to be just that. Wasn't there another kind of closeness that came with that kind of intimacy? I felt it for her, or did I? It was quick, but her presence was now with me. It seemed I somehow carried her in my inner being.

I prayed for hot water as I flipped the tap—hot water to wash away the jumble of confusion inside of me.

But in the midst of the confusion I identified another feeling. It was a bizarre sense of revenge. It was a payback to PC Cru for all their impossible rules. I somehow laughed; if they could only see me now. But wasn't I becoming what they said I would become? Hopelessly lost.

Did it really matter?

#

I was two days late in submitting my paper and told myself that this could not happen again. I needed to be on time with my homework, no matter what.

Over the following days, I tried to keep the girl out of my mind, making an intentional effort to watch the other girls on the beach and at school, fishing for an image that would push hers away. But she was like a broken jack-in-the-box that wouldn't stay down. The moment that sharp pang of intense pleasure shot through me as I lay on top of her kept reliving itself. Something held me to her, kept me looking for her every day, but I never saw her.

Finally I mustered the courage to go knock on her door. I banged my fist against the peeling green paint, simultaneously excited and terrified of what might appear on the other side.

"Hello," said a brown-haired girl in jeans.

"Uh, excuse me. I'm, uh, I'm looking for this girl who lives here. I met her a few weeks ago. Is she home?"

"What girl? Andy, check the eggs, will ya?" she yelled over her shoulder.

"Sorry, what were you saying?"

"Isn't there another girl who lives here?"

"Lots of girls live here," she said.

"I don't know her name, but she's about so tall." I held my hand just under my chin, where her head had rested when she pressed herself against me. The soft summer evening smell of her hair came rushing back into my nose. "She has long blond hair that comes about to the middle of her back."

"You remember her well." The girl laughed pleasantly. "But I'm sorry, she doesn't live here anymore. Two days ago she took off with a couple of surfer guys and they headed to Huntington Beach in Southern California."

"Oh." The girl started to close the door, and I asked quickly, "What was her name?"

"Cherry or something like that."

"Thanks," I said and turned away, now having a name to the first girl I ever made love to, if that was her name, yet she had disappeared, just like that.

The closing door echoed hollowly behind me.

#

One evening about a week after my experience with Cherry, I was in my apartment trying to advance on some homework. I was leaning back on the couch, legs stretched out, resting on a wooden box that doubled as a footrest and coffee table.

I was taking a Philosophy course, a subject that had never captured my interest; I was always a basketball guy, more or less fitting the stereotype of your average jock. I liked to do things without thinking about it too much.

The metal knocker clapped in three firm beats, resounding through the thin door.

I went to the door and a girl was standing there who looked like so many of the other girls in Santa Cruz and San Francisco. They all looked basically the same: stringy blond hair hanging down the back or partially covered in a headscarf, or held by a headband, brilliantly colored tie-dyed t-shirts outlining braless breasts, hip-hugging bell bottom pants dragging on the ground, and sandals.

"Hello," she said. "Cherry told me about you."

I wondered what Cherry had said and felt a strange mix of emotions; guilt for my sinful act, and shame for my quick performance.

"Can I come in?" She asked.

"Sure." I led her into the small living area and moved the philosophy reading on top of a foot-high stack of textbooks and random papers that were on the floor.

We sat down next to each other.

"What's that?" She pointed to the pile as she plopped down next to me on the couch, her breast brushing my shoulder.

"Nothing much." The feeling of her warm body against mine pushed philosophical musings back into the nether regions of my brain where they usually stayed.

"I saw you at the beach a couple days ago. You looked pretty good out there on your surfboard. You can really ride the waves well." She moved closer to me and traced her finger gently across my forehead.

"I like to surf, but I don't have a lot of time for it. School and stuff, you know."

"School keeps you busy?"

"Yeah, I'm on the basketball team, so we have practice and games all the time. I transferred here last year, and I lost some credits in the process. Plus, I have to work pretty hard to make up for some classes I failed my freshman year."

"I'm Flower."

Here was another one of those crazy pseudonyms that all the girls seemed to be adopting, like Ocean, Liberty, Rainbow, and Freedom. Where they came up with their names, I didn't know.

"I'm Robert," I said.

"I know. Remember, Cherry told me about you."

"Ah . . . yeah . . . ah, Cherry, a free spirit."

She smiled and whispered, "Isn't that what life's all about, a free spirit . . . and free-love?"

32

The next morning I found a note on the kitchen counter.

Thanks for the night. See you around. Flower.

Again there was the pang of guilt, but I told myself that this was nothing more than the voice of PC Cru playing games in my head, so I decided to suppress that and move on with this new life I had found.

And then there were more girls, not usually knocking on my door.

I began going to love-ins in San Francisco, to music concerts in open parks, and coffee houses where folk music was played, and some Eastern religion gatherings. I went to those places to hang out and escape into a different world. Those events became a diversion from the routine of work and school, and I felt freedom like nothing ever experienced at PC Cru. My hair grew long and I wore bell bottom pants, tie-dye t-shirts and sandals, and I blended in with the surfers and hippies.

It was the time of the "Summer of Love" where teenagers from all over America were flooding to San Francisco, and Santa Cruz got the over-flow. They lived without restrictions, throwing off the morals and taboos of society, living in a counter-culture with a new set of forms. Hashish and LSD were abundant and reality was whatever you wanted it to be. I became lost in a world of ideals, of freedom and peace and love.

I flowed with the experience, except for the drugs. I was an athlete and wanted to stay at the top of my game. And, there was an internal voice telling me not to cross that line, for if I did, I might go beyond the point of no return. That terrified me.

At some of those events I met girls. Or, I should say, that's where they came to me.

Sometimes they stayed with me, maybe for a few days or even a week. Some were runaways from the Midwest, making their way to San Francisco, looking for a place to crash for a night or two. Others were from the local scene. I would see them around, and they would come back with me to my apartment. Most seemed lonely and we would do our act together, our dance, and then they would move on. Not that I wanted any of them to really stay.

Every time I slept with someone, I found myself bound to her in an incredible force of passion and intimacy. And yet afterward, although we had shared this intense baring of our bodies, I realized that I hardly knew her.

Each girl left behind a bare couch or bed amongst scattered papers and clothes, a half filled water glass by the sink, the imprint of a head on the pillow next to mine. Those were the only tokens I held of a fleeting presence in my life.

Each girl took something of my soul with her, like precious stone by precious stone being removed, leaving behind a deep, dark, empty pit.

If life was a scale, the frequent moments of physical pleasure I was experiencing could in no way balance out the empty heaviness that was there most of the time.

33

The alarm rang, and I rolled over, knocking an open container of deodorant onto the floor as I groped for the off button. The sheets twisted around my legs, and when I sat up to untangle them, I noticed that the other side of the bed was empty. There was a note on the pillow.

Thanks—you're fantastic!

And that was it. Where was the ultimate meaning in this? Where was the true lasting intimacy I needed? My soul demanded something more.

I dropped the note into the wastebasket and stumbled drowsily into the bathroom in my boxers, I splashed cold water on my face, and dried off with the still-damp towel the girl had left crumpled on the counter. I couldn't remember her name.

I went into my living area and picked up a handout that my philosophy teacher had given the students the previous week. I hadn't touched it yet, and we were supposed to discuss it in class tomorrow. I scanned the title: Arthur Schopenhauer, Selected readings from On the Basis of Morality' and On the Vanity of Existence.

Sinking onto the couch, I picked up the Schopenhauer excerpts I had thrown aside the night before and began reading. I lifted the first page to turn it over when something halfway down caught my eye. My mind had been wandering, skipping through the paragraphs without absorbing the content.

The greatest wisdom consists in enjoying the present and making this enjoyment the goal of life, because the present is all that is real and everything else merely imaginary. But you could just as well call this mode of life the greatest folly: for that which in a moment ceases to exist, which vanishes as completely as a dream, cannot be worth any serious effort.

We shall do best to think of life…as a process of disillusionment.

"A process of disillusionment." Maybe that's what had happened at PC Cru. Something about the whole system struck me as strange, but I hadn't been able to put my finger on it. All I knew was that it hadn't turned out to be what I thought it was.

Now the same feeling pestered me again. All the talk of free love, but what was it really? A succession of one-night stands that, for all the pleasure they offered, left me with empty hands a few hours later?

I started the article over at the beginning. Maybe philosophy could tell me something after all.

Every moment of our life belongs to the present only for a moment; then it belongs forever to the past. Every evening we are poorer by a day. We would perhaps grow frantic at the sight of this ebbing away of our short span of time were we not secretly conscious in the profoundest depths of our being that we share in the inexhaustible well of eternity, of which we can forever draw new life and renewed time.

This was making sense. That week I spent at Morro Bay I had looked up at the stars and had seen the vastness of the universe and felt so small and finite, yet I had also felt the 'inexhaustible well of eternity'. Maybe that explained this recurring spiritual longing inside that I couldn't explain.

After class that afternoon, I stepped across the threshold of a university library for the first time in my life. I wanted to read more of this Schopenhauer guy who wrote exactly about everything I was feeling. The professor said that Schopenhauer had started the 'Pessimist' school of philosophy and he borrowed heavily from the book of Ecclesiastes in the Bible.

The library had a Bible somewhere back in the religion section. I took it over to a desk at the end of the wall between two rows of books, and searched for a while to find the book of Ecclesiastes.

Vanity of vanities, said the Preacher, all is vanity. I have seen all the works that are done under the sun; and, behold, all is vanity and vexation of spirit.

For what has man from all his labor, and from the troubling of his heart, in which he has labored under the sun? For all his days are sorrows, and his labor sadness; yea, his heart does not take rest in the night. This is also vanity.

That evening, I went straight home after work and read. I had to slog through some of the philosophical stuff, but every so often I would stumble across a section that would set the neurons firing in my brain. A couple days later, I dug an old Bible out of a box in the closet and looked up Ecclesiastes to see what else it had to say. When the questions and confusion got too intense, I grabbed my surfboard and headed for the waves I understood and could manage.

I was longing for spiritual things and wondered if I hadn't missed something at PC Cru? Strange as it was, I couldn't help wondering what it would be like back at PC Cru. Although I'd hardly been in touch with Eddie and Leyland since I left, their friendship still seemed valuable.

I remembered Mr. Grazer's words on the day that I left: "Robert, Christianity is a belief system, something to be learned and followed. A true believer is saved and sanctified and this is demonstrated through a life of holiness. Unless it is learned and followed it is frustrated and ultimately lost. Living by this system allows believers to be healed of their moral and spiritual ailments."

Maybe I was running away from the light, and that was why I felt distant from God. And I felt morally and spiritually sick. But if I went back, could I find God? And would the God that I found fill my emptiness?

I thought I could live without him, but could I? Really?

I grabbed a jacket and headed out to the beach. Sitting down next to a large rock that blocked out the wind, I remembered the end of the book of Ecclesiastes that I had read earlier in the day:

Now all has been heard; here is the conclusion of the matter: Fear God and keep his commandments, for this is the whole duty of man. For God will bring every deed into judgment, including every hidden thing, whether it is good or evil.

I believed in God, or at least I thought I did. But if God didn't exist then each person's life was like the waves of the sea: churning with force, following a given direction and then fading quietly into nothingness on the shore.

I wanted my life to have ultimate meaning, and I couldn't see a way to find that apart from God. Yet I saw that every deed was judged and there was a deep separation between God and me. Then I thought, if I obey the rules and do my best to live up to the expectations, maybe I could earn their approval at PC Cru, and then prove myself to God so that he would accept me too.

I decided the only hope I had was to return to PC Cru, or at least that thought kept going through my mind.

CHAPTER 34

Present Day

I follow the Pacific Coast Highway from Morro Bay to Monterey. It is one of America's great scenic drives with rugged sea cliffs and pounding surf. It is a pleasure to drive the Porsche on this winding coastal road.

When I get to Santa Cruz I turn off the highway and drive through residential and commercial streets until coming to the Santa Cruz lighthouse. After parking the car I walk over to the area where you can see the surfers. Large swells are coming off the Pacific, and a group of surfers wait on their surfboards. They wear wetsuits. I know from experience how cold the water can be here in Northern California.

They sit on their surfboards, legs dangling in the water while anticipating the swells, trying to choose the perfect wave for the perfect ride. The waves come in at an angle here. If you catch one and are unlucky, you can crash against the cliff, but if you stay wide, you can ride the wave for almost a mile, one of the longest rides anywhere in California.

This is where I lived for two years. I have mixed emotions about those years. The religious system I was in had led to death, but so did this other world. This is where I experienced the counterculture, which was something that blindsided most of us at that time.

As I reflect on this, I realize that many social and religious institutions in the 1950's and early 1960's had been living in an idealistically narrow bubble just ready to be popped. Our general culture came from three primary television sources: ABC, NBC and CBS. They formed our view of the world and established the things we valued: a house, a car, a job, and a happy family.

But it wasn't all that idealistic. For instance, all the admired singers and movie stars smoked cigarettes, and therefore most adults copied their behavior. Smoking was admired and accepted as normal by the society. And, as a result, a lot of people died of lung cancer.

Conformity characterized the culture, and things became highly materialistic.

In that time, the churches we attended formed our religious views and told us how to work our way to God. At the same time, our religious institutions were uninformed about the philosophical changes taking place in society. A new worldview based on relativism was emerging and the old order was about to crumble. Babylon, as I like to call this new philosophy, was about to take the place of the old order. But then again, this Babylon philosophy isn't all that new.

My feeling is that many of the religious institutions, one of which I was a part, were built on inadequate presuppositions. Some people naively lived within these religious constructs, whereas others used them for their own benefit.

They weren't ready for the counter-culture tidal wave that was coming, along with its philosophical underpinnings. It's interesting that once it came, some religious leaders adapted their institutions, not for the sake of truth, but for the purpose of keeping their positions of power and control over their flocks.

For those of us imprisoned by these legalistic institutions we had two choices, either to conform or to get out. We were like canaries confined to small cages. If we became free we didn't know how to survive outside because we were not given the tools. So the choice was, stay in the cage and die, or escape the cage and die.

That's what was happening to me when I had lived in Santa Cruz. I had drifted outside the restrictive boundaries of PC Cru into the wide open world of the California counterculture. As a result, my morality had become relative.

My generation of the 60's, the baby-boomers, is the one that resurrected an old idea from 2,300 BC Babylon, that every person is their own god and their own morality. "Free-Love" and "Make Love Not War" were not just superficial slogans but expressed a deeper philosophical belief. It is the ideology that there is no right or wrong, only how you interpret actions as right or wrong.

Unfortunately, this philosophy doesn't satisfy the deeper human longings and it only leads to chaos and confusion.

When I think about it, the so called "Free-Love" was not all that free, for we paid a heavy price. We lost our souls and we lost the meaning of intimate and lasting relationships.

In my parents generation they fell in love, got married, and then had sex. In my generation many people fell in love, had sex, and then got married. The generation of today has sex, then sees if there is a feeling, and then waits for what will happen. Maybe I was ahead of the times, for that's how I was functioning when I lived in Santa Cruz. It's tragic, for we have lost the ability to love, and to make the commitments that accompany true love.

My thoughts shift back to my surroundings. Standing above the cliff,

I watch the surfers. Surfing is something I've missed over the years—that brief moment of existential joy, the thrill of feeling nature sweep you along on the face of a wave.

I envy the young surfers down there and for a split second consider renting a surfboard. But with years of no practice I would only set myself up for looking like a fool. I laugh at myself. I had looked foolish enough just trying to keep up with Monique as she glided down the ski slopes like a butterfly. I wish she could be here with me, to see this and to talk about culture, and religion. She had such good insights into these things.

For a moment, my soul feels empty as I sense deep grief and loss. I look at the big waves rising up and down, as sorrow rises up within me. I have to ride those waves of pain. I remember how Monique shared how Christ understood pain, because he experienced every single one on earth, never denying the feeling . . . even though I wish there was a way for me to avoid them.

Leaving the lighthouse, I drive around and search for the apartment where I lived so many years ago. It is still there, only painted a different color. So was the apartment down the street where I had been with Cherry or whatever her name was, "the first one." I thought about that brief almost humorous moment of encountering her. Funny yes, but it was also the moment where the canary left the narrow cage. I thought he had tasted freedom but that was an illusion.

In reality it was vanity that led to emptiness, but those events drove me to seek deeper things. Indeed that was a significant turning point in my search for truth.

I gaze at the run down apartment where I had lived. The place had provided me with fleeting pleasure and it gave me an alternative to the legalistic world that was destroying me. But neither the Pharisees of Pasadena, nor the Babylonian garden of delights can fulfill you, for in the end the deeper philosophical questions are not answered.

But can I blame everything on them? How much responsibility rests on me for taking the path of death? That's another thing my generation perfected . . . to not take responsibility for failures, but to blame others.

I go to my rental car and head north, to look for Ronita Jansen.

CHAPTER 35

Junior: 1967-1968

My first year in Santa Cruz ended, and I picked up thirty credits at Cabrillo College. I passed, with mostly C's. It marginally improved my grade point average, but not by much—the fifteen units of F from PC Cru still sitting there. There just wasn't any time for serious studying, with surfing, basketball, work at the gas station, and the endless progression of girls.

With the girls I lost count, and I knew they were keeping me from getting better grades. I expended a lot of mental and emotional energy, not getting much sleep, and I carried a lot of guilt.

One warm Friday evening in late Spring I escaped my apartment for a stroll along the boardwalk. In a few weeks my second year of Junior College would be finished, and I wondered where I would go from here. I knew I would have to make a decision.

My stepfather kept telling me that I needed to stay in school, because the Vietnam War was getting really bad, and the U.S. government was drafting more and more young men. I still didn't understand all that. It raised so many emotions in people. There were now regular anti-war demonstrations taking place in San Francisco, Chicago, New York and other cities. There were also a lot of politicians and church people who were calling the demonstrators a bunch of 'commie lovers' and things like that. All that war stuff was far away, and mostly I didn't care one way or the other. Fundamentally, I just didn't want any army people telling me to march here or there, to tell me what I could or couldn't do.

I was now twenty years old, and a prime age for being taken into the army and sent to Vietnam. There were around half a million soldiers there, with hundreds of dead ones being shipped back every week.

There were a lot of other things happening, but they didn't impact me directly. Some weeks before, a colored guy, the Reverend Martin Luther King Jr. was shot by someone. It was causing a lot of tension between the coloreds and the whites.

Closer to home, over in the valley, a guy by the name of César Chávez started something called the United Farm Workers Association. All the Mexican workers were striking, and fruit was rotting in the fields. Some people said we were going to starve.

I read about the women's liberation movement, causing trouble all over the place. And it seemed a lot of young people were going eastern and joining groups like the Hare Krishna's, who shaved their heads and wore sandals and yellow colored robes. They chanted and begged for money out on the streets—Buddhists or Hindus, or something like that.

People began to flock to Eastern religions. When I talked with some of them they used terms like "collective consciousness" and "collective oneness" and taught that everything in the universe is one, starting with some kind of impersonal force, matter or energy. But I wondered, if the origin of the universe is intrinsically impersonal, then how do we explain personality? These people said that any experience of personality is ultimately an illusion, including any inclination toward morals. Laws are arbitrary and every person has to make up their own rules and construct their own belief system.

I could only see chaos as a result if everyone made up their own laws, and the way they were thinking made everyone their own god. Doesn't the fact that we can't escape this unique sense of personality point to a higher personality? To say it was an illusion was a denial of reality, although they would argue that there is no reality.

During that year a lot was happening politically. The main thing was that President Johnson announced that he wasn't going to run for a second term. I guess he just gave up, and I didn't much blame him with all this discontent.

But politics were not on my mind. I was wondering what I would do next year when I was finished with Cabrillo College.

One evening I went out to think. I found a bench close to the road running parallel to the boardwalk. In the background I could hear music blaring from a radio inside a hot-dog stand, *Sitting on the Dock of the Bay* by Otis Redding. I could relate to the song. Especially the part that said, "I wish this loneliness would leave me alone." It's amazing how you can be so lonely in the middle of such a busy place, like Santa Cruz on a weekend.

Weekends usually offered the freest entertainment, with hordes of people flocking into Santa Cruz looking for a little excitement to liven up their relatively mundane lives. Teenagers cruised slowly in their hot-rods down the packed one-way street, showing off their stuff, rolling down their windows to chat back and forth in the stop and go traffic.

I had been staring off into space when I felt a tap on my shoulder. Six girls stood in front of me.

"'Scuse us," the designated speaker said. "We're trying to find a place to park. Do you know where we might find a spot?"

"Down the street to the left." I explained the rest of the way, then asked, "Where you from?"

"Visalia," she responded, jerking her thumb backward. "Over in the valley."

I recognized the name. An agricultural town dominated by Mexican workers and American greasers more interested in hot rods than surfboards. It had a reputation for being somewhat on the rough side.

A low-riding 1963 Chevy with shiny chrome rims and oversized tires pulled up to the curb. The passenger door opened, and a tall, heavyset guy got out. Comb lines streaked through the grease in his wavy black hair, and a black leather jacket lent him a sufficiently intimidating presence.

He walked straight up to me and, with no introduction, delivered a hard shove to my shoulder. I tripped backward and stumbled, trying to catch my balance.

"You been messing with my chick?" he threatened, his eyes darkening.

My stomach tightened, and I could feel every muscle in my body tensing.

In a ferocious tone, the girl who had been talking to me answered, "Buddy, he ain't been messing with nobody. We were just asking him directions."

Buddy leaned closer to me, blowing a blast of warm alcohol breath into my face. "You been messing with my chick?" Both his hands thudded against my chest before I could respond, knocking the wind out of me as I fell backward onto the bench.

"I don't even know who your chick is," I spat as soon as I got my breath back.

"I'm gonna beat the shit out of you." He wasn't joking.

I popped up from the bench and backed away, but he leaped toward me and grabbed a fistful of my shirt. Pressing his knuckles against my chin, he lowered his voice and spoke through clenched teeth. "No one touches my girl."

I had never fought before, but my arm shot out instinctively, and I palmed Buddy's face like a basketball. He reached up to yank my arm away, but before his fists closed around it, I unleashed a hard kick into his groin, so hard that his feet left the ground. I nailed him with a second vicious thrust, and he fell to the ground, clutching himself in agony.

Stepping away in surprise at the strength of my own hands and legs, I couldn't believe what I had just done—until two policemen came running up, drawing clubs from their belts. I ducked, shielding my head with my hands. Out of the corner of my eye, I saw Buddy get up and charge one of the policemen. He didn't stand a chance. Thirty seconds later, he lay on his face, arms wrenched behind his back as the policeman snapped handcuffs on his wrists.

I watched in stunned disbelief, and almost jumped when the other policeman came over and clamped my wrists in cold metal as well. Despite previous slight encounters with the law, I had never had an opportunity to think of myself as a real criminal.

Then they frisked us both.

A police van pulled up, and they loaded us into the back. Buddy sat leaning forward, his head hung between his legs. Groaning, he repeated, "Oooh, you kicked me so hard."

The van hit a bump, and I unsuccessfully tried to brace myself with my feet. My tailbone cracked against the unpadded bench.

Buddy didn't look up at me until we approached the police station and the vehicle slowed. Then, lifting his head for a moment, he said, "Hey man. I need your help. You start talking to the two policemen when we get out of the van, and I'm gonna take off running. I can outrun these guys."

The key clinked in the lock, and the bright lights of the police station flooded the back of the van. Buddy began to stand up, then collapsed in pain, falling onto the floor of the van. The policeman pulled him out and set him on his feet, producing a horrific moan.

They moved us into the police station. There were no formalities at the front desk other than emptying our pockets and taking our valuables and belts. Moving us down a narrow hall, a policeman opened a solid metal door and said to me, "Inside."

Buddy started to move, but the policeman said, "Not you. Him," pointing to me. At that point he removed my handcuffs.

I walked in, and with a loud *clunk*, the door shut behind me. I froze. I had only ever heard the hollow clanging of prison doors in movies.

I don't know how long I stood there motionless before I heard a noise in the corner. I started slightly. I hadn't noticed anyone else in the dim light.

"What'a you in here for?" a scratchy voice rasped.

My eyes focused slowly, making out the figure of a man slouched on the bench. A dark five-day growth of beard lent him a somewhat sinister appearance. His shirt hung askew, dribbles of dried tobacco spit clustered just under the collar.

"I got in a fight," I answered.

"Yeah? Me too," the man said. He shifted his legs to reveal a ragged tear across the knee of his pants. "A guy jumped me, and I stabbed him. He died but it was goddamn self-defense. You gotta look out for yourself. The story of life. Don't forget. Think of yourself first." He rested his head in the corner and fell asleep with his mouth open, revealing a gaping hole where his two front teeth should have been.

Moving like a robot, I managed to sit down on the bench as far away as possible from the murderer. I pressed my hands between my knees to stop the shaking.

The clack of dress shoe soles on a concrete floor broke into my consciousness. The warden unlocked the door, and a man in a business suit appeared. "I'm the Santa Cruz District Attorney. Can you please come with me?"

He led me to the front desk, and a man handed my wallet and belt across the counter. "You can have these back. We aren't going to press any charges."

"Charges?" My voice rang in my ears.

"The two policemen saw everything—that you were attacked, and did what you had to do to protect yourself."

"I've never been in a fight before," I heard myself say.

"You did well, but don't make a habit of it. You can go."

"Thank you, sir." I shoved my wallet into my pocket, and began threading my belt through the belt loops.

"I don't want you to go back to the Boardwalk tonight. Go home or go somewhere else, but we don't want to see you down there," the attorney said sternly.

"Yes sir."

A policeman drove me back to my car.

I knew I wouldn't be able to sleep if I went back to my apartment, so I drove north on Highway 1 along the coast until I came to a small state park. Taking a jacket from the back seat, I walked toward the beach.

A cool wind blew off the Pacific Ocean, whipping my jacket around me. I could hear waves crashing far out and rumbling toward the shore.

I walked over some sand dunes, and down to the beach, and then made my way to some large rocks that jutted out into the dark ocean. A sliver of a moon illuminated the clouds giving an ominous feel to the heavens.

The tide was at its height, and extremely large breakers were rumbling in toward the shore like raging spirits intent on grabbing you and sucking you in. In the darkness of night they were frightening, but I sensed something even more evil. In reflecting back on PC Cru, and then my life since leaving PC Cru, I imagined myself swimming out into the blue ocean, and that the religion world and the California culture were two different tides. And, as I swam they were coming at me from both sides, closing in upon me, both competing with each other for my soul, and both intent on rising up to engulf me, to stifle and drown, a pale death.

I stood on the rocks and sea spray from the crashing waves hit my face. I stared out at the massive expanse of black sea, almost indiscernible from the night sky. Tilting my head backward, I searched for the constellations that I'd been studying in astronomy class.

The stars seemed to spell out Schopenhauer's words: imagine

The vanity of existence is revealed in the infiniteness of time and space contrasted with the finiteness of the individual in both.

Infinite, finite—how could I begin to get my mind around such abstract concepts?

But I didn't need to understand them to sense that, standing beneath stars and a God I could never reach, standing in front of that vast expanse of water that plunged deeper than Mount Everest rose high—that in light of these things, my six-foot-five form was very, very small.

Where could I find the spiritual answers? The only place seemed to be PC Cru.

CHAPTER 36

Present Day

By the end of the day I arrive in San Francisco and spend the night at the Mark Hopkins Hotel, a historic landmark. I am exhausted, as jetlag is taking over. I go straight to bed and sleep through the night.

In the morning I wonder if I might squeeze in a day to see the sites and do some shopping. It would be interesting to see how things have changed. I know there were no more love-ins at Golden Gate Park and the Haight-Ashbury area is no longer a gathering place for hippies and runaways.

Instead, parts of the city have become a hedonistic metropolis, where God is perceived to be dead and the creature is worshiped rather than the creator. It has become like Narcissus worshiping his own likeness. It is a logical outcome of the door we opened in the late 1960's.

I know I only have two days before going south, so sightseeing and shopping have to be put on the back burner. In reality, something else is pulling more strongly on my soul. I'd like to find Ronita.

I check out of the hotel, go to the Porsche and tap a destination into the GPS. It leads me through San Francisco, across the Golden Gate Bridge and into Oakland. It turns out to be a pretty rough area of the city with boarded up shops, graffiti everywhere. I see my destination even before the GPS tells me I have arrived.

A shop ahead on the right has a sign that reads, Black History Book Store. There is an empty place in front of the store so I park, lock the car and go inside.

The store has shelves full of books and there are a couple of round tables with chairs where coffee could be served. A couple of computers are off in one corner. There is no one in the store except for a man who is seated at one of the tables. He is reading a book and has a mug of coffee in front of him.

I approach him and ask, "Is it possible to speak to Leroy, who runs the store?"

"You looking at him," he says. He is a black man with gray curly hair. He is wearing jeans and a gray t-shirt. His arms and chest are huge like he spends most of his time in the gym.

"My name is Robert Macon," I tell him. "I called you about a week ago."

He looks up from his book. "You the dude that calls me from Paris?"

I smile. "Yes, from Paris."

He glances out toward the street and says, "That your car?"

I nod.

"You crazy to leave a car like that out there. Around here it's gonna last about three minutes before someone borrows it. Lucky it's in front of my store because no one will mess with it."

Leroy stands up and makes his way over to the counter by his cash register. He's about my height but much broader.

"What you want with this Ronita?" He asks.

"I was a friend. You know how it is. You get to a point in life where you're curious to know what happened to people you knew in the past."

He looks at me and grins. "Most of the people from my past are either in jail or dead."

I'm not sure how to respond and say, "Sorry to hear that."

"How's it that a white boy became friends with a black girl, so much so that he's willing to pay money to find her?"

"She's just one of several people I'm hoping to find. You know, just that curiosity about old acquaintances and their story." He doesn't need to know everything.

I had found his store on the internet, knowing that Oakland might be a good starting point. His website says, "Everything about Black History: events, places, people and everything that ever happened in Oakland." On the website there was a lot of information about marches, protest movements, and the Black Panthers. The website claims that the Black History Bookstore knows the bio of everyone who had been a member of the Black Panthers, so I thought this might be a good starting point. I had called from Paris and gave him my request, and he said he might be able to help . . . for a price.

I agreed.

"Did you find her?" I ask.

"Maybe," he says. "It was a long time ago. She was here in Oakland with her brother, but not for long."

"Why not?" I ask.

"He was a Panther and a small group of them was extending themselves from the main leadership, you might say."

"Extending" I ask.

"Uh huh. They went out on their own and tried to rob a bank. Ronita's brother was one of them and he was shot and killed when they ran into the police. You can't blame the Panther leadership for not being happy, so they said they didn't know those guys. The Panther's were already getting big pressure from the law."

"Do you know what happened to Ronita?" I ask.

"You got the money?" he asked.

I reach into my pocket and pull out an envelope. It contains several hundred dollars.

He takes the envelope, looks inside, pulls open a drawer and hands me a piece of paper. "She was only here a few months and then she headed back south. No reason to stick around here after what happened to her brother."

I look at the paper and on it is written an address in San Marino, California.

"San Marino? The one near Los Angeles?" I ask.

"Yeah, down south somewhere," he says.

"Are you sure about this?" I raise the paper.

He turns to me his muscles bulging. "Look man, it was a long time ago that she went down there. But we got a network of people. I sent out a bunch of emails and someone from down south remembered her, at least where she used to work. Try that address."

I glance outside and see three black guys getting close to my rental car. They are dressed in black and wear black bandanas on their heads, and are carrying some sort of tools.

Leroy moves his large frame to the front door, and opens it and goes outside. He says something that I can't discern and the three guys look in at me, and then they move down the street.

He turns to me with a grim look on his face and says, "You crazy to come here with that car. It ain't safe and I'd advise you to get out of here pretty quick. And keep moving because of carjacking."

"Thanks for the address," I tell him.

He nods and then glances right and left.

I get into the Porsche. The three guys are just up the sidewalk and are staring in my direction.

I drive away wondering if in fact there was real danger or was he just trying to get rid of me?

Ronita in San Marino doesn't make any sense.

CHAPTER 37

Senior: 1968-1969

I made a tough decision to return as a student to PC Cru, but I knew I needed to be there.

My life in Santa Cruz was leading me nowhere, only to unhappiness. The lifestyle there gave nothing to fulfill the deepest needs of the soul. Part of me never wanted to see PC Cru again. But there was a much stronger motivation at play in that I ached to find a religious solution to fill my longing for God, and this seemed to be the only place where I could turn.

I stood before the PC Cru registrar.

He said, "I'm not sure how we're going to work this out," sweeping his hand across the pile of transcripts in front of him. "When you were here at Pasadena Purity-Christian for the first time, you majored in Physical Education. At Cabrillo College you majored in Sociology. And you have classes in Astronomy and Philosophy and Math. Is that correct?"

I nodded. My classes were all over the map but my best grades were in Math.

"You have one semester of completed credits from our institution, four full semesters from Cabrillo Junior College, plus summer classes there. However, you also have fifteen failed credits from here, and all of your other grades are just passing. That means that you are going to have to work extremely hard to get your GPA high enough to meet the require-ment for graduation." He folded his hands on his desk and peered at me through thick, black glasses.

"I understand." The hard wooden slats of the chair dug into my back.

"We need to answer two important questions. What do you want to major in now, and what classes are you going to take this semester? In this decision, we have to consider that your transcripts are a mishmash of classes, and it may be difficult to match them to our course requirements. You are also missing something. You still need to take all the advance level religion courses expected of students here."

With every word, I wanted to slump lower under the impossibility of it all. I felt like I was standing in front of a looming brick wall, and he just kept adding more and more layers on top.

But I had to prove myself.

I decided on a Sociology major. According to the schedule the registrar laid out for me, to graduate I would need a year and a half of studies, plus a heavy load of classes during the following summer.

We talked about finances. That seemed to be what he was interested in most. I needed to get a job to pay the school tuition. Going to a private Christian college wasn't cheap, but I had made my choice. I had saved some money in Santa Cruz and would work to make up what was missing. This was the place where I had to prove to myself that I could make it, socially, academically and spiritually.

Walking out of the administration building, I almost felt as if I had never been there before. I hardly recognized any faces, and the students looked so different from the people I'd been around in Santa Cruz. Their beehive hairdos and cotton dresses lagged behind the times by about fifteen years. No girl at PC Cru wore pants, much less bell-bottoms, and flowers were found in gardens, not on clothes or in hair.

The housing department assigned me a roommate, a junior music major named Bob Harrington. He seemed nice enough, but after living on my own for the last two years, it would take awhile to get used to sharing my space.

Eddie was in a different building than me, with a roommate I didn't know. I had written to him to let him know I would be back.

I went from the administration building to their dorm, found their room, and knocked on the door.

"Come in," I heard a voice say.

I walked in. Eddie was lying on his bed throwing a golf ball up in the air and catching it.

"Hey, Robert. How you doing?" Eddie said. He got up from the bed and shook my hand.

"OK. I'm back. How about you?"

"Oh, same old thing." He looked me in the eyes. "Gonna give it another go, huh?"

"Yeah. Gotta prove myself."

"Good luck." An undertone of mocking hovered beneath the well-wishing words.

"Who's still around?" I asked, scanning the room.

Eddie sat down in the chair, and rested his feet on the unmade bed. He thought for a minute and then started naming names, counting on his fingers.

"Do you remember Donald Bonen?" Eddie asked.

"Yeah, how could I forget?"

"He graduated, and then married Elizabeth the Homecoming queen."

"It was predictable. What's he doing?"

"Youth pastor in a church. Working his way up the church hierarchy."

"I wish him luck," I paused. "Do you know what happened to Pamela Owens?"

Eddie laughed. "You're an old dog. You still have the hot's for her?"

"No. I moved on a bit." I didn't want to tell him what life had been like in Santa Cruz.

"She graduated and took a job as a secretary in L.A. I think she's got a boyfriend, or several boyfriends. The underground rumor is that she is willing to share herself, if you know what I mean?" His eyes twinkled. "I remember that she was interested in you. We can track her down if you want?"

"No, thanks." In my Freshman year she had been an obsession for me, at times filling my mind, yet we had never really spoken to each other. Just to see her had sent my emotions racing, and any glance from her caused me to blush. Now those feelings were gone. Back then I had fantasies about her and she had been an imaginary escape from my miserable life. Now, she was just another girl.

It's a strange thing how you can become infatuated by someone, where you desire them above everything else, and then later you feel nothing. Then, the same intense feeling can be transferred to someone else, and then someone else.

"What about Leyland?" Eddie hadn't mentioned him.

"Tulsa."

"He moved back there?" I exclaimed. "Why?"

"His parents thought California was too wild for him. Some rumors from the big-wigs made their way back over there, and they had to shut them down before they became anything more. It wasn't a problem since his dad is at the top. Personally," Eddie added, folding his arms behind his head, "I don't think California was too wild for him—it was the other way around: he was way too wild for California."

We laughed, knowing Leyland.

"Do you hear from him? How's he doing?" I asked.

"Pretty miserable. They have a short leash on him. Get this—his only social activity is singing in the church choir. Other than that he works at a desk in the denomination headquarters, doing administration things

The picture of Leyland in a choir robe, standing at the front of the church with a bunch of gray-haired men and dyed-blond women, humored me for a moment before the reality struck me. "Wow, that's rough. And, how about you?"

"Oh, I do okay. I'm not around campus too much, but I still manage to keep a good face to the school. I'm well on track for graduating. Almost there. Can you believe that?"

"Hardly." It really did seem strange. "Are you still smoking?"

"Yeah. I found these smoker's breath-mints that work real well."

"Do they still kick you out for smoking?"

"For sure. The rules haven't changed. But you know, I try to be a good college citizen and all. Every now and then I slip a few to the right person here or there, and I come out clean. Hey get this—you won't believe it." A forgivable smugness filled his smile.

"What?"

He grinned. "You're looking at the current vice president of Circle K."

"No kidding. I thought they were a bunch of snobs."

"We are. But if you're in Circle K you get way better treatment from the teachers and administration. It's a small price to pay, not to mention that it sort of raises your status with the girls. Not like I've got a steady girlfriend or anything. You know my aversion to beehive hairdos."

Eddie hadn't changed a bit. He started tossing the golf ball from one hand to the other and asked, "Tell me, how was it out there in the world for the past two years?"

"Different. A lot of things going on." I scratched my neck. "But I felt like I needed to get close to God, so I came back here."

Eddie laughed. "You, get close to God? Too funny."

"No. I'm serious."

"I don't care; I still think that's funny."

I asked, "Do you know if Georgia Rose is still a student here?"

"Who?"

"Georgia Rose."

He raised his lips and stared at the ceiling for a few moments. "Never heard of her. Who was she?"

"Just a girl . . . someone I talked with about religion one time."

"You and religion," Eddie mocked.

For some reason my heart felt heavy. Some of the things Georgia had said about God's love and faith had come back to me while I was in Santa Cruz. Somehow I knew she was theologically misguided, but I would like to have another conversation with her.

Eddie said, "Look. I've got to go to a meeting—Circle K, you know. Maybe I'll see you around."

"Sure. Thanks."

I wandered slowly back to my room and started unpacking.

38

During my first week back I saw Coach Smyth but he failed to acknowledge me. I also saw Dr. Arlin and Mr. Grazer at various times, and they always stared at me with looks of contempt; something like, "We are watching you." I didn't care. I was there to prove myself.

With my resolution to work diligently at school, I was determined to make a good impression with the teachers, to stay focused and not let anything distract me from my goals.

I doubled my efforts, spending all my spare time in the library. I finished every reading assignment before the class in which it would be discussed. I started papers as soon as I knew about them, and made appointments to speak to the professors to get extra help when I felt like I didn't understand something.

The extra work paid off on exams with true/false and multiple-choice questions, but it seemed like no matter how hard I tried, I could never make more than passing grades on written papers and exams. I began to wonder how much longer I could maintain the motivation to keep my nose in the books. Why did I always have such problems on written assignments? Those grades were more subjective. A creeping suspicion slowly snuck up on me. Were they purposely giving me low grades for some strange reason?

But, I was determined to move on and show everyone that I could live by the rules and be a good guy for God. On the financial side I had just enough money to make it through the year, but knew I needed a part-time job.

I found one at a Bill's Gas Station on Fair Oaks Avenue on the west side of Pasadena.

#

"Here, I've got something for you." Bill struggled to open the top drawer of the rickety wooden desk. Reaching down, he pulled out a .38 special.

I gaped.

"The first chamber is empty; then you've got five bullets," he continued, as if it was a water gun or something.

"What do I do with it?" I asked, hoping he wouldn't tell me I'd have to use it.

"Carry it on you at all times. This is a rough neighborhood, and the place has been robbed before."

I hadn't expected such an exciting job when I applied for a night shift at Bill's Gas Station on Fair Oaks Avenue in Pasadena.

"Uh, how?" I asked. I had shot guns when I was growing up, but nothing more than a BB gun in my backyard or a hunting rifle with my step-dad out in the middle of nowhere. The idea of trotting around in the city with a weapon caught me by surprise.

"Stick it behind the belt in the small of your back," Bill replied.

I took the gun and carefully placed it between my belt and blue jeans, pulling my tie-dyed t-shirt down over it.

"Here's the safe," he said, pointing to a small slot in the wall. "Whenever you get more than fifty dollars cash, bring the overflow back here. It's a good idea to have as little money on you as possible.

"Come out to the register now, and I'll show you how everything works." He kicked the desk drawer shut, knocking a haphazard pile of papers onto the floor in the process. I closed the office door behind me, but the reek of cigarette smoke and damp drywall lingered in my nostrils.

He explained everything behind the counter and then went on to the gas pumps. "Now we're an independent, self-service station, but if you see a woman that looks like she needs help, you get out there and give her a hand, but whatever you do, leave the men alone. They can take care of themselves—and you don't want to cross the wrong guy the wrong way." He clapped me on the back with his broad hand, almost knocking the wind out of me. "You got it? That's a bit of stuff to remember, but I'm sure you'll do fine." His metal-toed boots struck the floor sharply, and then the little bell on the door rung a soft jingle as he walked out. "Hugo will be in at six in the morning to replace you," he called out to remind me.

A motorcycle engine roared loudly before fading off into the distance. I straightened my lightweight green army jacket, and wondered if I should trade it for something more like Bill's black leather.

Glancing at my watch, I took a deep breath and walked around the station a little, familiarizing myself with my new territory. I had Friday and Saturday shifts from ten p.m. until six a.m. That way I didn't have to sit around PC Cru over the weekend, when there was nothing to do. I had taken this job because I needed some extra money, but also because the school environment both stifled and bored me.

I settled in behind the counter and waited to see what the evening would bring.

Around midnight, business started to pick up. A steady stream of cars flowed in, and I began to observe a pattern. One person would fill up the tank while the other ran next door to the liquor store, returning a couple minutes later with a brown paper bag or two.

I was finishing pumping gas for a woman when a guy on the other side of the pump walked back with a six-pack of beer. "You want one?" he asked, holding out a can.

"Sure, thanks," I said. He tossed it over and drove away.

The liquor store closed at one, and traffic through the station died down, so I went to the office to relax. Leaning back in the torn vinyl chair, I put my feet up on the desk and sipped the beer.

I had to admit to myself, going back to PC Cru probably wasn't the smartest move. The spirituality that I was looking for continued to elude me, and I didn't fit in to the general climate there.

Now I couldn't afford to switch schools or majors again. I had accumulated a fairly significant collection of useless credits underneath a less-than-desirable grade point average. If I could hold myself together enough to stay at PC Cru for two years, I could walk away with a degree. Otherwise, it looked pretty hopeless.

Around 2 o'clock, I went back out to the front. A small pickup with a camper on the back was the only vehicle in sight. A Hispanic guy in a leather jacket and pants came in to pay. As he counted out the money, he asked, "You need some tires for your car?"

"My tires are OK," I replied.

"I got some new tires in the camper on the back of my pickup truck."

I put the cash in the drawer and looked up. "Where'd you get them?"

"You don't need to know," the man said. "But if you ever need anything for your car—tires, like I said, a new transmission, even a new engine. All you gotta do is let me know." He stuck out his hand, gold rings stacked on each finger like Life Savers. "My name's Sammy, and I can get you anything you want, mainly for cars, but hey—lawnmower, motorcycle, bicycle—you need something, you put in an order with me, and I'll take care of it. Everyone around here knows that you can count on Sammy." He grinned, flashing a gold tooth.

"Well, thanks for the offer. I'm good for today, though," I said.

"Okay, that's okay. I'm around here every few days, so if you think of something, I'll be back." He waved before driving away.

I hadn't realized that I'd dozed off until I heard the insistent honking of a horn. An older model black Ford sat outside. I went out and walked toward the car. The driver's side door opened. A long, shapely leg swung over the running board, and a tall colored woman with olive colored skin stepped out. The amazing thing was that she had deep blue eyes. I'd never seen that on a colored person before.

She told me to fill the tank. There were five other colored girls in the car.

Leaning against the car, she watched me without saying a word. I glanced in her direction long enough to take in the generous curves accentuated by her very short, slim-fitting red dress.

The pump clicked off, and I told her the amount.

Fingering a stack of bills, her shiny nails painted to match her dress clicked against each other. She flashed me a seductive smile, full lips parting to reveal brilliant white teeth. "Hey white boy. Why don't you get in the car with us?" Motioning to the other five similarly dressed colored passengers, she said, "We can show you a much better time than any white girl."

I laughed. "That would be a white boy's dream, but unfortunately I'm on duty for another couple hours."

"Well, another time then. Too bad, this could have been your lucky day."

A shiver crawled down my spine as she ran her fingers down my cheek. She slipped back into the car and shut the door.

The trace of her touch lingered on my skin. No. I fought back the feeling. I needed to stay focused, to get through school, and do the right things.

39

I began looking forward to the weekends, particularly enjoying the variety of people that I met at the gas station. The suburban, middle-class America where I'd grown up seemed relatively monochrome in comparison to my Technicolor job at Bill's. Whatever negative stereotypes I'd had about certain kinds of people faded as I got to know them on a personal basis.

The customers who came to Bill's were relaxed and friendly. A steady group of regulars flowed in and out, and before long, I found myself laughing and joking along with them. Every so often, some big, surly guy would try to intimidate me, but I quickly learned how to play the game, and let his attitude wear off like the rubber on his screeching tires.

One Sunday evening I had to drive back to Bill's gas station where I had left a textbook.

Parked next to the liquor store next to Bill's, I spotted the shiny black Ford from a few weeks ago and the red-dress girl walking toward it.

My steering wheel seemed to turn in of its own accord. Pulling up next to her, I rolled down my window. "Hey. Remember me? I'm the guy who works at Bill's."

"Sure, I remember you. The cutie white boy. What'ya up to?"

"Just cruising around."

"You come back to take my offer?"

"What offer?"

"Come on. You stupid? To meet a colored girl. You ever talked with one?"

"Ah . . . not really," I stated.

"Yeah, don't act like you don't know what I'm talking about."

I wasn't certain what she was taking about.

She paused for a moment. "Maybe we can talk?" Her deep blue eyes penetrated into my emotions.

"Um . . . sure. How?"

"You date girls?" She asked.

"Uh . . . yes."

"I seen you at Bill's and say, he looks like a nice boy, and maybe we can get to know each other."

This was all new to me. The coloreds were so different than the whites. And we were told that they were inferior to white people and we should not intermingle with them. But I was interested in her. And the thing that surprised me was how assertive and honest she was.

"I'd like to ah . . . spend time . . . with you," I stammered.

"Let's go to my place." She stated.

And she got in my car.

We drove several blocks away from Fair Oaks to an area with very rundown houses. She instructed me to pull into a driveway. I parked the car and we walked behind an old house that had broken windows repaired with strips of tape.

At that moment I wondered if I was doing the right thing. Was she setting me up to be mugged?

She led me to a small building in the back that looked like a large shed where she opened the door with a key and we went inside.

It was a small one room apartment, with a table, a couple of chairs and a bed against one wall. On another wall was a sink and counter and on the counter was one electric cooking element.

Next to the counter was an old waist high refrigerator.

She went to the refrigerator and pulled out a couple of cokes and served me one.

My legs were jittery from nerves, just being here. She was exotic and so beautiful.

She sat down and said, "My name is Ronita . . . Ronita Jansen."

"My name is Robert Macon," I said. I didn't know where we would take it from there. She seemed more vulnerable than before, less assertive and even younger.

"Are you from Pasadena?" I asked.

"We lived in L.A. and then here, my mama and me and my brother."

I wondered about her father and was hesitant to ask.

She said, "My mama now lives in L.A. and I am here in this place that belongs to some relatives. I kind of watch out for the property; that house in front isn't lived in much of the time. My brother lives in Oakland." She was quiet for a moment. "My father was Swedish, so somehow I got the blue eyes."

"Beautiful eyes", I commented, noticing that her features seemed like those from North Africa or maybe Ethiopia. But I didn't know much about ethnic origins.

She smiled a lovely white smile that melted my soul.

And we started to talk and the conversation flowed. We were talking about all kinds of things and we laughed a lot. It was so natural and I opened up to her like I thought would never be possible with another person, particularly a colored.

She asked me questions about where I came from, my life, and what I liked. We talked about basketball.

I told her I was twenty and she told me she was twenty-one. I thought she might even be older than that, because she seemed so sure of herself, but with colored people it was hard to tell their ages.

She told me she worked at a fast food restaurant. I remembered seeing it once. It was right in the middle of the colored area of West Pasadena and it was mostly colored people who ate there. And one day a week she did house cleaning for some rich people.

The time flew and I relaxed. In fact, I was feeling very good to be with her.

At a certain point I got up to go, but didn't want to go, and she came near me to say goodbye. I moved toward her to give her a hug or whatever I was supposed to do but the hug turned into a kiss and before I knew it we were on her bed.

I had never been with a colored girl before. In a dark room you'd think you wouldn't know the difference, but there was something unique. Was I even supposed to think like that?

We started slow, but from her I felt spontaneity, a spirit I didn't feel in the other girls.

When it was over and we talked and she snuggled close to me, resting in my arms, while running her hand over me. Her body was sleek, but that isn't what got to me. There was a silent connection taking place—the most intimate and beautiful thing I had ever experienced.

At seven o'clock in the morning, completely exhausted, I stumbled back to the dorm and collapsed into bed. I missed classes and woke up in the evening, and took a long, steaming shower. The smell and taste of Ronita flowed away with the water, leaving only an empty memory behind.

It took me three days to recover and most of the time I sat in class with feelings of regret and stupidity. I couldn't let this happen again. Most of all I felt dirty inside, sinful, and my long showers could not wash that feeling away. Yet Ronita was special. I wished I could be with her more, even all the time. But what would people in the world think, and particularly those at PC Cru? I knew I would be condemned, but did it really matter?

I even confessed my sins to God and promised to change my ways. I wanted to know God so badly, and vowed that I wouldn't do that kind of thing with women any more. But in the depths of my soul, I knew it was becoming impossible to change.

And underneath it all I knew that the experience with Ronita had been profound, something unique and I hungered for more.

And the worst thing of all was to think that I could never be seen in public with Ronita.

And in the end, wouldn't I end up hurting her? Or, had I already done so?

40

I existed in confusion and stayed away from Ronita's, wondering what to do with the relationship. I didn't have any answers.

In comparison with my experiences outside of the campus confines, the options at PC Cru seemed increasingly bland and restrictive. To get away, I joined a local industrial basketball league and tried to complete most of my studying during the quiet night hours at Bill's. Occasionally I went to the park on Saturday mornings to play with the colored guys. A few of the same guys were still around as when I was a freshman, and they were real happy to see me return. Now I found myself playing above their level.

At school, I only had one focus: getting good grades and graduating. The hopeless goal of being a good guy for God was put on the backburner.

I learned my subjects inside and out, and when teachers gave me low scores on exams, I debated with them, sometimes for hours, until they gave me all the points I felt I deserved.

But then I couldn't stand it anymore and I absolutely had to see Ronita. One evening I went back to her place, saw the light on in the window and knocked on the door.

After a series of reprimands that sounded like the language used by the colored basketball players on Saturday mornings, she invited me in, and her face softened. The evening consisted of a wonderful conversation and it ended like the previous time.

There was something extraordinary taking place, some kind of bonding that was beyond the physical. With the other girls I always felt I lost part of my soul, but with Ronita our souls fused together.

I again left with a deep sense of guilt and had the feeling I was not man enough to do the right thing, whatever that was, and I told myself not to come back again.

Yet, I kept returning.

41

On Monday morning I was walking fast to a class, when I heard the voice of a woman calling out behind me. "Excuse me, you're Robert Macon, right?"

"Yes," I said, turning around impatiently. I had reset my alarm a few too many times this morning, and didn't have a minute to spare if I wanted to make it class on time. Being late would mean some snide remark from my professor that I could easily do without.

"Mr. Grazer requested that you come to see him immediately after you're finished with classes today."

"Thanks a lot," I muttered and ran toward the class building.

What could it be this time? I wondered, wracking my brain for some obscure thing I might possibly have done.

Ronita, I suddenly thought. But how could they know?

I went to my class, but couldn't concentrate on anything the professor said, dreading the meeting with Mr. Grazer.

#

On the way to the administration building in the afternoon, I thought about all my encounters with Mr. Grazer and my stomach tightened.

When I got to his office I grit my teeth and opened the door.

The secretary motioned for me to go ahead into the office. It was empty. I sat down in the wooden chair. It would probably only take a few more visits before the wood would be molded to fit my form.

Mr. Grazer came in, sat down behind his desk and straightened his tie. Clearing his throat, he began, "I know that you have been away for a couple of years, and perhaps you have forgotten some of the rules. However, that does not mean that you are exempt from them." He cleared his throat and paused, offering me the opportunity to become aware of my violation and confess it.

I hadn't the slightest idea what I had done.

The expectant moment deflated along with the expression on his face. Resignedly, he continued, "The dress code, Robert. Granted, we have made some small adaptations. However, no student—you are a student, and a therefore not exempt from this—has the prerequisite to dress exactly however he or she chooses. The rules are there for a reason."

I looked down, double-checking to make sure I hadn't accidentally pulled on a pair of shorts or obliviously put on my sandals. Nope. Khakis and closed-toe shoes. So what was wrong?

"To refresh your memory, students are now permitted to wear t-shirts in the afternoon outside of classes, although at all other times collared shirts are required. We still firmly believe that an individual's choice of outward attire is a reflection of what is in his heart, and it also reflects badly on the institution if our students are seen wearing inappropriate attire."

"I'm not sure I understand," I said. "I have made every effort to adhere to the rules and to demonstrate that I can follow them."

"I've heard rumors that you dress like a hippie," he replied sharply.

"What do you mean?"

"A number of students reported seeing you in a tie-dyed t-shirt at various times. Also in an army jacket and stained, faded jeans."

"Oh, that was in the evening. I wear those clothes when I work at the gas station over on Fair Oaks."

"Excuse me, did you say Fair Oaks?" He leaned forward, squinting, and adjusted his glasses.

"Yes sir."

"One of our students is working at a gas station on Fair Oaks?" He shook his head in bewilderment. "Aren't you concerned about the image of you and our school? To have any association with *that* part of town?"

"It's a job, sir, and I need the money to pay for my courses."

It must have been a good choice of words, because Grazer sat silently for a moment, fingering his pen.

"I don't think that fits the norm for the kinds of place we would like for students to work. Certainly there are other options for employment in the area."

"It pays well and I have to work," I stated, looking him in the eye. It didn't seem necessary to mention that I had also been offered a job at a department store in an upscale area of Pasadena that was owned by a member of one of the local Purity-Christian Churches. "And I like the job," I added in a burst of confidence.

Grazer studied his pen, then lifted it and tapped it on the desk. "I understand that our students must make money to pay for their studies," he resigned. "But concerning your choice of clothing—we have to think about the image of the school. What are our students communicating to each other and to the world that is watching them? As Christians, we are supposed to stand apart and to set a good example. A tie-dyed t-shirt identifies you with the hippie movement, which stands for values and beliefs that are completely antithetical to everything that we in the Purity-Christian Church strive to represent."

"It's just a t-shirt with color," I insisted. "A friend gave it to me. And wearing it doesn't make me a hippie. I lived in northern California for the last two years; I met plenty of real hippies there, and I know for a fact that I am not one of them." I punctuated the last words firmly.

Mr. Grazer leaned back in his chair and focused on the wall behind me. Then he straightened and said, "In the future, we expect you to respect the dress code of this college and not wear that t-shirt when you are on campus. In addition, I would also like to remind you about our standards on hair length."

"I'll get a haircut," I said, ready to end the discussion before he found some new item to pick on. My hair happened to be somewhat longer than the buzz-cuts of the other male students on campus, but it was nowhere close to the shaggy manes the guys in San Francisco sported.

"Thank you. You may leave now." He looked me sternly in the eye, and I met his gaze without flinching.

Leaving the office, I muttered under my breath, "Sure I'll get a haircut—next year maybe."

42

I was deep in thought when I passed Coach Smyth and Miss Walker on my way to the gym the next afternoon. Smyth shot me a glare that could have split my head in half if I hadn't been prepared for it. It didn't surprise me that he and Dean Grazer were in cohorts. I grinned back at him, his assault leaving me unscathed.

A few steps behind them, Eddie appeared with two other guys, going in the same direction. I had hardly seen him all semester.

"Hey, Robert!" He clapped me on the shoulder.

"Where are you off to all spiffed up?" I asked in only partially-feigned shock, motioning to his dark blue blazer with the Circle K emblem embroidered on the left lapel. "And this?" I tugged on his tie.

"Hey," he said, retrieving the tie from my grasp and smoothing it down. "Don't you remember? I'm the vice-president of Circle K. On my way to a board meeting." He waved his companions on. "Go on ahead. I'll catch up in a minute."

"Don't tell me Smyth is going to your meeting," I said, watching as the two guys headed off.

"Yeah, special speaker—for learning about teamwork, how to lead a team or an organization. His area of expertise." Eddie laughed half-heartedly, knowing that my experience with Smyth had proven otherwise. "Besides that, he's coming as the representative of the sports department—we're organizing an alumni golf tournament in the spring. You know, the school's running a little tight on funds as always, and guys who play golf have money, right? So they come, we show them a good time, and then put the squeeze on—milk them good, you know." He pretended to milk a cow.

"Right." I changed the subject. "I haven't seen you around much."

"You neither. By the way, I'm moving off campus. Good PC Cru citizens are allowed to move out of the dorms, so I'm making my move. I had to get special permission from Mr. Grazer, but he signed off on it. Why don't you come over and see my place once I get moved in?"

"That would be great. Maybe you could give me a few tips on fitting into the system, which you seem to have figured out so well."

He laughed. "I don't fit the system, Robert—I never did, you know that. I've just learned how to use it."

I managed a grin. "So where's your apartment?"

He scribbled down his address on a piece of paper. "Here. I've got to run—can't be late for the meeting. I move at the end of the month. Oh yeah, and by the way, Smyth is an asshole," he added. He jogged off, barely avoiding tripping over his dress shoes.

I followed his gangly form until he disappeared into the building.

I felt disgusted when I thought about Eddie's comments about Coach Smyth, how they were organizing a golf tournament to "milk" the rich guys out of their money, as Eddie had put it. That's what Smyth seemed to be focused on, to keep money pumping into the school so he could keep his position. The rest of the time he was trying to gain favor with church officials. He made sure their sons were on the starting teams. He attended all the right events. He was always going out of his way to travel somewhere to be seen with the higher-ups, always with the girls' choir and Miss Walker traveling with him.

All of that came first. Students were at the bottom of his priority list.

43

I was happy when I was with Ronita. The only other places I felt happy was when I was playing basketball in the industrial league, and when I worked at Bill's Gas Station. I was now twenty-one years old. One day a van pulled in to get gas. It surprised me because on the side there were images of flames and the words, "REPENT OR GO TO HELL" Next to that it said, "Turn to God's Love!" And there was a big cross next to that.

A very big guy got out of the van. He was taller than me and broader. He had a beard, long frizzy shoulder length hair, and wore a t-shirt with the image of a hand on it, the index finger pointed upward. Under that were the words, "One Way." He wore jeans and sandals.

I stood by the office and watched him fill the van with gas and when he was finished I walked toward him to collect the money.

He reached into his pocket and pulled out a twenty dollar bill and when I gave him the change he asked, "Brother, are you saved?"

I took a half step back.

"If you ain't saved you're headed to hell," he said.

"How's that?" I asked. I knew what he was talking about, but I never had someone be so up front about it, outside of the church like this, so in your face.

He took a step toward me and I felt aggressed. In fact, it made me angry and it was like I wanted to hit him, but he was big, real big.

He said, "What do you mean, how's that? Don't you know you have to repent of your sins and experience God's love? Christ died on the cross for your sins and when you accept this act, he forgives you and wants you to respond to his love. So don't ignore that truth."

"You want to know more?" he asked.

"Ah . . . I guess," I stuttered."

"Have you heard of the Jesus Movement?"

"Sure, a bunch of crazy hippies proclaiming Jesus," I said, a bit too spontaneous.

"Watch it brother," he said, looking down at me. "We are followers of the Lord."

He leaned into his van and came out with a mix of different colored brochures. He picked out three of them and handed them to me.

"Read these," he commanded. And then he got in his van and drove away.

I took the brochures and headed for the trashcan but before getting there I read some words that said, "Christianity is about Christ. It is not about church buildings and a lot of do's and don't. It is about knowing Christ and following him."

That caught my attention. I went into the office and sat at the desk and read through all the brochures, in fact, a couple of times.

One of them was something called "The Four Spiritual Laws." I didn't like the word "Laws", because it seemed too much like "rules" and I was sick of rules. But when I read through it I found it to be something different. It was more like some core principles on how you can become a child of God.

Basically, the first spiritual law said that "God loves you and has a wonderful plan for your life." That was hard to accept, because in my denomination they always talked and sang about God's love, but behind it they preached that God was always unpleased with you if you didn't attain entire sanctification. But it would be really nice if God got involved in the planning of my life, because most of the time I felt hopeless when I thought about my future.

The other laws talked about being separated from God and how Christ bridges the gulf between God and man. And it says that by accepting this free gift from God, you can become a child of God.

Somehow it reminded me of things Georgia Rose had said when we talked together in the Soda Fountain at PC Cru. It seemed so simple and in some ways made sense, but something was missing. What about the command to be holy and live by the Purity-Christian rules?

On the back of one of them there was an address of a place called The Jesus Christ Light and Power House. It was in Westwood, close to UCLA. I saw that they had meetings every Thursday evening.

Rather than throw the brochures in the trashcan, I slipped them into one of my textbooks.

44

Christmas came and went, we had an unusually rainy January and February, and in March the weather cleared up. I turned twenty-one.
I continued to work at Bill's Gas Station while increasingly going to Ronita's place especially when I was feeling lonely. Sometimes we just talked and we saw that our worlds were far apart. At the same time she was more mature than me, not only street wise, but she seemed to know more than me with every topic we discussed. After all, she was a year older than me.

I felt something deep for her, very different than the kind of irrational infatuation I had for Pamela Owen during my freshman year. And somehow I believed Ronita had strong feelings for me. Maybe it was love, but I had been told so many times that it was very wrong to be romantic with a person of another race, especially a colored. One of our leaders even called it an abomination.

When I was with Ronita it felt anything but an abomination. At the same time it hurt me to know that I might be using her, like I was. And I felt bad that she was so poor.

Other than my times with Ronita, life became routine. Mr. Grazer called me into his office a few times to "see how you are doing," he said. I always felt great apprehension before seeing him wondering if he had learned about me and Ronita. Most of the time it was because I still wasn't meeting the dress code.

I went to the gym when I could, and was outplaying everyone on the court including the starters on the senior basketball team. Some of them asked me to join the team the next year. They even talked with Coach

Smyth about it, but he turned them down. He was still spending a lot of time visiting Purity-Christian churches on the weekends as the special speaker that accompanies the Women's Choir.

I went to Dr. Arlin's office once to try and test him on some religious ideas, but as I wasn't taking any of his classes, he didn't have time for me.

I occasionally reread the brochures that the large Jesus Movement guy had given me. On the Thursday before Good Friday I decided to go to Westwood and I found The Jesus Christ Light and Power House. It turned out to be an old fraternity house near UCLA that a Christian man had bought and turned into a kind of school. On weeknights they had studies.

When I got there I entered a large room. The place was packed with maybe a hundred or more young people sitting on the floor listening to a speaker. I got there at the end so I didn't really get the gist of what he was saying.

Some of the people there had long hair and looked like what I had seen in San Francisco. Others looked like they were students, most probably from UCLA.

When the speaker was finished the crowd began to clear out and a guy came up to me and asked, "First time here?"

"Yeah, what is this place?"

"Just a place where some Christians are living. Some are students at UCLA. Others are just here to study the Bible."

"The Jesus Movement?" I asked.

He laughed. "I guess we are part of it."

"What is it?"

"Just a common vision between many different Christians that Jesus is what's important. There are a lot of different expressions of this, but I guess that summarizes it."

We talked on but I was uneasy. I didn't know if it was a cult or what. I'd seen a lot of strange religions during my time in Santa Cruz and my visits to San Francisco.

"How'd you like to learn more?" he asked.

"How?"

"We're going to Oakland tomorrow to join up with some Jesus people. You're welcome to come along."

45

I spent the night sleeping on a mattress in a hallway in the Jesus Christ Light and Power House and on Friday we made the long drive to Oakland. I rode in a tightly packed van with some guys and girls that seemed about my age. The guy who invited me drove most of the way. His name was John Creasy.

The conversation was about normal things like sports and people they knew, but they also talked a lot about Jesus. It was a bit strange for me, and I mainly listened.

We arrived in Oakland on the Friday afternoon and I spent the night in a 'crash pad' sleeping in a room with five other guys, mattresses on the floor. On the Saturday morning we went to the campus of the University of California at Berkeley.

The goal was to join up with a group called the Christian World Liberation Front, or CWLF. We had a few hours to kill before meeting them so I strolled on my own around the Berkeley campus.

As we neared the Sproul Hall Steps I saw a crowd starting to form. There was a microphone and speakers set up at the top of the steps so I went to the bottom of the steps and sat down.

An attractive young woman went up to the microphone; she represented a feminist group. She began her speech and started to rant and rave about how the 'institution' was mistreating women.

She finally started to yell, "We must burn all symbols of the institution," thrusting her fist into the air as if smashing an invisible object. "Religion is a primary symbol of the oppression of women. We must destroy these symbols. I ask you to burn your Bibles!" She waved a Bible in the air and then cast it into a small trash can with a fire inside.

"And look at the clothing our culture forces us to wear. For centuries, we have conformed ourselves to men's desires instead of choosing what we want. Bras are a male-imposed binding that cover up who we are and restrict our freedom. Why are we letting someone else determine our appearance and our identity? Shake off the shackles, women, and unite against the oppression of men!" Leaning toward the crowd, she shook her wrists emphatically, and then spread her arms wide in an expression of release.

"Take it off!" someone shouted. "Take off your bra and burn it!"

Incited by the passion in her speech and her well-built form, I joined in. "Off with the bra! Free yourself!"

Other men followed along, and a chant began to rise, softly first, then increasingly louder, as if someone was slowly turning up the volume. "Take-it-off! Take-it-off!"

For a moment, the speaker stood paralyzed by the unexpected reaction. Her face twisted first into a knot of confusion, then fury, but the thunderous male voices continued.

Turning around briefly to look at the people behind me, I was just in time to see a female figure flying through the air in my direction. I ducked, shielding my head with my hands. The burn of fingernails scraping along my skin registered with my brain, and I flung my arms out, freeing them from the attack. With renewed vigor, the body jumped back on top of me, knocking me to the ground. Knees pressed into my chest, and two sweaty hands tightened around my neck in a stranglehold. Instinctively reaching up to defend myself, I grabbed her wrists and yanked them away, shifting her weight off of me and struggling back to my feet in the process. She wriggled and writhed, kicking at my legs, but I maintained a firm grip as microphones and men holding cameras appeared in front of our faces. On the side of one, large letters spelled out ABC, and on the other NBC.

At the same moment, a big colored guy took center stage, jumping up and down and screaming into the microphones, "I love the feminists, and I love women! I want them all to go out to work and support me. In my next life I'm coming back as a poodle dog, and you know what I'm going to do? I'm going to sit around in their laps and let them pet me. Yeah!"

The cameras turned toward the colored guy and the girls scrambled off.

I silently melted back into the crowd.

\#

My blood still pumping from the excitement, I wondered if they were going to show what happened on national TV. Would Mr. Grazer, or Coach Smyth or Dr. Arlin see it or anyone else at Purity-Christian College? What would be their reaction to see one of their students being manhandled by feminists in Berkeley? Or should it be woman-handled? They would have a low tolerance for this, for sure.

I made it back to the meeting point for the Christian World Liberation Front, saw John Creasy and went over to him. There were nearly fifty people congregating there.

John pointed out the leader of the CWLF, a guy called Jack Sparks. He was a small man who looked to be in his late fifties with long hair and a gray beard. He wore jeans and a t-shirt with "One Way" printed on it. There were a lot of hippy-looking guys and girls around him.

Jack Sparks led us across campus to a large building and we went inside where a few hundred people were seated. We spread out, taking seats wherever we could find them. I sat next to John.

On the wall were large banners that proclaimed Make Love—Not War and Destroy the System, and Change to Believe In, and SDC: Students for a Democratic Society.

There were large photos of Mao Tse Tung, Che Guevara and Fidel Castro smoking a cigar, and Lenin the communist.

"What is this?" I asked John.

"National convention of the SDC."

"That tells me a lot. What is the SDC and what does it have to do with the Christian World Liberation Front?"

"You never heard of the SDC?"

"Sure," I replied. "Anti-war, anti-government, blow up the system. I lived in Santa Cruz for two years."

John lowered his voice. "The SDC believes that the political system in the U.S. has totally failed to bring peace and hasn't addressed the social problems in our country. They want to create a society where the people really have a voice. They want change through revolution and for people to fight against the power of the government even if it means blowing up buildings."

He paused. "And they feel that private ownership leads to social evils and they want to spread all the wealth to everyone."

"You make it sound so academic," I stated. "A lot of people would just call them a bunch of radicals. So, what is this convention?"

"There are SDC representatives from all over the country here today, but even though it's their national convention, they say that their form of leadership doesn't exclude anyone in the decision-making process. So anyone who wants to get up at this meeting and express his or her views can do so."

"So, what does this have to do with Christianity?"

"That's why the CWLF is here," John said. "Just watch."

I looked around the room and just about every guy had long hair and beards, although some of the beards looked pretty pitiful. Some of the girls had their hair done up in Afros, like many of the colored people were now starting to wear their hair. Ronita had switched to an Afro. Only, the girls here weren't colored.

John pointed across the room. "I heard from one of the CWLF people that Jack and Alec, over there, are waiting for an opportunity to speak."

"To speak about what?" I asked, confused that Christians would even be with a bunch of radicals. At the same time, I was feeling excited, a sense of anticipation filling my chest.

"The CWLF guy said they were here to share the gospel," John said.

I opened my mouth in search of some comment, but a speaker had risen to the podium and began calling the meeting to order.

Over the next hour, the SDC members and other attendees discussed and debated topics ranging from the war in Vietnam and university research that supported the military-industrial complex, to racism and the idea of participatory democracy. A debate about the oppression of the Palestinians was warming up when Jack Sparks stood up and raised his hand. The chairman acknowledged him and opened the floor for him to speak.

John and I sat up.

"I'm Jack Sparks, the leader of the Christian World Liberation Front," he introduced himself. "We have an expert on the Middle East, Alec Linden, who is currently writing a book on that topic."

"Have you ever heard Alec?" John asked me.

"No, who is he?"

"Some radical Christian guy, like Sparks. Alec is one tough dude. He used to be a Mississippi river boat captain. These guys are leaders in the Jesus Movement."

"A river boat captain?" I asked.

"Listen," John said.

The chairman hesitated, turned to a couple of other guys on stage. One raised his hands and nodded his head and Jack motioned for Alec to come forward. Alec confidently strode up to the stage and took the platform."

"We live in extremely interesting times in which the Middle East is the focal point, where the tensions between the Palestinians and Israelis are setting the stage for a great conflict. To the north of the Middle East the Soviet Union is growing in power. To the east is China, the sleeping giant, with its army of tens of millions. And to the west is the vestige of the Roman Empire, ready to reemerge. A great battle will be fought by these forces in the territory we know as the Holy Land."

The room was quiet, everyone listening intently. I wondered where this Alec was going with this, not having heard anything like this before in my church. Sure we knew that Jesus was coming back to judge sinners, but all this stuff about the Middle East was new.

Alec looked across the room and lowered his voice. "It is not just a political battle, but a spiritual battle, one that will precede the second coming of Jesus Christ to this earth."

The chairman looked at the other guys seated on the stage and one of them was shaking his head back and forth. The chairman stood up and quickly walked over to the podium and spoke into the microphone.

"Thank you for your views," the chairman said. "Now we have to continue with the topic of the injustice to the Palestinians."

"I'm not finished," Alec protested. "They want me to speak." He swept the audience with his hand.

A number of people were yelling out, "Let him speak."

"Get off the stage now," the chairman commanded through tight lips. "Your point of view is not accepted around here."

"So much for free speech," Alec countered, leaning in to the microphone.

"Get off the stage or I'll kick your ass," the chairman challenged.

Alec looked him squarely in the eyes and shifted his feet into a boxer's position. "Try me," Alec said.

A surge of excitement shot through me, and I remembered the guy who had yelled out "Take it off!" at the rally earlier in the day. Jumping up on my chair, I shouted, "Free speech! Free speech!"

The other CWLF members immediately joined in. "Let him speak! Free speech!"

The room was breaking out into a wave of voices. Some were calling for Alec to get down, whereas the majority wanted him to continue speaking.

The CWLF people moved to the front of the room and sat down on the floor in front of the stage. "Free speech! Let him speak! Free speech! Let him speak! Jesus is Lord."

Alec, the ex-Mississippi riverboat captain turned evangelist-prophet, raised his fist in triumph and then stuck his index finger into the air. "One way!" he cried out.

John and I went to the front and sat down with the CWLF people, and joined in the chants.

We thundered our approval for Alec. "Free speech!" I continued to cry out. Others in the crowd took up the chant, while the chairman desperately tried to restore order.

I was having a great time.

"Quiet. Calm down, please." He put on his most authoritative voice, but the din of the chant rolled over it, burying him in obscurity. The room broke into chaos. Two guys tackled each other, sending their chairs flying.

Finally the core SDC members rallied together and stormed our protest. One by one they dragged us outside. I got dragged out by two guys. I really felt like getting into a fight with them, and would have had not one of the CWLF guys said to me, "No violence."

As I was dragged outside, I saw television cameras filming the scene.

I cried out, "We're being oppressed! Oppressed by the SDC!"

46

I stood outside the building, straightening my pants and rubbing my sore underarms where the guy's hands had dug in as he dragged me. Someone yelled out to Jack Sparks, "What's next?"

"Picket North Beach!" he responded thunderously.

"Right on!" A cheer went up from the regrouped supporters.

"What's going on?" I asked John. From my two years in Santa Cruz I learned some things about San Francisco. North Beach was where all the strip clubs were.

"I don't know," John replied. "I told you these guys are radical."

I was confused. I had never seen a Christianity like this, if you could even call it Christianity. These guys were getting a big kick out of confronting people. It was totally different than anything I had experienced in the Purity-Christian Church, where things seemed so confined. Here there was spontaneity, and they genuinely expressed their beliefs.

I was having fun.

The CWLF people didn't give me much time to contemplate my confusion. The aggression of the SDC had energized rather than discouraged them. My stomach growled loudly, but food seemed to be the farthest thing from their minds as our crowded cars headed over to the house of one of the members.

With poster-boards and black paint, we made signs in the backyard. A black arrow pointed to a cross with *One Way His Way* written underneath. *The Word. Not Flesh* and *Turn Strip Joints into Churche*s, read two others.

Finally someone thought to bring us food. Taking a break and stretching our sore backs, we stood around eating sandwiches while Jack Sparks explained the strategy for the evening.

In the evening we got into cars and crossed through Oakland, and then made our way across the Bay Bridge to San Francisco. At nine o'clock we grouped in a parking lot near North Beach.

Hoisting the *Let Jesus Clothe You in His Robe* sign someone had assigned to me, I marched along the street with the other fifty people. For an hour, we paraded up and down, some of the group singing Amazing Grace. By ten o'clock, a number of the strip club owners appeared in the doorways of their establishments to discover the reason for slow business that evening.

A man with a fierce expression stalked up to the front of the line and shouted, "Who's the leader?"

"Jesus!" someone yelled back.

"Jesus!" we all echoed.

The owner spat at us. "Nice try. I want someone to talk to."

"Talk with us," Jack Sparks said, as he and Alec Linden stepped forward.

"Get out of this place before I call all hellfire down on you." The owner's eyes bulged in his fury, and he could barely form his words in his mouth.

"We do what Jesus says," Sparks calmly replied.

"If you like your life, you better get out of here," the man challenged.

"Man does not live by flesh and blood, but by every word that comes forth out of the mouth of God," Sparks countered without backing down in the slightest.

The man stared at him like he was crazy. "Who the hell are you freaks?"

"The Christian World Liberation Front," Sparks announced.

"Yeah, I've heard of that—wacky Jesus movement, right? You guys are all kooks. Get the hell out of here," he scorned.

His mockery bounced off Jack Sparks like a little boy's fists off the chest of a professional boxer. Sparks smiled kindly. "We're here to bring the light to dark places, and we won't leave until the brightness of Jesus has shone into at least one of these buildings." He motioned to the rows of strip clubs and bars.

Alec joined in. "Let us come in your club and share the gospel, and then we'll move on from here. But," he added, holding up his finger, "all your strippers have to listen."

The owner grimaced and rolled his eyes. Then, shrugging his shoulders, probably realizing that we'd already irreversibly damaged his business for the evening, and eager to get us out as soon as possible, he said, "Okay," and led us through the entrance.

A small group went inside, John and I included.

A rush of déjà-vu washed over me, reminiscent of the Pink Pussycat when I was a freshman. Rhythmic music pounded at my body, softening resistance and arousing my senses.

It took a few moments for my eyes to adjust to the dark. Small, multi-colored spotlights were directed toward the stage.

Catching a glimpse of the stripper gyrating around a pole in moves of artificial ecstasy, I felt two powers at work in me, one pulling my eyes irresistibly to the girl's completely naked body, the other drawing them down to the floor, away from the tempting sight. The first power seemed to be gaining.

Unlike the girl at the Pink Pussycat, this one didn't have red stars pasted to her nipples.

John Creasy and I found empty seats, and suddenly bright lights flashed on. The stripper straightened the sensuous arch of her back, and squinted in shock.

I looked around. There were hardly any clients in the place. I suspected our picketing out front had scared them away. The few men seated at tables put their hands up, partly to protect their eyes from the light, though it looked more like they were hiding their faces.

"Ruby, get off the stage," the owner barked.

Grabbing a long string of feathers, and holding it around herself, she called in an angry rasp smoker's voice, "Jerry, what's going on?"

"Sit down, and listen to the good news," he said in a resigned tone, waving her down.

"The good news?" she cackled, wrinkling her upper lip in mockery.

"Just do what I say and take a seat. The other girls are coming too."

Shuffling across the side of the stage, she picked up a discarded silver-sequined robe on the way, and threw it over her shoulders. She climbed down the stairs and took a seat at a table, avoiding looking at any of us.

One of the customers started to get up to leave, but Jerry caught him by the shoulder and shoved him back down. "You ain't going no where. You gotta listen to this."

"I'll be back with the other girls," he said to Alec and Jack, and disappeared through a side door. After a few moments, five women in robes appeared, two of them walking with a decidedly defiant sway in their hips. The faces of the other three looked worn and tired. They sat down with Ruby, and the bartender came around with free gin and tonics for everyone.

I looked at my drink and tried to hide an impulsive smile at the irony of the situation. Here I was, sitting in a strip joint with alcohol in front of me, with a group of Christians. If only I could beam the image into Mr.

Grazer's office.

Alec stepped up on the stage, commanding attention with his powerful presence. Spreading his arms wide and holding his palms up questioningly, he asked, "How many of you are looking for love? Have you found it yet? Every heart desires to be loved, and yet many of us go through life unsatisfied, searching but never finding what we so desperately long for." He paused, giving his words time to penetrate the ears and hearts of his listeners.

"Let me tell you about Jesus, who came to earth to die for your sins and to offer you the promise of being loved forever. He is waiting to accept you."

"But there's one major problem." Alec looked around the room. "God is holy. We are not. And fundamentally we are separated from God because we fail to live up to his perfection."

He paused. "Let me ask you a question. If God is absolute perfection and holiness, how perfect do we have to be accepted by God?"

One man sitting at a table looked up at Alec and said, "Real good."

Alec nodded his head. "That's right, real good. In fact, it's to be absolutely real good all the time."

Alec pointed with his finger at himself and asked, "Am I absolutely perfect all the time?"

He pointed his finger at everyone in the room. "Are you able to live up to God's constant holiness every single breathing moment of your existence?"

The room was silent. Alec said, "The answer to both of those questions is, no. And therefore, we need help, and that's exactly what God did because he loves us. He loves you. He sent his son Jesus Christ to die for your sins, your shortcomings, so that you can have a relationship with him."

"Let me ask you. How many of your sins did Jesus Christ die for, when he was executed on a cross?"

It was quiet again and the same man by the table questioned, "All of them?"

"That's right, all of them. Past, present and future. And the good news is that when you tell him you are truly sorry for your failure to live up to his perfection, and when you accept that it is God who enables you to enter into a relationship with him and God alone through no human works, then God sees you through the holiness of Christ."

Alec looked down at the man by the table. "My brother, when you accept this free gift from God, then God sees you as holy and perfect and pure, and you enter into an eternal relationship with him as his child."

The man at the table hung his head and tears rolled down his face.

Alec looked at the man. "My friend, the Christian life is not one of struggle to achieve God's ongoing acceptance. It is a daily faith-rest in him. When we walk with God, then he takes the brokenness of our lives and heals us over time. And he does this because he loves you; I mean he really loves you. He said he will never leave you or forsake you. Trust him. He will guide you to maturity and to that ultimate perfection that comes when we see him face to face."

He finished, and I looked down at my glass. It was still full. I had completely forgotten the drink, listening mesmerized to Alec's words. I had never heard anyone describe God or Jesus as someone who simply loved me, without demanding all kinds of things that I could never give him.

A chair scraped across the floor, and I focused my lost gaze on John.

"Pretty amazing stuff, huh?" he said. "This is far out, and I mean really far out."

"Yeah," I said, somehow not feeling like conversation. Something inside of me had split open, releasing a tangled knot of thoughts and ideas. I needed to follow the threads, and see if I could separate them and make sense of all this.

"Alec's quite a preacher," John continued.

I looked up to see Alec moving over to the table where the man was sitting. Alec sat down next to him and began talking softly. A couple of the other customers moved to the table, as well as Ruby, the stripper. Alec began to pray and everyone bowed their heads.

Jack Sparks and the rest of the CWLF people got up to leave. Jerry stood at the door. I almost expected him to shake hands with the people who were leaving, just like Reverend Finch shaking hands at the end of the church service. Only Jerry didn't go that far. Nevertheless it seemed surreal.

John got up. "Are you coming? It looks like everyone's leaving now."

"Thanks, I think I'll just stay for awhile," I answered.

"Okay. Well, see you later." He waved kindly and turned to go.

The lights dimmed and the room emptied.

From what Alec had said, I wondered how many of my sins were forgiven, if I fully accepted what Christ had done. Just the past ones? Or, all of them? Did it mean I didn't have to try and win God's favor any more in order to be accepted by him? And, Alec said that God gave us a free gift. I wasn't sure I could accept all he said, but a lot of it was making sense.

Alec began to answer questions asked by the people around him.

After what seemed like a long time, Alec stood up, shook hands with everyone around and walked by my table. He beckoned to me. "Let's go. I think the message was received."

I nodded my head and got up. I got the message too.

My mind was racing. At PC Cru they used slogans like 'the old rugged cross' as means to get you to conform to their religious system of rules. And for the most part, it seemed like the girls wore crosses as symbols that they indeed achieved the standards.

But after listening to Alec I realized there was something debasing about doing this, like an affront to the true holiness of God. For the greatest wrong is to believe one can attain God's impeccable holiness through efforts. At PC Cru it was a religious system of Christ plus works, with a lot of emphasis on the works, and wearing a cross was like showing a badge that one belonged to this performance club.

I was experiencing a profound realization that I was far from God because of all the bad I had thought and done, and worst of all was to believe I could attain God's perfection through my own efforts . . . an impossibility. In reality God paid the penalty for my shortcomings through the horrible death of Jesus on the cross. God is the one who brings the reconciliation.

A lot of these Jesus People wore crosses, but I sensed it was for a different reason than those at PC Cru. For the Jesus People, the cross pointed to Christ's sacrifice and love, period.

This was more than just good news.

Something happened. It felt like a weight was lifted from my soul. It was an understanding that God would never leave me and that he loved me and that I didn't need to do things to gain his favor.

I was in a daze and had no idea where things would go from here.

And facing PC Cru was still a reality.

47

Two weeks after going to San Francisco to be with the CWLF, I was back on the wooden chair in Mr. Grazer's office. I feared that he might have seen me on TV, or even worse, heard that I had been in a strip joint in San Francisco.

"Robert. There was some trouble in the dorm on Saturday night, and you were implicated."

"What kind of trouble?" The wooden chair seemed unusually comfortable today.

"Some students went wild, and a number of expensive windows were broken. Several students identified you as the instigator." He raised his eyebrows in expectation.

Hearing this took away some of my anxiety, unless there was something more. "Would you mind telling me when it took place?" I asked, unperturbed by his subtle accusation. I'd had enough experience with his charges to not let them bother me.

"Saturday night."

"And at what time?" This was an interesting reversal of roles, having him on the opposite side of the interrogation process.

"Around 11 o'clock."

Shaking my head, I pressed my lips together and shrugged my shoulders. "Sorry, but you've got the wrong person. I wasn't there."

"They said it was you."

Couldn't he come up with a better argument? "Well, I guess they're mistaken."

"They are responsible students who said it. I'd believe them."

Various dried rings of coffee formed the imprint of his mug on the Formica surface covering the mahogany desk. "How did they identify me?"

"They recognized you." He rubbed his finger on one of the prints, partially erasing the stain. "You seem hesitant to identify yourself as the perpetrator—understandably so since any additional mark on your record will mean a final expulsion from the school. However, I'll give you the benefit of the doubt for the moment and ask how you intend to explain this one."

"Simple," I said. He had finished an entire coffee mark and moved on to the next one. "As I've mentioned to you before, I work the Friday and Saturday night shifts at Bill's Gas Station on Fair Oaks. The shift lasts from ten p.m. until six a.m. the following morning. Therefore, at 11 o'clock I was nowhere near campus, and if you have some concern about that, I'd be more than happy to give you Bill's number so that you can speak with him personally."

"You've told me you work all night in that part of town before." His finger halted its insistent movement. "Are you telling me the truth?"

I reached in my shirt pocket and fished out a business card. Laying it on his desk, I said, "If I was here on Saturday night breaking windows, then a lot of people were getting free gas at Bill's. Check it out."

An oily fingerprint on the card provided Bill's stamp of authenticity. Mr. Grazer picked it up gingerly, bracing the edges between his thumb and forefinger as he scrutinized it. Then he sighed in resignation. "You wouldn't be able to offer me any suggestions as to the identities of the individuals behind Saturday night's ruckus, would you?"

"Not a clue." I looked at the business card that he'd set back down. "Seems like you're having trouble getting the right information."

"Unfortunately, it's impossible to have enough staff to keep track of all student activity. When we encounter a problem we're often dependent on the reports of other students, which can occasionally be misinformed."

He paused for a moment and he lowered his voice. "Those who help in this regard are given special academic consideration."

I knew where he was going and thought about the fifteen credits of F that were on my transcripts. I felt like nodding my head, but somehow thought of Christ when he was tempted in the wilderness.

"I'm not your man," I said.

During my classes my mind wandered to many things. I thought back to the weekend in Berkeley; of listening to Jack and Alec: the fiery message at the convention and the powerful works of love and forgiveness at the strip joint. Then I thought about my last meeting with Mr. Grazer, and the looks I was getting from Coach Smyth. The only way I could find solace in all this was through basketball. I played with an intensity I had never had before. My team in the industrial league was undefeated, and that league had some of the best basketball players in Los Angeles.

After one game a man approached me.

"My name is McGregor," he said. He handed me a card with his name and underneath it was written, Professional Basketball Agent.

I had looked at him, confused.

"Have you ever thought about playing professionally?" He asked.

"You mean, like in the pros?" I asked.

"Europe. Things are opening up and there's a lot of money to be made."

"Me?"

"I've been watching you. You'd fit right in, just what they need. Someone that can play all positions making up for all the weaknesses in the team."

"I'm still in college."

"You got my card. Come and see me when you are finished, or even before." He laughed and walked away.

I didn't think I was that good, but to play professionally in Europe would be a wonderful experience. But they were probably looking for people who had played for well-known universities and players that had university degrees. I put the thought out of my mind.

I rarely played ball at PC Cru, but the day before I had gone down to the gym when all the starters on the senior team were playing. After a few minutes of play I found that I was better than all of them.

And so my mind drifted during my classes.

I was awakened from my daydreaming when I heard the professor end the class. I shuffled out of the room and the professor stood by the door, handing out sheets of paper. I took one mindlessly, barely glancing at it when I set my pile of books down on the desk in my room. It said, Review Sheet for Final Exam

Final exams were next week. I had almost completely forgotten. I had been keeping up, spending my late nights at Bill's gas station to read my books and prepare my papers. I turned in all the required homework and papers, and passed the exams. I went to the library regularly, but, found I was checking out books on subjects that really interested me—history, psychology, and economics. Because of my interest in math I found myself reading a lot of books on finance and investing, but it was more out of curiosity because I knew I would never have any money to invest.

I studied hard, took the final exams, and passed all my classes, but my grade point average was not yet up to a level where I could graduate.

48

That summer I worked the day shift at Bill's Gas Station. One afternoon after work I decided to go to Ronita's place.

I felt best when I was with Ronita. She was the only girl I felt comfortable with. In fact, she was the only girl I really wanted to be with. She was the only girl I was thinking about. She was kind to me, and there was something that clicked between us that was more than physical.

I wondered what it was that made it different from the other relationships I had experienced. For one thing, when I was with her I could be myself. So often when I was around other people, and especially girls, I felt like I was an actor playing a part, wanting the audience to accept me.

Maybe that's what attracted me so much to her. She accepted me. And I liked her personality and would never want to change her. At the same time I had a desire to support her to become whatever she was meant to become.

Normally I went to her place at night, but now I had a clear view of the neighborhood. They were old wooden houses, badly in need of paint, and abundant trash in most of the yards. There were broken and boarded windows.

Normally I didn't see all of that.

I parked my car, walked up to the front door and knocked. A minute later the door opened.

"You early today," she said. "You ain't been here for a while."

"Final exams. Can I come in?" I asked.

She seemed to hesitate and then opened the door. I walked in. With a quick glance, I saw a couple of cardboard boxes in the middle of the room.

"What you want?" she asked again.

"I was hoping we could talk," I said. "Would that be ok?" On the wall was a poster I hadn't seen before. It was of a colored woman with a large Afro. Underneath was a slogan: Black is Beautiful.

She said. "Have a seat."

I didn't sit down and said, "I'm wondering if we could go somewhere, just to talk."

She looked hesitant, and then said, "Sure, where?"

"Just, please come."

We got in my car and she was quiet. I drove to the coffee shop near the Purity-Christian Church, close to the college campus.

Ronita seemed uneasy.

"What we doing here?" she asked.

"I'd just like to do something different, if that's alright. Just as friends. There's something I need to say."

"This ain't exactly the right side of town for me."

"It's about time I did what's right," I stated.

We found an empty table. All eyes were looking at us. I didn't care what they were thinking.

The waitress seemed hesitant.

"You like apple pie?" I asked Ronita.

"Love it," she said.

I ordered two apple pies, each with a scoop of vanilla ice cream.

It came quickly, and we talked. I tried to ignore the stares of all the people around us.

We made small talk, but it felt good to be with her. She asked me what I had been doing and I told her that I had finished my exams. I told her about the basketball league and meeting the agent and the offer to play in Europe.

She was happy for me, but I sensed something was holding her back like being timid, like there was something she wanted to tell me, but she wouldn't.

When we were finished I paid the bill, and we walked out to the parking lot. I went over to the passenger side to open the door for her.

She let out a small laugh but there was a weight in her voice. "That's the first time a man has done that for me, unless he was inside the car."

I said, "Ronita, I want to tell you that I am so thankful to know you. And, I've been doing a lot of thinking. I want to apologize if I ever hurt you, and I'm sorry if I've used you." Then I noticed that her eyes were red and her face was drawn. "What's going on?" I asked.

"I'm moving," she said.

"Why? What's going on?"

"My brother." She spoke quietly.

"What about your brother?"

"He joined the Black Panthers. He's been getting into trouble and I want to go up there to see if I can help him."

I had heard of the Black Panthers, a radical group of colored people who hated whites. "Why?" I asked, confused.

"I been listening to them, to my brother, and they make a lot of sense. The white man just uses black people." Her face turned away from me and her voice became almost a whisper. "White men just want to sleep around with black women and they could care less about the consequences. White man just want to get his moment of pleasure . . . there's no future." Tears came down her face.

I didn't know what she was talking about. It made me feel guilty when she said that, yet was there truth in what she said?

I countered, "Ronita, I'm sorry from the deepest part of my being if I've hurt you. But, it's more than that." I didn't know how to explain what was going on inside my head. "It may sound strange to you, but from the honest part of my heart I can say I feel more toward you than I ever felt for any girl."

"How old are you, boy?" she asked.

"Twenty-one."

"I'm older than you," she said, "and there's an even bigger difference than age . . . color."

"Because you're colored and I'm not."

"Don't use the word 'colored' around me no more. I had a white father who left my mother when I was young, therefore the blue eyes. Jansen was his name; Swedish. But I'm black and proud to be it. Black is beautiful."

I thought of the poster on the wall back at her place. "I think you're the most beautiful person I've ever known," I said.

We continued to stand by the car. "What do you know?" she challenged.

"It's just what I feel," I said.

I looked over and saw more tears on her face. I didn't know what to do. "I'm sorry for what I did to you," I said.

She sniffled. "How do you think it feels like to be poor and I mean really poor? With no education I can't get a real job? How do I get money to eat and some day to feed my family? The Black Panthers said they would look out for me."

I stood there feeling empty, watching her wipe tears from her face with her delicate fingers.

"I'm sorry," was all I could say.

She began to contort, sobs arising from her chest. I wanted to reach out to her.

After a few minutes I said, "Ronita, do you think you and I could ever make it in the world together? I feel close to you, more than any other girl."

"Me too . . . to you," she said. "Our spirits touched . . . and I didn't feel that with any other man, not the same way."

"That's why I would just like to be with you," I said. "Do you think it would work?"

She shifted and leaned in against me. I put my arms around her and hugged her for the longest time. I leaned back against the car to support our weight.

Finally she whispered. "No. Whitey would never accept it. You would be looked down upon. Blacks wouldn't like it either. Who would hire us if we tried to get jobs, if they found out we was together? It just won't work."

That made me feel angry. "I don't care."

"Listen to me. It just won't work."

I stood there knowing she was probably right. I knew I loved her, if I knew what love was. And I think she loved me, too. Yet the gap was too wide, and it was killing me inside.

I had lost track of time when she kissed me on the cheek and said, "We gotta go."

"Why?" I asked.

"I gotta finish packin'. And I don't want you coming in or we might do something that's gonna make it even harder between us."

I released her, and she leaned up against me again. She gave me another kiss on the cheek and said, "We better go."

I looked into her beautiful deep blue eyes and said, "I'll always remember you,"

She gently pushed me and we separated. I dug for the keys in my pocket feeling like my heart was about to crack.

When I looked up, standing about two car lengths away were Mr. Grazer and Champ Smyth. They were with two women, and I recognized that one of them was Coach Smyth's wife.

They just stood and stared, anger on their faces.

I looked at them for a moment and then got into my car and drove away.

49

The evening after I took Ronita back to her place, my industrial league basketball team had a game. I played with intensity, trying to drive confusing thoughts and feelings from my mind. I was angry that Ronita was moving away; I was angry at society for not accepting our relationship; and I was especially angry with Coach Smyth and Mr. Grazer for the way they had looked at me, for their sick intervention into that delicate moment with Ronita.

I took out my anger on the other players. I blocked shots, rebounded, led the fast break and made points. We played against an excellent team, and won by seventeen points.

During the game I noticed that McGregor, the basketball agent, was in the stands. After the game he came up to me.

"Do you remember me?" he asked.

"For sure. You're Mr. McGregor, the agent," I replied confidently.

"Have you given it any more thought about coming to Europe?"

"A little, but I'm still trying to finish school." As I said that, I realized what an impossibility finishing school was. Morally I was low and felt I didn't have the motivation to face another class at Purity-Christian College. And who knows what Coach Smyth and Mr. Grazer would be thinking after seeing me with Ronita today. Did they have a rule against being kissed by a black person? It sickened my stomach to think about it.

"Look. You're good," he said.

"Just okay," I replied.

"No, really. You're an excellent ball player. Do you have a minute? I'd like to speak with you."

He directed me to the side of the court and lowered his voice. "Look, I place a lot of players on teams in Europe. But, I'm also testing the possibilities of Asia. In two weeks I have a team of all-stars that will tour in Asia for three weeks to play in tournaments against the best national teams out there. I've got one spot left on the team, and I'd like to offer it to you. Seriously. I'd like you to think about it."

"To Asia?" I stammered. About all I knew about Asia was Vietnam, and I didn't even know much about that. This was out of the clear blue sky.

"Then, after Asia most of my players will move on to Europe to start the season over there. In fact, several teams over there that are looking for a player like you, someone who is a good all around player. Do you want to play in Europe? I know I can sign you with a team."

"Asia? Europe? In two weeks. I don't even have a passport."

He smiled. "Teams are starting to pay good money for American players. I'll keep the slot open for you until the end of the week. After that I need to fill it with someone else. Please think about it. Do you still have my card?"

"Yes . . . but . . ."

He handed me another card. "Don't lose it. Call me," he said.

50

The metal screen door rattled as I held it open and banged the brass knocker just below the spy-hole. Scuffmarks formed a stripe of gray across the bottom of the once-white paint. The sticky odor of sweat and trash rose up from the alley one story below the iron grate platform on which I stood. Footsteps came toward me from inside and paused a moment before I heard the deadbolt click.

"Hey, Robert, how are you?" Eddie greeted me, gripping my shoulder with one hand and taking the cigarette out of his mouth with the other.

"Okay. Just stopped in to say hello, but I can't stay long," I said.

"Well at least come in for a minute. How long ago was it that I invited you? Doesn't matter really. How you doing?" He stepped aside and motioned for me to enter the living room.

"Good, real good."

"Hey, sit down, will ya?"

I swept a pile of crumbs off the cushion before I lowered myself onto the couch. "Congratulations," I said.

"For what?" He went to a recliner, sat down and it opened up as he leaned back.

"For graduating," I said.

"What a relief," he said. "I'm so happy to get out of that place. You gotta be nuts to stay there for four years." He looked at me. "Oh, sorry. You still got a ways to go."

"It's okay," I said. "Now that you're out, what are you going to do?"

He raised his hands up in the air. "Who knows? Maybe play some golf."

"What about all those money making projects you used to do? I'm sure you have some new ideas."

He smiled. "Honestly, no. Just surviving." He took a cigarette paper out of a small box on the table, dropped a pinch of tobacco into it and rolled it up. "Want a smoke?" he asked, raising his eyebrows and holding it toward me.

"No, thanks. I never could stand the smell. Looks like you found your freedom."

"Yeah, don't have to keep those guys happy anymore." He let out a raspy laugh that turned to a cough. "Hey, you wanna see something?"

Leaving the recliner sprawled open, he swung his legs over the arm and stood up. I followed him into the back room.

Translucent curtains hung over a large window facing a courtyard. Two spotlights mounted on small tables shone down on a large square tray with black dirt. Eddie squatted beside them, pressing his fingers into the soil, and pointing out small green plants that resembled small artichoke plants with spiky leaves. I realized what it was, recognizing the smell in the apartment—the same smell that was at the love-in in Golden Gate Park.

"So you're growing your own?" I asked.

"Best quality in town. Sure you don't want a drag?"

"Thanks, but I really have to get some things done."

"Come on, sit a bit."

We went back to the living room and sat down.

"Want to hear some insider information?" He asked.

"What do you mean by 'insider'?"

"You're looking at an insider in the Purity-Christian system. Through Circle K and the rich donors, I am now part of the club. You want to hear something?"

"Sure."

"You remember Donald Bonen and Elizabeth?"

"Of course." How could I forget how he had been so controlling, while gaining favor from teachers and the administration?

"He was a youth pastor, but really had his eye on working into the church hierarchy in Tulsa. Well, it seems Elizabeth came home early from work one day, and found him in bed with another person."

"No kidding! Donald Bonen?"

"Yeah . . . only the other person wasn't a woman. It was a man." Eddie laughed.

"I can't believe it!"

"You should believe it. The one given rule you always have to keep in mind in that church is that everything is candy coated on the outside, but a lot of rottenness within . . . so people crack. In this institution things are never what they appear to be."

"I sense it," I stated.

"If you know that, then you can not only survive, but you can also play the system."

I thought about what he said. It gave me a hollow feeling, knowing that I couldn't be that kind of actor. "I'm late. I better run."

I walked to the front door and Eddie quickly followed.

"Wait, there's something else I found out," he said.

"What's that?"

"Do you remember when the PC Cru girl's choir came to our church in San Diego when we were still in high school?"

"Yeah." I smiled, remembering Eddie and I crouched under the seats in front of us switching shoes, and the girls singing off-key when they went up front.

"Do you remember how no one came forward at the altar call?"

"I remember."

"Dr. Arlin has been preaching altar calls for thirty years. He was very proud of that. Then that night in San Diego it was the very first time no one came forward. He had a reputation for saving backsliders and then, all of a sudden, his perfect score was finished. That information went through the church hierarchy like wildfire. I found out he was furious."

"Because no one came forward?"

"Yeah. The congregation wasn't really into the altar call because they were laughing at the girls. Coach Smyth and Miss Walker found that out, and you ended up taking the blame."

I felt even emptier. Was that the reason the professors didn't like me? "Why me?"

"You did the greatest wrong possible. You offended their pride. From that point on they turned against you and then everything you did was seen as a justification for condemning you. They saw you as an evil backslider, impossible to be redeemed and on the road to hell. No matter what you did, even if you just innocently looked at them, they interpreted it as rebellion. In fact, they saw you as an attack on their pride and power."

"That's totally unjustified," I exclaimed. "I tried so hard to live up to their rules, to please them, at least in the beginning."

"But you never bowed to their oppression, not really," Eddie stated.

"I guess not," I realized.

"But why me and not you? You were also there when we switched the shoes."

"I don't know. I'm guessing it was because I was a preacher's kid, but I think it was because you were so big, and you looked kind of vulnerable—an easy target."

"Vulnerable?"

"Well, yeah. Naïve or just out of it. Something like that. But, you aren't like that any more. Something's changed in you." He paused. "And there's another thing,"

"More?"

"Oh, yeah," he exclaimed. "A lot more. You know Coach Smyth and Miss Walker?"

"Of course."

"Things aren't going very well between Coach Smyth and his wife."

"So?"

"Think about it. Where does Smyth spend every weekend."

"Traveling with the Women's Choir."

"You got it," Eddie confirmed.

"Come on," I said. "Is that true?"

Eddie laughed. "I don't know if it's true or not, but isn't that a good theory? Wouldn't blame him. Would you turn down her body?"

"I don't like beehive hairdos." I smiled.

"Put a bag over the hairdo and just shut your eyes," he said. "Robert, you've got to finally take out a girl. Everyone's going to think you're a homo."

"Yeah. Good idea. Maybe you can set me up with a girl some day."

I imagined him setting me up with one of the typical, uptight Purity-Christian Crusader girls, and it sent shivers down my spine.

Eddie's words rang in my head: insider information. Dr. Arlin, Smyth, Miss Walker; a funny teenager's prank that touched the pride of these perfect, sanctified people. And they turned against me. All those years of their condescending looks, the years of attempting to live up to their standards, but always failing.

We had hurt their pride and pride is the greatest weakness of anyone who sees themselves as righteous and sanctified in their own eyes. Hurting their pride was the deepest wound that could be inflicted upon them.

I felt a pain in my heart, and I didn't know what to do with it. "I feel sick," was all I could say.

"I understand. I wasn't sure I should tell you, but I thought you should know. The problem is, you never learned to play the system," Eddie stated. "Are you sure you don't want a drag?"

"No, thanks. I'd better be going."

Eddie sank back down into his chair, and took a deep drag from the joint. "See you around," he said, looking up at the ceiling. His eyes began to glaze over.

"Later," I called. The steps shook under my weight. I walked through the stinky alley, and coming out to the sidewalk on the main street I took a deep breath of fresh air.

51

A week after going to Eddie's place I walked onto the Pasadena College campus for one last look. No one was around. An anticipatory stillness hung in the air. In three weeks, summer vacation would end, and swarms of students would come crowding back, filling the dormitories and classrooms, the cafeteria and the chapel. I could hear their voices, the laughter of girls as a boy walked past, the thud of textbooks on desks, and Mr. Grazer's heavy "Robert Macon" as I entered his office or occasionally met him while walking across campus. The sounds faded into the recesses of my memory, replaced by the empty echo of silence.

I saw a couple of girls walking together, giggling. They wore long dresses and their hair was in the traditional PC Cru bouffant style. I reflected on an event that had taken place last week called Woodstock, where half a million counter-culture partygoers waded through the mud for four days to enjoy music and marijuana. Compared to Woodstock and where the general culture was going, being at PC Cru was like visiting a foreign planet.

Up in San Francisco the so-called "Summer of Love" had turned bad. The thousands of runaways who had flocked to the west coast now found themselves homeless and destitute. Venereal disease and Hepatitis C were rampant. Drug addiction and crime were on the rise and there were numerous drug overdoses. Pimps were enslaving the young girls, forcing them into prostitution. The protest movement was becoming vicious and violent.

The great idealism of free-love and peace had crashed, and perhaps hundreds of thousands of young people were lost in the wreckage, maybe more. I had participated in some of that, but considered myself lucky.

In July Neil Armstrong was the first man to walk on the moon. I wondered if Purity-Christian College would be the next place they would land.

I was wearing jeans, leather sandals, my tie-dye t-shirt and I hadn't had a hair cut all summer. My hair was well below the collar line and I knew I was far out of the dress-code norms at PC Cru. I didn't relate well to this place. Nor, did I relate to the general culture, or the counter-culture. None provided what I really needed, and I knew that my journey was headed in a different direction.

My feet took me to the gym entrance. Slipping in through an unlocked side door, I sat down in one of the wooden chairs and looked out over the basketball court. I imagined the blank faces of the coming year's students, first stretching out in long lines to sign up for classes, then listening to the droning of the fall revival speaker. They would file in alone, lumps of clay of different shapes and sizes; they would leave in one form, molded into almost indistinguishable objects.

Would there be another one like me? A stubborn block of mud that they couldn't conform to their image? Or Eddie, squeezing his way through but still holding onto his original nature? Or Leyland, who was steamrolled by the system? What would happen to them? I wondered how many more students were caught up in colleges like PC Cru and the religious systems behind them.

I wanted to give PC Cru one last goodbye, and never see it again. I had made my final decision to leave knowing I had wasted my time at this school. With the fifteen credits of 'F' that I received my Freshman year, I understood it was a heavy load to bear. No matter how hard I tried I just never seemed to get my grade-point average back to an acceptable level.

It was something I would have to live with the rest of my life.

But now I was going halfway around the globe to play basketball. After the Asia tour I would go to Europe, and have a choice of teams in France and Italy. I needed new sights, other experiences, and a different world. My parents were supportive. I was only twenty-one, and I had a lot of living in front of me.

The offer from McGregor was exceptional, out of the clear blue sky. It was nothing I had asked for or deserved. Sure, I didn't make it through college, but maybe I needed time to step back from all of that.

I thought of the girls—a blur of faces and bodies, of loneliness, of treating something intimate as something banal. There was Ronita. I didn't have the strength to fight the system of prejudice around us, and wished that someday that would no longer be a barrier. And, I was thankful for Georgia Rose, who pointed me to a new understanding.

The school system had not been good for me. More than that I could say that it was me that had not been good for me. I had done some pretty stupid things, but now I had a chance to move on.

I looked at McGregor's offer as a free gift, like what Alec Linden had described: acceptance and a new beginning, and I would take it. It gave me the feeling that an invisible hand was looking out for me and I hoped to learn more. For me, it was a living example of God's grace.

Wandering over to the Sports Department, I walked into the empty office of Coach Smyth's secretary. Piles of sheet music sat on her desk. The PC Cru Women's Choir would be back soon enough.

A thud came from the direction of Smyth's office and then I heard some strange sounds. I whirled around to face the door. It was closed. I tiptoed over to it, put my ear against the wood, and then opened it a crack. The sight before me froze my feet to the ground.

A man lay on top of a woman, both of them sprawled over the desk. Her buttons were undone down the entire front of her dress and his pants were down to his ancles. They were in the act, and he was grunting like a pig.

My hand slid off the door handle, and the door swung slowly open. It creaked on its hinges. Miss Walker's head turned in my direction, and she screamed. Smyth jerked up off of her and looked at me, fury flashing across in his face in a flame of brilliant crimson.

The heat melted the ice under my feet, and all the fear and intimidation he had tried to drill into me disappeared. I looked him directly in the eye and laughed. "Just came to say good-bye. You were right, Smyth, I definitely do not fit your system."

"You bastard!" he shouted, shaking with rage, attempting to pull up his pants.

I laughed again. "Perhaps I am, but at least I'm not a hypocrite about it."

I took one last look at their shocked faces, quickly turned around, and retreated from the building.

I felt disbelief and disappointment. This is a man who held his players and students to unreasonably high standards, to be perfect to merit God's blessing. In reality, his way of living was there to impress people by relying on human abilities rather than God's grace.

This I now understood. I didn't blame Smyth so much for having the desires of a man, but more for his two-facedness and for the hypocrisy and false pride of others in this institution. In fact, this institution was nothing more than a system of using human efforts to obtain God's blessing for their own glory.

The thing is, Eddie had deducted this about Smyth and Miss Walker. Surely others at the school, like professors, administrators and pastors knew about this. Yet they turned a blind eye. As long as Smyth held students to the standards of their legalistic religious system, then any of his shortcomings were overlooked.

How many others lived double-standard lives while proudly calling themselves sanctified and holy? How many others were doing what Smyth was doing?

These thoughts and realities were rushing through my brain and I couldn't get out of this place fast enough. I walked quickly toward the parking lot and saw Mr. Grazer and Dr. Arlin walking side by side talking, coming in my direction. It looked like they were lost in a deep topic and didn't notice me.

My mind flashed back to what Eddie had told me about these men, and I understood more than ever that they were blind to their own hypocrisy.

When they approached, I said, "Hello Mr. Grazer, Dr. Arlin. Nice day, huh?"

Their heads popped up in surprise. Mr. Grazer stared at me for a moment. "You don't belong on this campus," he spluttered, "To be like that with that Negro girl."

"You're right," I said, thinking of the passport and one-way airplane ticket sitting on the front seat of my car. In one week I will be gone.

"I know I'm right," he answered indignantly.

I smiled and looked him in the eye. "Look Grazer. I've got no argument with you. I absolutely don't belong here at PC Cru."

I passed them by and began to walk in the direction of my car when I heard Dr. Arlin say, "Robert Macon, you are going to hell."

I looked back and said, "You guys should know. You own the place."

#

I'm twenty-one years old and it's the end of August 1969, and I'm nervous, even terrified. I've never been in an airplane before.

A week ago I was visiting PC Cru for the last time and now I am headed toward Honolulu. From there I go to Hong Kong to join up with McGregor's basketball team. After a tour in Asia, I will go to Europe to play professional basketball. The thought of that makes me even more nervous.

I feel the rumble of the jet engines as they force this metal monster down the runway of Los Angeles International Airport. In a moment we are suddenly in the air and climbing above the dark blue Pacific Ocean. My fear turns to wonder and thrill.

For a long time I stare out the window until California disappears behind me and everything becomes endless blue, above and below. I then recline my seat and recall what has happened over the past four years. I play it through like a movie, scene by scene . . . my story.

After playing it through, I realize those memories are extremely painful to bear. For sure there are a lot of funny things that happened and I learned a lot and grew as a person. But, in the end I know that PC Cru and the outside world in California have caused a deep internal ache. And my personal choices throughout that time did not help. I can't dwell on those events, for they eat me up inside.

I begin to think of other things and attempt to purge the memories from my mind. I don't know how my story will evolve from here. All I know is that I'm twenty one years old and there is still a lot more to come.

The one thing I realize is that God is with me and I am his child. Georgia Rose planted the seed, and then there was the 'chance' meeting with the Jesus Movement guy at Bill's Gas Station when he handed me the brochures. And then Alec Linden had proclaimed a message of grace. With faith I accepted that message and it is making a difference.

There is now no pressure to perform in order to win God's favor and the guilt imposed on me by PC Cru is gone. God loves me unconditionally.

Besides this truth, all I know is that I am flying across the vast blue Pacific Ocean, leaving the pale suffocating world of PC Cru and California behind . . . maybe never to return.

CHAPTER 52

After leaving the Black History Book Store, I drive to the Oakland airport, leave the Porsche with the rental agency and catch a flight to Los Angeles. This time the rental agency didn't have a Porsche and I was ready to try something different, so I drive away in a bright red Corvette. It has forty-eight miles on the odometer. It's a car I always wanted to try and we don't see many in Paris.

I spend the night at the same hotel near the airport and in the morning drive to Pasadena following the thick slow traffic.

I eventually find the old PC Cru campus and park the car in front of the main administration building. Some years ago I learned that the denomination had sold the property and then moved the school to a new location in San Diego, on a site that overlooks the Pacific Ocean. I will drive to San Diego to see the new campus, but first want to visit the old PC Cru.

I wander around the old campus which is now some kind of missionary training institution. There are young students everywhere and I feel conspicuously out of place. All the buildings are still there. Whoever is running the place was doing a fairly good job of keeping them maintained.

I eventually return in the direction of the rental car and pause at the old fountain. I look down at a thin layer of green slime coating the stagnant surface. I drop a small rock into the slime and a hole opens up, momentarily revealing the brown water underneath before the slime closes back around it.

For some reason revisiting the campus doesn't raise the feelings that I thought they would. Maybe too many years had passed? Maybe the ghosts I had carried weren't all that important. Maybe all the experiences of the past years had indeed given me a new perspective and had helped me overcome the pain that had been handed out by this school.

Years ago when I left this place I had walked away with a penalty on my college transcripts that I could never overcome. It was a Sword of Damocles always hanging above me. But then going to Europe and seeing new sites and meeting people allowed me to see the world from a new perspective. But a university degree always eluded me.

I played professional basketball in a number of countries and learned about different cultures. After I had signed with a team in Paris I learned that the president of the basketball club was also the director of the École des Hautes Études Commerciales de Paris, or HEC. I didn't know it at the time, but it is one of the top business schools in the world and the selection process to get into the school is highly competitive.

One evening I shared with him the story of my transcripts. He laughed and said, "C'est ridicule! Le système éducatif américain est aberrant"; that is, "This is ridiculous! The American education system is absurd".

His administrative assistant obtained the transcripts from my U.S. schools and then wiped out all the bad grades and then they admitted me into the school. Our basketball team, Racing Paris had just won the European championship and I think the director wanted to keep me around.

On one level this made me realize that success often has more to do with who you know rather than what you know. But I've always think of this as an illustration of the grace of God. His redemptive act is the only basis for approaching him. When we realize that and repent of our shortcomings, He forgives our sins and they are wiped clean before him. As far as the HEC, the administrative assistant had in one quick stroke of the pen wiped out the condemning grades once and for all.

And I consider it divine providence that I ended up in Paris and met the director of the HEC. It showed me that God can lead and redeem. For indeed my life was in the pits when I left PC Cru and there wasn't much hope.

After two years of very hard studies I obtained a License or Bachelor's Degree from the HEC. Then I went to INSEAD, another top ranked business school where I received an MBA. It was there that I met my business partner and we started our hedge fund. It turned out that I was quite good in math and he and I worked well together and we turned our company into success. It is now one of the best performing hedge funds in Europe.

Shortly after starting the hedge fund I met Monique and it was instant love. Monique was of Huguenot origins and a Psychiatrist. She was a believer in God, put her faith in him, and that further strengthened my faith.

I joined her church, a small Huguenot-Protestant congregation in Paris. And through our travels all over the world we met believers from many Christian backgrounds. This has caused me to identify with Christ's world-wide church.

We never had children, but during our travels we saw needs and began to support some orphanages in poorer countries. We often called those orphans, "our children."

In Paris, our home for many years has been a large penthouse apartment on a quiet street not far from the Avenue des Champs-Élysées.

Besides work and travels I became the major investor in the Racing Paris Basketball Club which has a team that plays in the French first division. The team almost always makes it to the European championships. The club has many junior and lower division teams.

I still play on a senior team, very senior, with guys my age. I can jump up and touch the rim, almost. We tend to pass and shoot much more than we run and rebound, sort of like slow-motion basketball. In fact, every guy on my team is a high percentage three point shooter. We figure that from there, it is a shorter distance to get back to the defensive end, and therefore we use a lot less energy.

My parents ended up moving to Europe where they lived in our small chateau in the South of France and helped run the vineyard. My step father's construction skills were invaluable in leading the restoration of a number of old buildings on the property dating from the Middle-Ages. They became part of a group of English speaking expatriates living in the South of France and enjoyed their time there until the end of their days.

But over the years I carried emotional hurts that sometimes raised themselves at the oddest times. On the outside one can have the demeanor of maturity and control. Yet on the inside one can have feelings of insecurity, inferiority and brokenness. And even if one holds to a Christian worldview where you can experience the healing power of God, there are times that the inner person can be broken and fallen. Monique said that healing can be a long process.

Often these emotions seemed to connect back to PC Cru, to their hypocrisy and how the staff had treated me and others. But I couldn't always make the connection between PC Cru and my feelings. Before she died Monique encouraged me to go back to California and see these places and find people, including Ronita Jansen, and Eddie Bailey and Georgia Rose. Monique said to talk with them, that it would help the healing process.

In Monique's book she says that hurts from the past can be like scars. They heal but may always be there, and they may be sensitive when provoked. But they don't need to control you. Her book advocates exploration of events of the past and analysis of emotional reactions to them.

So, I followed her advice and am surprised how I am now feeling while standing here in front of the old PC Cru campus. It is as though the negative emotions are gone, or at least they have found a place of resolve. Maybe I had been foolish to carry those feelings for all those years? Yet I know the true confrontation is yet to come, for the beast had moved to a beach front location in San Diego.

I've seen enough here. I have a meeting with Eddie Bailey, and tomorrow is Homecoming.

I go back to the car and drive through Pasadena. Before heading to San Diego I will first swing by San Marino to the address that Leroy in Oakland had given me.

I wonder if the address is something Leroy had fabricated, just to get some money from me, or would it in fact lead me to Ronita? And if I were to meet her, would she remember me and what would she say?

Am I stupid to even attempt this quest?

53

From Pasadena it was a short drive to San Marino. Somehow I keep thinking that Leroy is leading me on a wild goose chase. San Marino is a very upscale community with spacious homes, many in traditional Spanish style. Most are situated on large properties with green lawns, trees and flowers. The streets are lined with tall palm trees. It was a town known for old-money wealth. What in the world is Ronita doing here?

I drive past the Huntington Gardens, where Eddie had fished for change out of the fountains, and then past Cal-Tech, a technical university that attracts some of the finest scientific minds from around the world. Then I go down a tree lined street and find the address. The house is set far back from the street, almost completely hidden because of the bushes and trees. I turn onto a long driveway and then stop the car in a large circular parking area in front of the house.

It is a Spanish style structure with a three car garage to one side. There are some rooms on top of the garage and stairs going up to them on one side of the house. Next to that is a large paved area and there is a basketball hoop. I approach an arched polished wooden door and am feeling foolish as I rang the door bell. This seems completely absurd.

After a couple of minutes the door opens and a woman looks at me inquisitively. Perhaps she is between thirty five or forty years old. She has brown hair, dark olive skin and green eyes. I have the impression her origins are from North Africa or somewhere in southern Europe. She's wearing a pink cotton dress, and is tall and slender and attractive.

"Excuse me," I say, "but I was given this address by someone. The information may be wrong, but I'm looking for someone named Ronita Jansen."

"May I ask who you are?" She says.

"My name is Robert Macon. I live in Paris but made a trip here to try and find some people I used to know."

When I said Robert Macon her eyelids blinked and she stepped back a bit. For a moment I sense something like shock or even fear in her eyes.

She then straightens herself and says, "Please come in."

She leads me through a charming foyer and then into a large living room with an impressive carved beamed ceiling. There is an impressive fireplace and in one corner of the room is an antique table and on it is a picture of four people; the woman, a tall blond haired blue eyed man next to her and two teenagers, a girl who looks to be eighteen and a tall boy about fifteen.

Then she leads me through some French doors to a cozy patio. Beyond the patio is an oval shaped swimming pool. Further back there is a lawn and then in the back is another building that looks like a small guest house.

"Could you please wait here for a moment?" She says pointing to a cushioned chair next to a round patio table. Then she leaves.

I sit down and wait. As the minutes tick off I wonder what I've gotten myself into. After more than ten minutes she returns. Her eyes are red. She carries an envelope and hands it to me.

"Please read this," she says sitting down in a chair on the opposite side of the table. She stares at me.

I open the envelope, take out a letter and began to read:

Dear Dina,

As years go by I want to tell you something that I should have shared many years ago. I don't know how to say it other than to say it outright.
When I was seventeen years old I met a very nice young man who was twenty. I told him I was one year older than him. He was white. Back then, interracial relationships were looked down upon by both races, but there was something very special between us. I felt I could be myself around him and sensed he felt free with me. I loved him but never told him. I sensed he had

the same feelings for me.

We had an affair and I became pregnant, but I knew this relationship would never be accepted by his side or mine. So I went off to Oakland to join up with my brother, and you know what happened up there.
After that I came back to Pasadena where you were born. And then I had to support my beautiful little daughter and took different jobs and we ended up in San Marino.
I'm so sorry I have held this from you for so many years. It has been a hard burden to bear, not telling you the full truth. But back then there was the color barrier and I felt shame and I had so little and there were so many emotions and feelings I wanted to hide. I just tried to be brave and get on with life and support my daughter. But not telling you was a great sin.
I'm proud of what you have become.
Your father's name is Robert Maykon and he was a student at Purity-Christian College.
Please forgive me. May God bless you. I love you,

Mama

I finish reading, put the letter on the table, drop my head and take a deep breath. It is like I was hit by a club. My chest tightened and my mind raced. If this was true, the woman in front of me was my daughter.

I glance at her. Indeed she is beautiful with the light filtering through the trees and reflecting off her brown hair. I see a resemblance to Ronita but also something a little more familiar.

A tear rolls down her face. "She never told me," she whispers.

"I'm sorry. Truly sorry," I say, searching for words.

I keep looking at her, wondering if this is a nightmare. I feel shock, all of a sudden engulfed by a block of ice. I cross my hands and put them below the table to hide them. My body tightens and I bend forward.

She looks down as though she is talking to the table. "Mama died a few years ago, a series of strokes over time and then a big one that finally took her. I found the letter tucked into her Bible," She delicately picked up the letter and fondly held it in her hands. Her eyes turn toward me again. "We tried to find you."

"You did?"

"My husband contacted the school, which is no longer in Pasadena and they weren't helpful."

I nodded.

"He got a lawyer and eventually the school said they never had a Robert Maykon as a student. We tried a lot of other means to find you, but it was like you had never existed.

"It's Macon, with a 'c'." I spell it for her. "After your mother went to Oakland I went to Europe and have never been back to California since then,"

"That explains it," she exclaims.

Her eyes drift past me and fix themselves on something in the distance. I wait some time until she looks back at me.

I search for words. "I believe you have a family . . . the photograph on the table in the living room.

She nods. "James my husband and a daughter, Janette who's a freshman at UCLA and a son, Dan. He's a junior in high school."

Things become quiet, an awkward moment of not knowing what to say. She intently fixes her eyes on me, looking at my hands and then my face, like the mystery of discovering a long lost photo that one has never seen.

"I'm so sorry to hear about Ronita . . . your mother. I've thought about her over the years wondering what happened to her but never thinking that she had a child, like this. I never imagined . . . I'm stunned."

I put my hand to my forehead.

"Are you alright?" She asks, looking at me intently.

I try to control myself and fold my hands back together and slightly shake my head. "Please tell me more."

More tears roll down her face. She breaths deeply, a couple of times, and says, It's a strange thing to learn you have a father who you know nothing about, a stranger."

"I didn't expect this. It's almost unreal," I confess.

I feel helpless, again wondering if what she said is true, but it had to be. My mind was racing to find connections and conclusions, yet I didn't know what words to say and feel paralyzed. Nothing prepared me for this and I sit frozen to my chair.

There is more silence between us, to the point of being uncomfortable. I finally ask, "Can you tell me what happened to Ronita when she came back to Pasadena?"

She peers at the letter in her hands. "As you have seen from the letter, she gave birth and as a single mother she had to support me. She took any job she could find and eventually became a nanny and housekeeper to the Williams, the family in this house, on the condition that she could bring me."

"The Williams were a wonderful couple. We lived in the small apartment above the garage and we never left and they practically took me and my mother into the family. After I graduated from university I married James, their son."

A tear rolls down her face and she wipes it with the back of her fingers. "And you? Tell me of you. You mentioned Paris."

I wait a moment not knowing where to begin. How do you absorb the sudden knowledge that you have a daughter and son-in-law and grandchildren? How do you share decades of personal history?

I begin, "After Ronita left for Oakland and because of other circumstances, I left for Europe and played professional basketball in a number of countries, for fifteen years."

Her eyes brighten. "Dan would like that. He's crazy about basketball and is already the best on his high school team."

"He looks tall on the picture in the living room. His father looks tall."

She nods. "He is." She looks at me and asks, "So you stayed in Europe?"

"Yes. I ended up in Paris where I finished university and started a company. Then I got married to a wonderful French woman. She died some months ago."

"I'm so sorry to hear that," she says. "Did you have children."

"No,"

Dina gently puts the letter back in the envelope. And then she begins to cry, weeping, her chest shaking up and down.

"I'm sorry," I say, my words sounding hollow. Clumsily I reach across the table and touch her hand, wanting to ease the pain.

She gently pulls her hand away from me.

"It's too sudden," she sobs, "like this, out of the clear blue sky . . . a shock. I need time to think.

"I understand," I tell her.

I hear a sound in the living room and a young male voice cries out, "Mom, are you home. There's a cool car in the driveway."

A teenager comes through the French doors and walks onto the patio. He is carrying a backpack and a basketball is cradled under his left arm. He is tall, maybe an inch or two taller than me. He has green eyes and he looks like a younger version of me.

He looks at his mother and says, "Mom, what's wrong?"

"Nothing," she says. She takes a deep breath and wipes the back of her hand across her face.

"But . . . what's going on?"

"It's nothing Dan," she says. She regains her composure and turns to me and says, "Can you please go. This has all been too sudden and I need time to talk to my family." She rises from her chair.

I nod and get up at the same time. "May I call you?" I ask.

"Maybe. Give me a day or two. We'll see."

The teenager has a puzzled look on his face and goes to her side as though trying to protect her.

She turns to her son and says, "Thank you Dan. It's okay. We were just talking about your grandmother."

We go back through the living room and into the foyer where she goes to a desk and writes something on a piece of paper and then hands it to me. It is a telephone number.

"I'm not sure," she states.

I nod

As the boy is there I don't know what to say so just thank her for her time and then go back to the Corvette. What I had learned over the last hour seems unreal and my whole being feels numb. I go in the car, get in, start it and then drive slowly down the driveway. In the rear view mirror I see Dina and Dan watching me drive away. Dina's eyes are wide, eyebrows raised, eyes fixed on my car. Dan is turning to his mother, his arms out from his body with his palms held upward.

54

My goal had been to go to San Diego to meet with Eddie Bailey and to attend some of the homecoming events at Purity-Christian University, which had previously been called a "college."

But, after what I just experienced in San Marino I'm considering dropping the whole thing.

I take my time driving to San Diego trying to gain control of my emotions. It was unreal what happened in San Marino. My mental state is fragile enough. I am still grieving the death of Monique. And now this.

My body is tight with emotions. Feelings of disgrace and regret rush through my soul. In Ronita's letter she said she was seventeen when she met me. I am horrified and ashamed. At the time of our relationship I certainly didn't know that. In today's world I would be arrested and put into prison and then be classified as a molester for the rest of my days.

But in Ronita's letter she said she had told me that she was older than me. Indeed in all our hours of conversation she had definitely been more insightful and mature than me.

My mind is racing, thinking of the past, of Ronita being an unmarried teenage mother, of all those years on her own and how she had to take care of her daughter. And Dina had to grow up without a father. I am feeling shame. I imagine how they were poor while I had assumed a life of luxury in Europe.

It was somewhat consoling to learn that Ronita had ended up working for a nice couple. Dina now seemed to be in a good situation with a happy family. But I understood that there were years of struggle for them and for this I am feeling great dishonor.

I find myself blaming PC Cru and their treatment of me and their attitude toward blacks. In my rationalization I'm trying to convince myself that it was the school's fault this happened. But I have serious reservations. The fact is, I carry the ultimate responsible for this, for I had made the choices. The responsibility ultimately rests on me.

Years ago Ronita told me that her father had left her and her mother when she was young. Hadn't I done the same thing?

And for this I am truly sorry, more than sorry, feeling a deep sense of guilt for the choices I had made and the lives I ruined.

I saw the pain Dina was feeling when I left her house and I regret that I went there. Her life was fine before I showed up. My appearance was an emotional lightning bolt she didn't need. I think of the piece of paper in my pocket with the telephone number she had given me and I question if I should give her a call. Probably not. I'm wavering and wish I could have some wise counsel.

Maybe I'll call Dina in a day or two. Maybe never. Maybe I should just drift away and leave them at peace without further shaking up their lives. But I already had.

I decide to head on to San Diego, to have some time to think and pray. Then, in a day or two I'd decide on whether to call her.

At the same time, my heart isn't motivated to go to San Diego, to meet Eddie Bailey, and worst of all to go to the Purity-Christian University homecoming. What did I expect to learn, really? What was I thinking?

In the back of my mind I consider to get on an airplane and head back to Paris. At this point I don't need more emotion and need time to absorb what happened in San Marino.

But I decide to press on hearing Monique's advice to visit places, talk with people and be ready to face the unexpected.

55

Ispend a terrible night at a nice hotel in San Diego and the following morning go to the fitness room and spend an hour on a cross trainer. Then I go back to my room, shower and change into jeans and a t-shirt. Coffee and a continental breakfast are brought to my room.

After eating I go for a walk in the center of San Diego. Things have changed since the last time I was here and I observe many more modern high rise buildings. It's hard to recognize the city, but that's not what I'm really thinking about.

The walk gives me time to reflect and I'm still not sure what to do.

I have lunch in a downtown coffee shop and decide that I will go ahead and meet with Eddie. I came a long way and it might be good to see him after all these years. Yet my heart is not fully into it.

I decide to give myself another day to process things. Perhaps I would also attend one or two of the events at the university.

Without doing this I may leave some necessary stones unturned. It is still important for me to reconcile with the past, no matter what it means. But I'm not sure I can take another day like yesterday.

I go back to the hotel, and change to a dark blue shirt, beige slacks, light tan hand made Italian shoes, and a gray and blue tailor made sport coat. I figure that homecoming is not a suit and tie affair, but I put on a blue silk tie that Monique had bought for me at a boutique in Paris.

I go the Corvette and drive through San Diego toward the Purity-Christian University campus. My meeting with Eddie Bailey is at five o'clock and I have a few hours before then, so I decide to find out if there are any homecoming activities to attend. Eddie couldn't meet until five because he was busy managing the homecoming golf tournament.

I find the campus and park the car in a visitor's parking space. Three students walk past, a guy and two girls.

As I get out of the car the guy slows down and says, "Neat car."

"Thanks," I reply.

"Are you an alumni?" One of the girls asks. She speaks with the same gravelly-whiney voice as Brandy.

"Sort of. If they would call me that?" I smile.

They give me an inquisitive look.

"Would you be able to tell me how to get to the Student Union?" I ask.

"We'll show you the way if you take us for a ride," one girl replies. She giggles.

I smile and walk next to them and ask, "How do you like the school?"

"The beach is great," the guy says.

"Is that why you chose the school?" I ask.

"Well that, and the school belongs to our denomination," he says.

We walk onto the campus and talk about San Diego and they describe it's attractions for students. They say nothing about their studies, which I guess would be consistent with many university students.

I enquire, "You know, when I was here we had to sign something called the Community Covenant. Do students still have to do that?"

They look at me inquisitively.

The boy turns to the girls and says, "Wasn't that the paper we had to sign about what you can and can't do?"

"I guess," one of the girls responds. She turns to me and asks, "What's behind your question?"

"Oh, I don't know," I respond, "I was just wondering if the school has a lot of rules for the students."

All three of them laughed.

The boy says, "They've got more rules than dogs have fleas."

"So, are you able to live with that?" I ask.

"Most of them, I guess," he answers.

I don't press the topic and we talk about other things.

We walk some more and the guy points out the student union, and I head for it. It is a blue building and on the front I see a large canvas banner that says, *'Welcome to Homecoming."*

On another banner there are the words, *'Sea Lions'* with a strange image that is a combination of an African lion surrounded by a wave from the sea. Something here doesn't fit logic with an animal from the African savannah sitting happily in a wave of the Pacific Ocean. But, it shows you how bizarre a symbol can become. And like any branded logo it can carry immense spiritual and cultural meaning, thereby forming an identity.

I find it interesting that the student-body no longer call themselves the 'Crusaders', but rather the Sea Lions. I guess the word Crusaders was deemed inappropriate at some point, from a religiously-politically-incorrect point of view, if you could call it that. The almost holy term, 'Purity-Christian College Crusaders' or PC Cru was discarded by the roadside, now replaced by an African lion that lives in the Pacific Ocean.

In the student union I notice adults of different ages standing in groups shaking hands and talking with raised voices and laughing. I don't recognize anyone.

There are some tables where alumni can register for various events, and some tables have leaflets with information about the homecoming. The previous evening there was a formal dinner and this evening there will be the homecoming basketball game. Perhaps I will attend. It's tough to pass up a basketball game.

Today is Saturday, a day with many special events for the alumni that included a boat ride around San Diego bay and various meetings and seminars at the school. An all day golf tournament is scheduled and on a brochure I see Eddie Bailey's name.

I have time to kill so pick out a seminar. It is entitled, "Purity-Christian University: Forming World Citizens in the Holiness Tradition." From the supporting information it seems to be a seminar designed to convince parents to send their students to this institution.

I ask for directions and eventually find my way to a large conference room. It is full of students and older adults. I assume the students were encouraged by their faculty to attend the seminar, instead of going to the beach. The students do not have happy faces.

A man walks to the podium and people stop talking.

He announces, "My name is Doctor Breedie and I am the head of the theology department."

He starts by giving an overview of the seminar and explains that he had become head of the department after Dr. Arlin had passed away to join his maker. Dr. Breedie tells the audience that he had been a student of Dr. Arlin and had been deeply influenced by him. Many in the crowd are nodding their heads, and they smile and seem to be pleased.

Dr. Breedie continues and informs us how the school molds students to become the religious, social and business leaders of the future.

He says, "We stand on a foundation of the Articles of Faith of the Purity-Christian denomination and believe these are the basis of being a Christian and of contributing to the church and to the world, for these principles give purpose to enact the Christian lifestyle."

"Many of you will know this truth from the Articles of Faith." He holds up a piece of paper, waves it a bit, and then reads from it. "Without purposeful endeavor one's grace can be ultimately lost."

He looks up. "This is core to the teaching of this institution. This truth teaches our students to lead lives of purposeful endeavor, that is, to take personal initiative in their religious duties, and not lead lives of slothfulness that will ultimately lead to backsliding and loss of salvation. It is a foundation for turning out the future generation, for servicing the kingdom and our church."

He continues and explains the schools position on sanctification and living holy lives and then he asks if there are any questions.

No hands are raised, and I suspect people are more interested in getting out into the California sunshine than listening to a rather boring lecture on theology.

I have a question and raise my hand. Dr. Breedie acknowledges me and has a smile.

I ask, "When I attended PC Cru, Dr. Arlin and other teachers taught that you were saved and then at a later point you became sanctified. Does the school still teach this?"

He shifts back and forth. "Ah, yes . . . ah, sanctification is a process we obtain as Christians. It is the divine act of a free gift from God that we realized through our purposeful endeavor expressed by holiness living. So the principles are the same, while it may be communicated differently because of the unique needs of each generation. But without holiness one cannot enter into eternal grace."

His answer is vague and doesn't answer my question.

I raise my hand again.

He points at me and nods.

I ask, "At PC Cru we were taught that holiness was a state of sinless perfection to be achieved in this lifetime. To exemplify what holiness is, we were given certain standards to be lived up to, some defined, some implied. As I understand it, if you achieved those standards, then it was a sign that you were holy. In other words, if you attained a certain level of behavior then you were accepted by God. Is that what purposeful endeavor represents? And, are the teachings the same as when I was at PC Cru?"

He shifts again and looks at the audience. The audience is motionless and silence fills the room. Some people are looking at me with frowns.

Dr. Breedie waits a moment, clears his throat, and says, "Well, I very much appreciate your question which is fundamental. Holiness is achieved through purposeful endeavor and certain Biblically based guidelines have been formulated in the foundations of the Purity-Christian denomination. They are also alluded to in the Community Covenant that all students at this school have signed. This is what sets this school above most other educational institutions. Our students leave this school with a sense of purpose for serving the church and the world."

I realize he used a lot of words to sidestep my question again and I wonder how far to pursue this. I decide to make another try and ask, "I honestly apologize if I'm belaboring this, but it might be an important factor in considering whether to send a child or grandchild to this university. Can I be confident that all the teachers and staff at this school have obtained entire and absolute sanctification through their purposeful endeavor?"

He picks up the papers in front of him and looks out at the audience. "Well yes. You can be confident of that."

"So they are perfect and will never manifest sin, and I can entrust a child to them?" I ask.

"Absolutely," he says.

He looks at his watch and then apologizes to the audience for running overtime and then adjourns the meeting.

As I leave the building some adults look at me with frowns on their faces. People keep their distance as they walk past me.

56

I walk around the campus and realize it is indeed in a magnificent location, on a cliff next to the ocean. The day is sunny and warm, but there is a fog bank ominously approaching from the west.
I reflect about the seminar with Dr. Breedie. The condescending way he answered my questions makes me feel belittled and it brings back some of the same feeling I had experienced at PC Cru. I wonder if there is something wrong with me.

At the same time it makes me realize that things have not really changed. If their concept of purposeful endeavor and achieving holiness is the foundation of their belief, then to reach God and stay in relationship with him is a matter of human effort, an impossibility to say the least. Rather than meet God based entirely with God's grace, this is nothing more than a religion of works.

The three students I had met earlier said there were a lot of rules and I'm sure there were a lot of unwritten rules that went along with those that were written. Ultimately those rules were established by the leaders of this institution.

In my years of travel and in observing different political systems, I've noticed that laws and rules are often a means for keeping an elite group of people in power. In this institution the students were taught to achieve certain standards that ultimately served the institution, at least from what Dr. Breedie had said.

Even more concerning was Dr. Breedie's statement that the teachers of this school were sinless and perfect. It meant they had no flaws, no short-comings and with their idea of purposeful endeavor, they ultimately felt they approached a holy God through their own efforts.

All of this makes me sad for I have come to the realization that when Christ died on the cross for my sins he died for all of them. When I accepted that, I believe I was made sanctified before God. While in this lifetime I may be growing in my faith, there is still a brokenness that continually needs God's grace.

And through this I understand that God's purpose is always to bring us back to him and his love.

For me, the essential thing is to walk in a relationship with God, not that I always do it perfectly. True spirituality is not a misguided attempt to live up to a set of man-made rules. That's what Alec Linden had said so many years ago at that very unusual event at North Beach in San Francisco. And that's what Georgia Rose had said even before that.

If Dr. Breedie and the other faculty at this school proudly proclaim they are sinless and holy because they live up to the man made rules in the Community Covenant, then this is deception and a great affront to the true holiness of an almighty God. I am sad that this ethos had perpetuated itself from one generation to the next. The hypocritical philosophy of Dr. Arlin and Mr. Grazer has been transferred to the next generation.

I walk over to an amphitheatre where I am to meet Eddie Bailey. In front of the amphitheatre there is a structure built like a Greek temple. Beyond that is an unobstructed view of the Pacific Ocean. I see that the fog is moving closer.

San Marino and Dina still weigh heavy on my soul.

#

I sit down and wait while watching students come and go and then see an older man walking in my direction. I recognize him. He looks smaller, slightly hunched, like life had taken something away. It is Eddie Bailey.

He sees me and smiles. "Robert?"

"Good to see you," I say. Emotions fill my soul, not only from seeing him, but also from the thoughts of everything that had happened back then.

"Good to see you too." We shake hands and he slaps me on the shoulder, and he says, "Sorry I could only meet now, but I've had activities all day long because of homecoming, including a golf tournament for the alumni."

He sits down next to me and we look out at the ocean and the fog moving in.

Some years ago I ran into a fellow PC Cru student in Paris and he gave me some updates about people from our time. I learned that after Eddie graduated, he had spent over twenty years in a cannabis-haze doing odd jobs here and there while living in a small apartment in Pasadena. That made me sad, as Eddie was probably the most industrious and creative guy I ever knew. He could have gone a long way in the business world, or any world for that matter. But for some reason that didn't happen.

Instead, Eddie took a job with Purity-Christian University.

Eddie commences to describe his responsibilities at the school. For the last ten years he had been a fund raiser, working with the alumni. He tells me he goes around the country meeting donors and playing a lot of golf.

"It's a good gig," he says.

After so many years of no communications between us, it is difficult to know where to begin. I thought I had some specific questions for him, but after the events in San Marino I feel like I'm walking in a void.

There is a moment of silence and then he says, "You know, it's funny. You're the one guy I could always be honest with, because you had no stakes in the system. And I owe you."

"What do you mean?"

"I took some things for granted back then," he declares. "You turned out to be the fall guy. It was only afterwards as I began to understand how they needed someone to place the blame. You took it. Leyland and I and others did things that earned the same treatment as you, but they placed us in a different system of justice."

"Still, being a preacher's kid wasn't all that easy," I say.

"I think you're right. When you are within a religious system, it's always a lot harder for the preacher's kids and missionary kids than for the normal kids. There's an abundance of performance expectations."

Having met many preachers' kids over the years I know he is right.

He begins to update me on some of the people from our past.

Donald Bonen had died of AIDS, infected with the disease before all the life-supporting drugs were available. The school hushed up any association with him.

Leyland McGrath had graduated from university, got a job working for the denomination headquarters in Tulsa, got married, had a couple of kids, and then died of leukemia.

Some of the students in our class are now professors or administrators at the school, and many are donors to the school.

Pamela Owens married a lawyer and left the church.

Dr. Arlin and Mr. Grazer had died from various old age problems.

Coach Smyth is still alive, in his mid eighties. Eddie explains that at halftime of the homecoming game this evening the school is going to give him an award for lifelong service.

In hearing that, I am determined to attend.

Eddie tells me there were many other students like me who were promised basketball scholarships by Coach Smyth, and when they got to the school he didn't deliver. Winning games wasn't the most important thing for Smyth, although his teams needed to have a decent record. What was important was that the right egos were stroked.

I ask Eddie about Miss Walker.

He laughs and says, "Some of the big wigs began to be suspicious that Smyth and Miss Walker may have had inappropriate encounters, but there was no evidence. She moved on to another school, and after that Smyth always seemed to surround himself with interesting ladies. The thing is, the guy had tremendous political leverage and there is no way that anyone could touch him. He still has amazing power around this place."

"Sad," I state.

He nods.

"Has anything changed since they moved the school down here?" I ask.

"What do you mean?" He questions.

"The rules, the theology, how they treat students, holiness . . . things like that."

He looks both ways and we are out of hearing distance of anyone. "Robert, I've always been honest with you and there are few people I can really talk with. You want me to be honest with your question?"

"Yes, if you can."

Eddie looks again in both directions and lowers his voice. "Holiness now has to do with prosperity. If you are holy then God blesses you with wealth. Having wealth is an example of that blessing. As a result, those in the church that have wealth are honored far and above those who do not. Wealth becomes the Holy Grail that everyone seeks, although they would totally deny it if they heard me say it like that."

"That's a strange way of thinking," I state.

"I guess," he said. Then he laughs. "But it sure makes my job a lot easier."

"What do you mean?" I ask.

"I go out and meet the wealthy alumni. I put a guilt-trip on them that God has blessed them and therefore they have to give a chunk back to the school. It works."

I look around the campus and observe that it is very well kept—a jewel sitting on the hill above the pacific. Maybe Eddie's insights are right. In their new system, it is wealth and externals that are important. This causes me to think of a teaching of Jesus where he calls the hypocrites whitewashed tombs which appear beautiful on the outside, but inside are full of dead men's bones and wickedness.

I shift the topic.

"Do you remember someone named Georgia Rose?" I ask.

He frowns. "No. Not really."

"She only attended PC Cru for one year, our freshman year."

"I don't remember her. Why?"

"She was my turning point."

"A girl at the college was your turning point? I can't believe that. I didn't think you were around a single girl during your entire time there, except for that one crazy girl your freshman year. I thought you might even be gay."

I smile. "I think there may have been at least one girl. Maybe more, but at my age the memory fails." I chuckle to myself. If he only knew the truth. And then a sense of guilt shoots through me as I think of Ronita. "Georgia was the one who first opened my mind to the idea of the grace of God."

"Why do you need her to open your mind to religion? Didn't the Purity-Christian Church do enough of that? They talk about God's grace all the time." Eddie states.

"As a slogan yes, but there was a difference in the way she explained it."

"You still into this God thing?" He asks.

"Yes, in a Jesus Movement kind of way. Do you remember the end of the sixties? That's where my spiritual journey began."

"Jesus freak. Good for you." He pats me on the shoulder.

"It's just a different way, for instance from what I heard at Dr. Breedie's seminar earlier today."

"His eyes widen. "You're not the guy, who was asking the questions, are you?"

"What do you mean?" I ask.

"The school is buzzing right now. Some older guy got into a theological debate with Dr. Breedie. They say he was a heretic. That was you?"

"I just asked a few questions out of curiosity. It wasn't to get into an argument."

"That isn't the way they took it," he states. "They're ready to throw you off the campus, maybe burn you at the stake," he says. His head turns one way and then the other.

He asks, "Did you give your name?"

"No. It was just a few simple questions."

He stood up. "Look I've got to go."

"Can't be seen with the heretic?" I ask.

"Robert, I'm glad to see you, but I've got to think of the system. Remember the number one rule. Don't rock the system . . . use it."

He pats me on the back, starts to walk away and then turns back to me. He smiles and says, "Do you remember when we were still in high school and the PC Cru girls' choir came to church and we switched their shoes around?"

I laugh. "That was really funny, wasn't it?"

Eddie grins from ear to ear. "Two high school guys doing pranks. Would you do it again?"

"For sure," I proclaim.

"Your coming here has made my day," he says. He punches me on the arm and walks away.

I ponder that event that happened so many years ago when we switched the shoes. It was a wonderful experience. Yet, isn't it fascinating how one small and seemingly insignificant happening can influence one's trajectory in life? Indeed our prank had upset the pride of Dr. Arlin and Coach Smyth, men who claimed to be without pride and sin. And that set the institution against me in a serious way. As a result my life ended up going in a rather unusual direction.

The fog moves in and it is becoming difficult to see the buildings at the far end of the campus. I look toward the ocean, and it appears as a clammy gray pale tide.

I reflect on whether the people here would ever see clarity beyond the murky controlling theological engulfing their lives. Would this narrow church-system continue to be propagated from generation to generation, where externals are more important than attitudes of the heart, and true faith in God?

I watch the fog begin to drift through the columns of the Greek temple and wonder if the campus police will escort me to my car?

57

In the evening I find the gym, sit in the bleachers, and watch the homecoming game. The teams are mediocre at best. There isn't one player on the floor good enough to play on my Racing Paris team back home.

The opposing team was well chosen for the Purity-Christian team is ahead by ten points at half time. The alumni and students are delighted.

The homecoming king and queen are crowned at half time, and then the master of ceremonies announces that Dr. Joseph Whitney the president of the university will make a special announcement.

Dr. Whitney walks to the center of the floor and speaks into a wireless microphone.

He says, "Ladies and gentlemen, this evening we are here to honor someone who for many years has made a major contribution to this institution. He faithfully coached the men's basketball team to a league championship and he has been a great leader to the thousands of students who have attended this school. He has been a living example of the holiness standards of our denomination and the church. I'd like to invite Coach Champ Smyth to come forward."

The crowd gives him a standing ovation. I remain seated.

An elderly man walks from one side of the court into the center. He has the same gait and I would recognize him anywhere. He shakes hands with Dr. Whitney and waves at the crowd.

A student runs from the sidelines carrying a plaque and hands it to Dr. Whitney, and then he hands it to Smyth. The applause becomes louder.

Dr. Whitney gives the microphone to Coach Smyth.

Smyth looked at the crowd and says. "Thank you so much for this award. I'd like to simply say that it has been a great honor to serve this institution that has stood for the highest spiritual and moral values. We can be proud of the administration and professors who exemplify lives of sanctification and holiness upon which the precepts of this school are based. Thank you and I wish you blessings."

There is more applause.

Then they leave the court and the teams come back.

The second half is much like the first, although more of the bench players are getting into the game. The Purity-Christian team wins by seven points.

The crowd slowly leaves the stadium and I stay behind. I must admit that it was actually fun to see the game. I love this sport.

The disturbing thing was to see Smyth be honored with the award. He had lied to many young men with promises of athletic scholarships and he demanded from them higher standards that he was able to live by.

The award is in fact a slap in the face to Miss Walker and any other women he had been with. But then I think of what I had done to Ronita and acknowledge that I am no better than Smyth.

Maybe the difference is in the hypocrisy?

I feel disappointment and realize there is nothing more for me to learn by being here.

I leave the gym and walk past a small crowd of people and see President Whitney and Dr. Breedie standing together. Dr. Breedie notices me and he takes a step backward.

Coach Smyth is standing to the side of Dr. Whitney. Smyth turns his head and sees me and there is a brief moment of some kind of recognition, but I can see that he isn't sure who I am.

He holds out his hand to me like a politician with a smile on his face. Maybe he is wondering what class I would have been in or whether I had been one of his basketball players.

"Nice to see you," he says, but it isn't followed with a name.

I shake his hand and simply say, "Robert Macon." I feel like asking him about Miss Walker, but refrain myself. What good would that do?

He stands still for a moment and then his eyes narrow and he quickly jerks his hand from mine. He becomes rigid. His eyes narrow and it seems like intense hate fills his face.

He knows I am someone who has seen his hypocrisy.

I look at Dr. Whitney whose eyes are wide with surprise. Dr. Breedie turns to Dr. Whitney as though he wants to tell him something, but then he refrains, probably because I am standing there.

No one moves and during that time I think about how their system perpetuates itself from one generation to the next, people just living by a culture. They freely use words like truth, but are in fact blinded to the truth because of traditions and legalism. And they make converts who become greater children of hell than themselves. Great guilt falls upon them, for they destroy souls.

I nod to them realizing I have learned something about false and true religion, as well as something more personal. As Monique said, the scar may exist, but it no longer needs to control one's emotions.

I walk away and go back to the car and head toward the hotel. A thick fog fills the streets and slows my drive.

EPILOGUE

The following morning I agonize about calling Dina. In my hedge fund company in Paris I used to make dozens of phone calls every day to some of the leading bankers in the world. Often they were tough calls dealing with difficult issues.

Now, this call to Dina is the toughest of them all.

It rings three times and then a female voice answers, "Hello."

I recognize her voice. "Dina, this is Robert . . . Robert Macon."

There is a moment of silence and then she says, "I'm glad you called."

"About the other day, I'm so sorry if it was a shock," I say. For me it was totally unexpected, for certainly my entire being quivers with after shocks.

"Yes," she answers, "but I spoke with my family. They want to meet you." She pauses. "I want to meet you."

"Me too," I say. "But I don't want to impose."

"No. No, please come," she implores.

"When?" I ask.

"Today. Now."

#

I drive north on Highway 101 past Camp Pendleton. There are soldiers training for battle, as they had many years before. I admire them for defending the freedom of this nation.

I listen to a music station that is playing the same kind of music that Brandy had called "cool" when we drove toward San Luis Obispo.

On the piece of paper I had given Brandy I had written the words, "If you need a job, call this number and give my name."

The telephone number is that of a woman I know in New York, one of the most professional job recruiters one can find. We have used her many times for finding people to work for our hedge fund company. If Brandy calls and gives my name, I'm sure this lady will try to help. She'll most likely call me for background information.

I wonder if Brandy will find a track that will lead her to fulfillment in life? Maybe not. But, I'm of the opinion that redemption is possible. I'm an example.

In listening to the music and thinking of Brandy, I reflect on how the culture around us shapes us and defines who we are. In my times we listened to the Beach Boys and songs like "California Girls" and "I Get Around." And that's what we did. Our values were California girls and just getting around. Now the songs have changed, yet they continue to define people's values . . . or one could say that the popular songs are a mirror image of the underlying philosophical presuppositions of the moment.

I switch to a classical station that is playing Bach, which is much closer to my mind-set and better integrates with the magnificent view of the Pacific Ocean. The coastal fog is gone and the tides no longer pale.

The top is down on the Corvette and the warm wind rustles through my hair. This is definitely a contrast to the old Chevrolet that I first drove north on this road. Back then I was nervous about going to a new school. Now I feel anxious because of other reasons.

I'm running through different scenarios in my head of what it will be like to meet Dina and her family . . . my family, if I could even believe that. I find myself imagining and making mental plans.

What if they reject me and accuse me of evil and immoral conduct? I have to accept that, for who else holds the blame. What if they accuse me of abandonment? I'd like to think that I would have stayed with Ronita had I known she was pregnant, but am I sure about that?

There are so many things that could go wrong when I meet this family and my mind is calculating . . . but maybe calculations and reason don't work here and I just need to go on intuition and honesty.

I think about what could happen if they accept me and we establish a good relationship. That is what I want, to be the member of a family.

In that case, maybe I'll buy a place over here, in San Marino, to be close to them. But then, maybe I'm jumping the gun and just need to get to know them first.

Dan is a basketball player and I like that. What will he think to learn that his grandfather is the partial owner of a top rate basketball team in Europe? Maybe I'll bring him over to see my team play? Maybe he could even play on my team some day? But again, I better not get ahead of myself.

And, to have a granddaughter. What is she like? And, a son-in-law. This is all too much to comprehend.

If they allow it, I would hope to make up for many lost years and to find the redemption that I know is possible.

I wonder how it will go when I meet them, and somehow I hear Monique's voice in the background with a sweet reassuring laugh telling me to just be myself. I miss her. Inside me there is a hole where Monique should be. How I wish I could share all these events with her.

Years ago I drove up this highway as a naïve young guy who was heading off to meet the two beasts, the Pharisees of Pasadena, and then the Babylon of delights. One was a legalistic religious system and the other a counter culture gone crazy. Both led to death. And after those encounters I found a third way full of grace and life.

But I can't blame everything on the two beasts, for I also had an enemy within, an innate rebellion that was leading to self destruction. What changed me most was experiencing God's love, as he led me through the years. Time and time again he has been good to me.

And that makes me think of Georgia Rose, the third person I want to find. Mainly I'd like to thank her for her words and her character that triggered my quest to find truth.

I will keep looking for her and some day hope to find her, but if not, I will always think of her as a visiting angel. In the Bible it says something about angels being ministering spirits sent to serve those who will inherit salvation. Indeed, that is what she was for me.

I drive through Los Angeles and take the freeway to San Marino and drive into the courtyard in front of Dina's house.

I get out of the car and see Dan over by the basketball hoop. He is practicing hook shots, but he stops when he sees me. I walk in his direction and signal for him to toss me the ball. He passes it to me.

After a couple of dribbles I fire off a long shot, almost three point range. It swishes through the net.

Dan says, "Wow," and he looks at me, eyes wide. It was a lucky shot but luck happens, and it's a good thing to have when you start out a new relationship with a grandson.

I look toward the front door. Dina is standing there. She must have heard my car when I drove in.

She is smiling.

Destinée Media

This is a Destinée Media publication. Destinée aims to bring a fresh perspective to living, culture and worldviews. We thank you for your interest in our materials and hope that you find them both relevant and challenging.

For more information please go to www.destineemedia.com

If you have any afterthoughts on Pale Tides we invite you to see comments from other readers and welcome your ideas in the discussion. Please go to the author's website at: www.casstell.com

www.ingramcontent.com/pod-product-compliance
Lightning Source LLC
Chambersburg PA
CBHW032017050726
47590CB00006B/2214